The Cat Trap

The Cat Trap

K.T. McCaffrey

ROBERT HALE · LONDON

Typeset in 10½/13pt Sabon
Printed and bound in Great Britain by
Biddles Limited, King's Lynn

For my good friend, Laz Costello

When lovely woman stoops to folly,
And finds too late that men betray.
What charm can soothe her melancholy?
What art can wash her guilt away?

The Vicar of Wakefield
OLIVER GOLDSMITH

The tattoo instrument issues a low whining sound. Menacing. Subversive. A cluster of needles penetrate the dermis layer on the woman's forehead, stopping short of fracturing the underlying fat stratum. The recipient remains unaware of proceedings, oblivious to pain.

Tattoo artist Stewart Longworth cleans the ink-laden residue of blood from the emerging design and sighs. Times like this, he needs to remind himself that he's a professional. This is a commission, albeit a strange one, at odds with the photographic examples of body art adorning every square inch of the tattoo parlour's wall, illustrations that depict aspects of scarring, branding, piercing and skin implants, most of it not intended for the squeamish.

The design he is labouring on has not been selected from his catalogue of stock designs; it's not one of the hackneyed emblems that most people are familiar with, not the ubiquitous anchor, the English rose, the cherub, the arrow-pierced heart, the skull and crossbones or such like. Neither is it one of the rude comic ad-libs his clients sometimes select in a rash moment. He'd seen it happen: the customer who, on a mad whim, insists on having the cartoon depiction of pigs in rut alongside the caption *Makin' Bacon* only to discover, a few days later that it isn't all that damn funny.

The emerging design is, if anything, beyond banality, it offends his sense of the aesthetic. Yet, he prides himself on his ability to comply with, and satisfy, his customers' needs, safe in the knowledge that his creative skills will redeem the end product, irrespective of their appalling taste. He confers his tattoo machine with the kind of respect a conventional artist bestows on his, or her, paintbrushes.

He is an artist, true, but that doesn't mean he lacks appreciation of the monetary worth of his labours. His fees for special commissions are substantial but unfortunately he doesn't get enough of them to provide a decent living. As a 24-year old healthy heterosexual, he likes to partake of the good life, indulge his fondness for women, recreational drugs, clothes and travel, excesses that cost more than he earns, excesses that force him to prostitute his art from time to time.

There's something familiar about the woman who has commissioned the tattoo, something that makes him think he's seen her before. He can't place her identity, her dark shades doing their job effectively, but he has an inkling that she's connected to the high profile charity business. A good-looking woman, late-thirties to early-forties, she is not the person being pierced, but she is present in his studio. Along with two female companions, she sits rather formally on a couch to one side of his work area observing his every move.

Through no fault of his, the design looks flat and lifeless, not at all typical of his work. He had tried to steer the woman in a different direction, suggesting various typefaces, indicating examples of intricate, decorative lettering. He'd enthused about his ability to render all manner of Celtic, Gothic and Art Nouveau lettering but she wanted a sans typeface, opting for Helvetica in the end, the plainest font in his catalogue. To make matters worse she'd insisted that he confined the use of inks to permanent black, and that he shave the recipient's head.

He punches the final little holes in the subject's forehead and watches the needles deposit Indian ink into the waiting receptacles. The skin will remain defiled for life. The tranquillized recipient, a woman in her mid thirties, has a good figure and a pretty face, though a tad on the coarse side for his taste. Her clothes display designer logos, yet she lacks the sophistication of the three women on his couch. They haven't told him why they want the younger woman's forehead tattooed and he's been paid enough not to ask.

He eases his foot off the power, shuts off the machine and beckons the women to inspect the finished work. There's no disguising their smirks of satisfaction as they watch him clean away the last residue of blood. As though transfixed, they stare at the plain black capital letters, characters that spell out a single word: S L U T.

CHAPTER 1

mma Boylan had managed to avoid contact with Bob Crosby for three days on the trot. Her plan – to keep out of his way for another forty-eight hours – came unstuck when he collared her in the canteen during the morning coffee break. Which was why she now sat in his office, the object of his enquiring gaze. 'You've been avoiding me, Emma,' he said. It was a question.

'Not true,' she lied, unconvincingly. 'Been chasing my tail on a number of fronts – you know how it is.'

Crosby smiled. 'Yeah, I know *exactly* how it is.' At 53, and just shy of six feet tall, Crosby was overweight, had a heavy face etched with impressive intelligence and kind eyes. He retained a scattering of grey hair atop a high domed crown. More than anybody at the *Post*, he knew Emma; he'd hired her a decade earlier as a cub reporter and had, over the intervening years, come to value her resourcefulness. Her instincts for sniffing out good stories, and the importance she attached to corroborating facts, made his job as editor that bit easier. There had been skirmishes along the way – she could be stubborn, he could be impossible – but a trusting friendship had evolved.

'What did you want to see me about?' Emma asked.

'Rumours!'

'Oh, the classic Fleetwood Mac album?'

'Very funny,' Crosby snorted, amused by the quip but unwilling to concede as much. 'No, I'm talking about the rumour that has you quitting your job here, leaving us....'

'You know better than to listen to rumours, Bob.'

'Indeed I do. But this one came from a usually reliable source.'

A quick decision was called for: Emma must bluff Crosby or come clean with the truth. Were this conversation taking place forty-eight hours later she'd have an answer for him, by then she'd have made a decision on the job offer she'd received. She'd been headhunted by the newest grouping to emerge on the political landscape, the Social Alliance Party, or SAP, an acronym that amused the media, appealed to detractors and appalled its founder-leader, Maurice Elliott. Elliott had dangled the job of media manager in front of her. 'Yours for the taking,' he'd offered. 'You've a week to think about it.'

Two days of that timeframe remained.

'Well?' Crosby prompted. 'You going to tell me or not?'

'It's true, Bob. I *have* been offered a job. I would've talked to you sooner but ... well, I haven't made a decision.'

Crosby's face was inscrutable. 'Who's making the offer?'

'What's the rumour mill saying?'

Crosby relaxed, the mask slipped. He smiled. 'That's my Emma, always ready to answer a question with another question. I'm told a certain business tycoon and tin-pot politician has made an approach.'

'You mean Maurice Elliott, right?'

'The very man. I dismissed it though, thinking you'd never abandon journalism to work for a serial philanderer like Elliott.'

'Envious of him, are you?'

'Envious! Don't make me laugh, the man is rich, fair enough, but his lifestyle, hey, you can have it. If even half what we hear is true, Elliott has shagged everything from here to Timbuktu and back again. I'd be surprised – no, *shocked* – if you of all people allowed yourself to become his mouthpiece.'

'All will be revealed the day after tomorrow,' Emma said, stung by the 'mouthpiece' remark but determined not to let it show.

'Bad career move, Emma, but I can't stop you if ... wait a minute, this is not a question of salary?'

Now it was Emma's turn to smile. 'You think I can be bought?'

'Well, no, of course not but I—'

'Just kidding, Bob. My decision doesn't hinge on salary ... well, at least not salary alone, but since you brought up the subject ...'

'I'll see you right, Emma, but I'm not getting into a Dutch auction.'

'It's all right, Bob; like I said, it's not *just* about money.'

'I'd appreciate if you'd talk to me before making a final decision,' Crosby said, ushering her out of his office.

Back at her own desk, Emma thought about her editorial boss's promise to look at her salary. She'd told him her decision didn't depend on money. And that was true – to an extent. She was far more concerned with the bigger picture. It was time to take stock of her life. It was springtime and like nature's renewal process the time was ripe for her to make a fresh start. She had reached a crossroads, split from her husband, thrown aside a marriage that had survived ten years. Her union with Vinny Bailey had simply run its course, leaving nothing in its wake except the shells of two people who'd once loved each other. The marriage could have plodded along indefinitely, but the emergence of a romantic interest in her life hastened the inevitable. This new liaison had developed over a longish period of time, a period that mirrored a corresponding decline in the state of her marriage.

Emma looked at the words appearing on her monitor, words her fingertips generated by tapping on a keyboard, words that would appear in tomorrow's edition of the *Post*. While this process of writing continued almost unconsciously, her mind wandered hither and thither, mulling over events that had shaped her recent past.

If there really were fifty ways to leave your lover, as the song suggested, then why hadn't she been able to find just one that didn't inflict pain and grief? Leaving Vinny had upset a lot of people. Telling him had been the worst part. He'd cried and begged her to reconsider, but she'd been firm. It was over. Her parents, who'd been particularly fond of Vinny, were gutted. Vinny's father too, who'd been enraptured by her, appeared shattered. She felt lousy about that; she'd no wish to hurt anyone, but it was her life and she was determined to take control of it. Was she being selfish? Yes, probably, but what were the alternatives?

Maurice Elliott's offer had got her juices flowing. Working for a political party would open up new horizons, pose new challenges, rejuvenate her appetite for the cut and thrust of media jostling. And yet, she wasn't quite so sure about quitting her job with the *Post*. Crosby's derogatory remarks about her prospective employer bothered her. Elliott's reputation as a womanizer was legendary, but she liked to believe that what a person did in his or her leisure time was, within reason, that person's own business.

She still had two days to wrestle with the pros and cons of what the change of employment would entail. With her fortieth birthday looming on the horizon (just two and a half years away) she needed to take some mature decisions. Not that she felt or, for that matter, looked all that mature. Even so, she feared her figure had begun to show signs of slippage, especially on the three Bs: *boobs, belly* and *bum* – and this, in spite of a health-food diet regime and occasional visits to the gym. Her face – people said she was pretty – had not as yet shown any major negative indications of mileage. She worked hard to keep it that way, investing time and a sizeable chunk of her wages at the MAC counter in the Brown Thomas store. She took advice from the beauticians there, learning how to employ make-up cleverly and, on a good day, offered the world a confident smile. Her crowning glory, an abundance of golden-brown hair, framed her heart-shaped face to perfection and deflected attention away from what she considered to be her least attractive attribute – a splattering of freckles across her nose.

She read the words she'd brought up on the screen and sighed. Technically, the meaning and syntax were fine, but it was a soulless piece of prose with all the passion of an undertaker's after-dinner speech. In the normal course of events she would bin it, start again, reconstruct the article, look for clever similes, invest a spark of energy into the words and create a dynamic. Yeah, right, but not today, today she couldn't dredge up enough enthusiasm to even try.

There was a degree of irony to her situation that hadn't escaped her. It stemmed from a constant conflict that had bedevilled her marriage. Many of her investigative projects were concerned with the sleazy world of crime and corruption. She had, on occasions, put her personal safety on the line, a factor that had greatly agitated Vinny. He'd wanted her to switch from investigative journalism to something safer, but she'd refused to budge.

And now, with her marriage on the scrap heap, she was contemplating giving up the very job that had caused so much friction. There was, however, one major difference: nobody was forcing her hand this time, the decision to leave or stay was down to her alone, no one else.

And what of the new man in her life?

She had told him of course, but he didn't wish to influence her one way or another. 'Do what you feel is right,' had been his advice, his attitude in marked contrast to Vinny's overly protective and suffocating anxiety. She decided she would press him on the subject when they met later, gauge from his comments how he really felt about it. Another thought struck her: she would call him on the mobile, get him to agree to meet her after work. They would eat out – low-calorie, low-fat fare for her, the whole works for him – and wash it down with a bottle of house wine while discussing the question of her employment, see if he let something slip, something that would let her know how he was thinking. With a smile on her face she punched the numbers that would put her in touch with him.

CHAPTER 2

It had been three months since Detective Inspector Jim Connolly had visited the house he'd once shared with Iseult. He checked his watch before pressing the doorbell. Midday exactly. Sun shone down from an uncluttered sky bestowing a benevolence that left him unmoved today. Iseult had asked him to meet her at twelve o'clock. It had been the first time they'd spoken to each other since the separation and she'd refused to say why she wanted to see him except to stress the importance of showing up on the stroke of noon.

Connolly considered the time stipulation quite unnecessary; he had always been a stickler for punctuality, today would be no different. It was something of an Irish trait to regard time and its observance in a casual manner. Arriving at a party or get-together at the exact pre-arranged time would be seen as odd behaviour indeed. Connolly didn't hold with this practice. The midday angelus bell rang in nearby St Catherine's as he pulled up to the gateway. Turning into the driveway, a blue Volvo almost collided with him as it sped away from the house. He swerved just in time. It happened so fast that he'd been unable to observe the driver in any detail.

Standing on the front porch, a twin-pillared structure that owed no allegiance to any order of architecture, he dismissed the incident, still trying to figure why Iseult had requested his presence.

A high-noon showdown perhaps?

No, she'd never arrange anything so melodramatic, not her style at all.

He wondered if his summons might be some kind of wind-up; today was after all 1 April, April Fools' Day. He dismissed the thought; even at the best of times, when their relationship had been operating on an almost tolerable level, Iseult never indulged in such frivolity. Her take on humour was sharp, spiteful and vicious. If a school for stand-up cruelty existed, she'd be leader of the pack.

He had never felt comfortable with this house. It represented the first tangible evidence that his life with the lovely Iseult Smyth-O'Brien would be no picnic. Eleven years ago, on the return from their honeymoon, her first act had been to bring him to see the house. Its location, a city suburb whose demographics placed it among the most affluent in the country, alarmed him. He'd thought she wanted him to buy it and begun to explain that a detective's salary would never stretch to such extravagance. His assumptions had been incorrect: the house was already theirs. 'It's *Daddy*'s wedding present,' she'd proclaimed proudly. 'Surprise, surprise!'

It had been a seminal moment, one that lived on in his brain and still rankled.

He jabbed the doorbell three times in rapid succession, the old resentments bubbling up inside of him. He wanted to get this over with, get away from here, away from the bitter memories he associated with the place.

Should I let myself in?

He still had the key to the house on his keyring. It occurred to him that Iseult would have changed the lock but he tried the key anyway. It worked. He pushed the door open and stepped into the hallway. 'Anyone home?' he called out.

There was no answer. He moved to the kitchen, called out again. Still no answer. Venturing upstairs, he noticed that the carpets on the stairs and landing had been changed and that new pictures adorned the walls. The bathroom had been refurbished; brand new suite and tiles. It was as though he was in a different house. The master bedroom, too, had been given a thorough makeover. The king-size bed had been turned at right angles to the position it occupied in his time. Walking around it brought back memories, some of them profound. Perversely, what little happiness they'd enjoyed had been realized between the sheets of this bed. Sadness welled up inside him; he never could understand why it had all gone so wrong, given the fact that, physically, they had been totally compatible, capable of indulging in bouts of wild, erotic passion, comfortable with each other's sexual needs.

There was a mark on the ceiling he used to stare at in the aftermath of their lovemaking. It vaguely resembled the letter 'g', so he'd christened it his post-coitus G-spot. Was it still there? He sat on the side of the bed, arched his head back and looked up. It was gone. Then he remembered; everything in the room had been repositioned.

He ran his fingers through his hair, smiling to himself at how easily he had been lured into the past. He got off the bed and began to smooth the indentation his body had made when he noticed something odd. The sheets and covering were not as they ought to be. Iseult had a specific way of making a bed, a habit she'd picked up from her mother who'd been a nurse. Instead of tucking the sheet beneath the mattress, she folded the material with mitre corners. She'd been fastidious about it. The sheets were now tucked beneath the mattress and none too tidily at that. What could have brought about such a departure from habitual practice?

Moving to the bedroom window, he gazed down at the sundappled grounds and the dissecting driveway that led to the front courtyard. Considering the time of year, the place looked really well. An unusually mild winter had given the lawn and surrounding hedgerow a head start on summer. Involuntarily, his eyes closed, his mind rewinding mentally, forcing him to revisit, re-experience a scene he'd witnessed from this very window.

He had arrived home late from work one night and found that Iseult was absent, an occurrence that had become a frequent aspect of their troubled marriage. He'd showered, gone to bed and dozed off when the sound of a car pulling into the driveway awoke him. He heard the car doors slam, heard Iseult and a man laugh and talk outside. It was obvious that both had been drinking. He'd got out of bed, gone to the window and watched them move unsteadily towards the front door, watched as they disappeared beneath the awning. Moments later, he'd heard a slow rhythmic sound: *thump, thump, thump*. He'd thought his ears were deceiving him, that such behaviour was anathema to Iseult. Lest there be any doubt about the significance of the sound, he identified the grunts and groans Iseult exuded when sexually aroused, sounds that until that moment he'd naïvely believed were exclusively reserved for him.

His body shuddered as the portal to that fraught time-dimension shut down. Too much pain remained lodged in the grim nostalgia, too much humiliation buried in the mind's imaginings; time to fast-forward to the present, to reality, to the here and now. He wanted to get out of this house. Returning downstairs, he put his hand on the front door latch, ready to leave, but hesitated. It was possible, he reasoned, that Iseult had been detained somewhere. He would give her another five minutes.

Like the master bedroom, the décor on the ground floor had been spruced up. Framed photographs that showed the two of them together had been removed from the sideboard. Effectively, Iseult had erased all trace of him. But curiosity – always a good quality in a cop – made him open a drawer at the base of the drinks cabinet. The family photographs had been stored here during his tenure in the house. It surprised him to discover that their wedding album remained in its usual place.

They'd looked the ideal couple on that momentous day; picture-perfect wedding, formal wear, the whole nine yards. Iseult looked beautiful. Stunning, in fact. Her face flawless, the head perched delicately above a long graceful neck, crowned with gold strands of hair, neatly swept back and held in place beneath a white veil of lace and crowned with a sparkling tiara. His own image, complete with top hat, high collar, and tails, looking towards the camera with eyes that, it seemed to him now, exuded pride. He'd been blessed with better than average looks. He was tall, had good hair – perfectly groomed – and took care to dress well at all times. He'd been 34 then but apart from the appearance of silver strands in his hair, he liked to think he hadn't changed all that much in the intervening years.

He was about to flick to another page of the album when a background noise caught his attention. A low humming sound. It had been evident since entering the house but it hadn't bothered him until now. It sounded a bit like a fridge or deep-freeze cabinet, yet different enough to attract his attention. He put the album back in the drawer and set about tracking down the source of the sound. The hum was more discernible in the kitchen. He inspected the cooker, opened the oven and dismissed it, crossed to the fridge, listened for a moment before ruling it out too. Perplexed, he took a look in the utility room, a small area next to the kitchen. The sound was more pronounced here. He went to the chest freezer thinking that at last he'd pinpointed the source. But he was wrong.

He approached the connecting door that led from the utility room to the garage. In that instant, he identified where the sound was coming from. He put his hand on the handle to open the door and noticed two things at once: the fitting was loose and the handle didn't work. Someone had jimmied the lock. He pushed the door open and stepped into the garage. Iseult's Audi was there, its engine purring, its windows totally fogged on the inside.

He dashed to the driver's door. 'Oh, Christ no,' he said aloud, wrenching it open. Through the haze he could see Iseult's body slumped over the steering wheel. The carbon monoxide fumes got to him immediately, choking him, stinging his eyes. He clamped his hand over his mouth and nose and managed to switch off the ignition. His breathing became more laboured by the second, his eyes now smarting badly. He stumbled towards the garage door, kicked open the small man-sized door within its framework and clambered outside. He gulped down a lungful of clean air and hurried back to Iseult. He pulled her from the car, laid her on the garage floor and examined the body. There was no sign of life, no response. He attempted the kiss of life, his lips covering hers in a cruel parody of past intimacies. 'Come on, Iseult,' he urged, 'breathe, breathe, breathe.' He struggled until exhaustion and the effect of poisonous air overcame him but her body remained limp, unresponsive, her eyes lifeless.

Badly shaken, he stood back from the body. It was then he noticed a length of black industrial hose fixed to the exhaust, its other extremity pushed through a small opening above the car's rear-door window. He jerked the hose free, threw it to the garage floor, watched it coil reptilian-like beneath the car as lingering fumes continued to spew from its killer aperture.

He needed to organize his thoughts, report the suicide to the appropriate authorities. In his capacity as detective, he'd been present at many death scenes, including gruesome murders and road crash fatalities, but this was different, *very* different His stomach churned, the urge to retch almost unbearable. 'Iseult,' he said aloud, 'what in Christ's name have you done?' As though in answer, his mobile phone sounded. He broke eye contact with his ex-wife to glance at the mobile's display panel; it was a number very familiar to him.

CHAPTER 3

'Jim, can you hear me?' Emma said, pressing the mobile to her ear.

'Yes, yes, Emma, I hear you … it's just that …'

'What Jim?'

'It's Iseult … she's dead. Iseult's dead. Suicide, looks like suicide. It's awful, just awful—'

'Oh, my God! When did this happen? How'd you find out?'

'I … I found her.'

'You—?'

'She called me, asked me to meet her in the house.'

'*She* called *you*? But … why would she do that?'

'I don't know, Emma. Out of the blue I got this call; she asked me to meet her … "see you at midday", she said. I got here but nobody was home.'

'Iseult wasn't there?'

'That's what I'm saying. I let myself in, had a look around. Place seemed empty … no sign of anyone. I heard a noise in the garage … had a look, found her in the car. Engine was running … got the fright of my life … tried to revive her but I was too late … she was dead.'

'Jesus Christ, that's terrible, really terrible. Where are you now?'

'I'm here … with the body. It's just happened. I was about to call the authorities when you rang.'

'Her father? Does he know?'

'No, no one knows. Like I said, I've just discovered her.'

'Oh Christ, why would she …? Is there anything I can do?'

'No, no, not really. I need to make some calls.'

'Yeah right, of course. Call me, call me as soon as—'

'Sure, Emma. Could take some time.'

'Yes, of course, I understand. Talk to you … whenever.'

Emma tried to visualize the scene. Detective Inspector Jim

Connolly, the man she loved, the man she'd left her husband for, standing next to the body of his ex-wife, his *dead* ex-wife. It was unnerving. She'd long felt an irrational resentment towards Jim's ex, but the realization that Iseult had taken her own life sent shudders through her. What little she knew about Iseult had been gleaned from remarks Connolly had let slip from time to time, insights into their hapless marriage. She'd slotted these insights together, jigsaw fashion, and conjured up an image of what it must have been like. From the start, it would appear the Connollys' union had been a disaster. Yet, when the detective had shown up on his parents' doorstep with Iseult, daughter of the wealthy and well-connected Smyth-O'Briens, the omens looked promising. Mother and Father described the proposed nuptials as being Heaven sent. Connolly was later to admit that the union had more likely been concocted in Hell. Living with Iseult, he claimed, had been akin to hanging on to one of those fairground mechanical bulls programmed to throw off those attempting to cling on. It was only when he discovered Iseult *in flagrante* did he accept the futility of prolonging the charade.

Before this marital upheaval, Emma had got to know Connolly; they had co-operated on a number of cases and had developed a trust and friendship. One case in particular had been pivotal in cementing their relationship. She'd been pregnant at the time with her first – and only – baby. To gain front-page banner headlines, she'd exposed herself to unnecessary risk. Disaster struck. In an encounter with the 'enemy' she'd been pushed down an escalator. She'd lost the baby. Too late, she'd learned that her priorities were misplaced.

In the days and weeks that followed, she'd drifted into a state of depression, returned to her parents' home, binged on food, piled on the weight and shut out the world. Connolly had been the one to get her to shake off the despondency. He'd visited her, persuaded her to help him with a new case. She embarked on her first ever crash diet and re-engaged with the world of investigative journalism. A strengthened friendship resulted, a friendship that blossomed into full-blown romance over time.

There was, however, a downside. Wasn't there always? In tandem with this burgeoning friendship, Emma's disillusionment vis-à-vis Vinny had been gathering apace. Losing the baby had been a catalyst for change; the rose-tinted glasses she'd hitherto viewed the world through had been shattered. In their stead, self-loathing and recrimination reigned supreme. Even now, six years later, the horror remained, the details forever present, never setting her free.

The escalator, yes, I am pushed. I tumble down, crashing into the steel-edged flight of steps, seeing the sunlit glass atrium flash on and off with dazzling speed, still falling, hurting, feeling sharp darts of pain, my body bouncing into shoppers. Blood, God Almighty! Blood on my face, blood in my eyes, a sea of blood. People surround me, a forest of legs, elongated arms, distorted hands reach down to me, and then, for a moment a face, a familiar face ... Vinny's face. The world swims out of focus. There is nothing, a void, no sound, just emptiness ... then, out of nowhere, the sound of squeaking trolley wheels. I travel through long corridors, through sets of swinging Perspex doors, into an alien world inhabited by people in white coats, green coats, face masks, starched uniforms. I am aware of pain, a great pain, but it is a far away thing, tearing at me in a different dimension. Blackness descends again, darker than the darkest night. From out of this void a distorted voice penetrates. The words are meaningless, little more than abstract sounds — uterus haemorrhage, pneumothorax, feotoplacental perfusion, severe trauma, suspected perineal weakness – just meaningless utterances. Sometime later, a kindly voice says, 'I'll send in your husband now if you like?' I hear myself reply, 'Please ... I would prefer ... I need, that is ... to be left on my own for a little while.'

Vinny put on a show of magnanimity, hiding his own hurt, never once hinting at attribution of blame for what had happened. She hated him for that, hated the look in his eyes that failed to cloak censure. The seeds of resentment had taken hold; she'd begun to hide things from him. At first, her sins were merely ones of omission. She'd neglected to let him know she was on the pill. He had wanted to get back into the baby-making business right away; she had no such desire. When he'd discovered her deception, a row ensued, a row that continued to reverberate to the very end.

Connolly's separation from Iseult helped Emma surrender to the feelings she'd suppressed for so long. She left Vinny. Their apartment went on the market and was snapped up within days, bringing in twenty times what they'd paid for it. Proceeds were split down the middle. Vinny moved to his father's house in Little Bray; she moved in with Connolly as a temporary measure. The plan had been to buy another apartment or small house, assert her independence, but sharing a bed with the detective had dulled her interest in pursuing that objective.

And now Connolly's ex was dead, something Emma was having difficulty getting her head around. Thinking about it, she decided she would go to the house, let Connolly know she was there for him. This was going to be a terrible time for both of them and it was important that they support each other. Emma would never have envisaged benefiting from such an occurrence, yet somewhere deep in the back of her mind, she believed that Iseult's demise would finally rid Jim Connolly of the monkey that had, until now, clung to his back.

seult Connolly's house had become a hive of activity by the time Emma pulled into the driveway. Police, medical personnel and forensic were in situ. She nosed her Hyundai into a space between a row of cars, got out and viewed the house that had figured so large in Connolly's troubled marriage, a stately two-storey redbrick screened by a high granite wall, part of the privileged enclave that lay between Dalkey and Killiney. It was the kind of house her ex would call a des-res with knobs on. The two-car garage attached to the west gable looked spacious enough to accommodate an average family. The front lawn, benefiting from its first mowing since winter, impregnated the air with the smell of freshly cut grass. Early April sunshine bathed the cultivated landscape, its brightness glistening off the border of daffodils lining the driveway.

Movement in the vicinity of the garage caught her eye. A small man-sized door, part of the garage's main door structure, stood partly ajar. Through it, Emma caught sight of camera lights and the bottom half of white-clad figures. She had to squint to get better focus but just as she identified the shape of a car, the small door closed. End of peep show.

As Emma entered the house's front porch a young garda officer, looking as though he'd just stepped into his policeman's uniform for the first time that morning, stopped her. 'Sorry, ma'am, no one's allowed access.'

Bending the truth, Emma explained that Detective Inspector Connolly had requested her presence. This confused him. He was about to check procedures through his walkie-talkie when a silver Mercedes entered the driveway at considerable speed. It veered erratically on to the lawn, barely avoiding the parked cars, sending clusters of daffodils in all directions before screeching to a halt mere inches from the porch steps. The officer, reverting to traffic-control mode, strode purposefully towards the offending vehicle. A big, red-faced man in a business suit emerged hurriedly from behind the wheel. Emma recognized Edmund Smyth-O'Brien. This was Iseult Connolly's father, a high-profile businessman, listed in the country's top fifty richest people. Right now he looked ready to explode.

'Where's Iseult?' he growled, in a voice that left little room for dissent. The officer's mouth groped for words as Smyth-O'Brien barrelled past him and up the steps.

Emma followed in the big man's slipstream, taking advantage of the policeman's momentary inaction. White-clad forensic personnel, subjecting the scene to minute inspection, glanced disapprovingly at the intruders but continued with their tasks. Smyth-O'Brien, obviously well acquainted with the house's interior, barged into the garage. 'Who's in charge?' he enquired, in an intimidating rasp.

Detective Inspector Jim Connolly looked apprehensively towards his ex-father-in-law and appeared startled by Emma's appearance. Next to him, Chief Superintendent Laz Rochford stood, an imposing man in his fifties with athletic build, chiselled facial features, deep-set eyes and close-cropped steel-grey hair. He flashed a withering glance in Emma's direction before clasping Smyth-O'Brien by the elbow in an attempt to usher him from the garage.

At first, the forensic crew obscured Iseult's body, but Emma caught sight of it when one of the white suits moved aside. Death always induced a queasy feeling in her stomach. This was no different. Iseult lay on the cold cement floor, hands by her side, a vacant stare in her open eyes. Emma remembered Connolly once describing Iseult's beauty as being akin to fine porcelain, adding the rider that she could be every bit as cold. Looking at the body now, it occurred to her that the unnatural repose resembled, more accurately, that of a wax dummy.

Connolly moved to Emma's side, a weary expression on his face. 'What are you doing here?' he asked in a hurried whisper.

'Thought you'd like some moral support,' she whispered back. 'Didn't expect this lot, though. How'd they get here so quickly?'

'They've been tipped off.'

Raised voices coming from Smyth-O'Brien and Rochford brought their hushed words to an end. Rochford appeared to be holding Smyth-O'Brien back from approaching the body.

'You're wrong, I tell you,' Smyth-O'Brien said stridently, 'Iseult would never do such a thing.' He lunged at the forensic technician who'd been photographing the body, grabbed him by the collar of his white overalls, shunted him out of the way before he hunkered down to inspect his daughter's body. 'She's been murdered, damn you,' he cried out bitterly. 'Don't you see? She's been murdered, I tell you ...'

Two technicians hauled him off the body. 'I'm sorry,' Rochford said, 'we can't let you interfere with the scene until we're through here.'

Smyth-O'Brien froze for a moment, then swung round and pointed his forefinger in Connolly's direction. '*You're* responsible,' he said, 'you're behind this whole charade, you're—'

Chief Superintendent Rochford intervened before Connolly could reply. 'Come now, Mr Smyth-O'Brien, this is a dreadful shock for you; let's go back inside the house ... we can talk there ... see what's to be done.'

Reluctantly, Smyth-O'Brien allowed Rochford to usher him from the garage, both men fixing Connolly with accusatorial glances as they exited.

'What am I missing?' Emma asked Connolly.

'Let's get out of here,' he said, moving towards the garage door. He opened the small inset door and placed his hand on her head to prevent it hitting the frame. Outside, an ambulance had pulled to a stop at the front porch, its driver in conversation with the garda officer. The sun had gone behind a bank of cloud and the first drops of an imminent shower spat down. Connolly closed the small door behind him. 'Look, Emma, I think it might be best if you were to leave.'

'Why?'

'There's more here than meets the eye.'

'What do you mean?'

'I don't know,' he replied with a shake of the head. 'Something's amiss here; something's not right.'

'Like what ... what are you saying?'

'There's a suggestion of suspicious circumstances—'

'Suspicious circumstances. Are you suggesting—?'

'—that it might not be suicide.'

'Not suicide? You've lost me ... What—?'

'Apparently, a 999 call was made ... a woman claimed that someone was being raped at this address. The call was logged at twelve o'clock midday.'

'But ... that's the time you were asked here.'

'Exactly.'

CHAPTER 5

The sight of Iseult's dead body had knocked her world out of kilter. It was as though something ominous, something malevolent, was out there waiting to devour her. Emma tried to imagine the horror Connolly must be feeling. A shudder travelled the length of her body. They would need each other's strength to get through the coming days. Her plan to dine with him in one of the chic eateries in Temple Bar was no longer an option; likewise, her plan to discuss her impending change of employment.

It was now eight o'clock, still no sign of him. Feeling restless, she forced herself up from the couch, switched off the television and moved to the lounge's main window. Four floors above ground level, the room afforded her a panoramic view of the River Liffey and its many bridges. Fading daylight had triggered the streetlights into their first phase of orange illumination. An April shower, highlighted in the jaundiced glow, fell softly on the quayside traffic. Triple glazed windows helped muffle the sound coming from the slow-moving trucks, buses and cars below her. Gulls criss-crossed the river and quays, taking pot shots at the vehicles, occasionally scoring splash-hits with their deposits. All this perpetual motion barely registered with Emma.

Her thoughts remained on Connolly. Not big on conspiracy theories, it seemed to her that something peculiar was afoot. Who, for instance, had called the police claiming that a rape was in progress in Iseult's house? And, wasn't it strange that the call should have been logged on the stroke of midday? She was still pondering the mysterious events when a sound from the landing distracted her. 'That you, Jim?' she called out.

There was no reply.

She could hear feet shuffling on the timber floor. Puzzled now, she opened the door. The sight made her gasp. Connolly had propped himself against the wall, a foolish grin on his face and a bag of chips clasped in his hand. The smell of booze overpowered the whiff coming from the fries. 'How are you?' he said, proffering the grease sodden bag in her face, 'Want one?'

'You're drunk,' she said in disbelief. Rarely had he abused alcohol and never, to her knowledge, had he eaten chips from a paper bag. 'Getting rat-arsed isn't going to solve anything.'

Connolly belched. 'Decided to have a few scoops ... then got peckish,' he said, popping another chip in his mouth.

Emma sighed. 'Can't blame you I suppose,' she said, 'finding Iseult—'

'Wasn't that at all,' he said, trying to eradicate the slurring. 'Got suspended ... had words with Rochford ... told him to shove his job.'

'Oh, for God's sake, Jim. I don't believe I'm hearing this; *you* of all people, what the hell were you playing at?'

'It's a long story,' he said, the words coming out: *izz-zah-longstorrry*.

Emma shook her head ruefully. 'Right, Jim, I'll brew some coffee.'

Plying him with caffeine, she restored a measure of equilibrium to his alcohol-doused brain. With patience, perseverance and not a little persuasion, she elicited a coherent account of what happened. It helped explain why he'd hit the booze. 'Tell me again what Iseult's father said?'

'Edmund Smyth-O'Brien claims Iseult called him this morning. She told him she'd been out horse riding and had come home before midday. She heard screams coming from the master bedroom, dashed upstairs and caught me in the act of raping Nuala Buckley.'

'Remind me again who Nuala Buckley is?'

'A friend of Iseult's ... and the daughter of Shane Buckley.'

'You mean *the* Shane Buckley, the racing tycoon?'

'The very man. But he and Nuala fell out years ago. He disapproved of her wayward lifestyle, threw her out when she became pregnant. She was hard up for cash so Iseult took her on for three days a week – supposedly to help with the housekeeping, but in reality it was just a pretext.'

'And Iseult told her father you raped this woman, right?'

'Yes, but get this: I'm supposed to have punched Nuala in the face, leaped off the bed and charged down the stairs after Iseult. I mean, for Christ's sake, can you see *me* doing something like that?'

'Of course not! What's supposed to have happened next?'

'Apparently, Iseult made her way to the garage, locked the connecting door and called *Daddy* on her mobile, implored him to come rescue her.'

'That's some story.'

Connolly snorted. 'Yeah, a regular *grim* fairy-tale.'

'It's pure daft. So, how did you and Rochford end up quarrelling?'

'A strange set of circumstances,' Connolly replied, his words more or less back to their normal cadence. 'They found bloodstains on the sheets, the lock on the garage door had been tampered with and my fingerprints were everywhere. An anonymous caller informed the police that a rape was in progress and, on top of that, Nuala Buckley has gone missing. So, I suppose it's hardly surprising that Rochford decided to suspend me.'

'When they track down this missing woman, she'll confirm your account; that'll put an end to this nonsense. It's obvious that Iseult concocted the whole thing to land you in trouble.'

Connolly shook his head. 'No, Emma, you're wrong. Iseult might very well despise me but she would never take her own life just to get at me.'

'What makes you so sure?'

'She loved herself far too much.'

'Am I missing something here?' Emma asked, her mind racing. 'If Iseult didn't commit suicide, then it follows she's been murdered. Yet, you say there was no one there except you … that can't be right, can it? I mean, someone else had to be present….'

'I checked the rooms, didn't see anybody.'

'Then, please, explain to me what happened?'

'I can't. I do have some ideas though.'

'Oh?'

'As I entered the driveway, a car shot past me on its way out.'

'So, there *was* someone there … before you arrived, yes? Did you get a look at the driver?'

'Not really. Could've been a woman; I didn't get a good look.'

'Was it the woman you're supposed to have raped?'

'Nuala Buckley? No, definitely not; Nuala is small, petite, cropped hair. The person I saw was larger and had longish hair.'

'You got the car registration, right?'

'Not a chance. I was far too busy swerving out of the way.'

'You didn't give chase?'

'No, I didn't. Under normal circumstances I probably would have, but I was preoccupied at the time, wondering what the hell Iseult wanted.'

Emma was about to probe further when the intercom rang. 'Hello,' she said into the speaker, 'who is it?'

'Detective Inspector Seán Grennan and Sergeant Tony Lidden. We'd like a word with Detective Inspector Connolly. May we come up?'

Emma covered the intercom with her hand, told Connolly who was at the door. He nodded and indicated that she should allow them come up. Moments later two men stood in her living-room. Grennan showed his ID to Emma before squaring up to Connolly. Nature had not been kind to Grennan; he had a puffy face, truncated neck, a tight crew-cut of smoky-grey hair and small piggy eyes. In his late forties, his thickset body was oddly proportioned: longish torso, short legs, no discernible waist, the kind of figure designed to challenge even the most resourceful tailor. His partner, Sergeant Lidden, a tall, weak-chinned man was younger, thirties or thereabouts, dressed like a Jehovah's Witness, all neat and tidy. He left the talking to Grennan.

Connolly offered to shake hands with Grennan, saying to Emma, 'I trained with this man in Templemore.'

Grennan studiously avoided Connolly's hand. 'I'm here to arrest you,' he said, in a thick midlands' accent.

Connolly looked puzzled. 'What are you talking about? I've spoken with the chief super and he knows that Iseult's death—'

''Tisn't Iseult's death we're bothered about at this juncture,' Grennan said, with a know-it-all smirk. 'We're here because of Nuala Buckley.'

'What?' Connolly said, his bewilderment turning to annoyance.

Grennan placed his hand on Connolly's shoulder. 'Under Section Four of the Criminal Justice Act 1984, I'm taking you in for questioning concerning grievous bodily harm inflicted on one Nuala Buckley.'

Emma moved to Connolly's side. 'Tell me this isn't for real?'

'He's just doing his job,' Connolly told her, 'It'll all be sorted out in a few hours. There's nothing to worry about, I haven't touched anybody.'

Emma listened, dumbfounded, as Grennan cautioned Connolly and led him from the room. 'Where are you taking him?' she asked.

It was Connolly who answered. 'Dun Laoghaire Garda Station.'

CHAPTER 6

he tabby, peering out from the picture, possessed what Emma considered an independence of spirit. One of several feline exhibits on the restaurant's walls, this particular cat's eyes, with pupils contracted to mere longitudinal slits, appeared to single her out for minute scrutiny. Emma liked cats. Growing up in a spacious old-world house in Slane, Co Meath, she'd been used to animals, especially cats. Her mother, Hazel, kept several cats at all times for the most practical of reasons; they ensured that the immediate vicinity remained off limits to the mice population. Many of those felines had been her pets, all of them independent, all with different attitudes. Cats, she'd discovered, didn't provide the slavish devotion of dogs but were aesthetically more appealing and, once you accepted them on their terms, capable of intriguing companionship. She broke eye contact with the framed image, emptied a sachet of brown sugar into her coffee, and returned her attention to the man sitting opposite her.

Breaking bread with Bob Crosby had in the past heralded awkward stories or exclusive scoops, usually the ones with litigation implications. On those occasions, Bob chose to talk to her away from the prying eyes, ears and keyboards of the paper's other journalists. From hard won experience, they'd learned that the *Post* represented the very personification of bitchy, competitive work environments. When it came to protecting a good story, the newsroom was nothing less than a den of thieves.

Crosby's venue for early morning *tête-à-tête* briefings seldom varied; he liked The Cat's Pyjamas, an up-market café on the Baggot Street junction with Fitzwilliam. The place was bright, clean and refrained from inflicting piped music on its clientele; service was efficient and unobtrusive. Morning trade was brisk, every table occupied, caffeine addicts imbibing their first fix, executive types grabbing a spot of breakfast before facing the rigours of the day, some reading morning papers or chatting quietly, while others, not totally released from their nocturnal slumber, sleep-walked through their collation. No one bothered Crosby or Emma. The only prying eyes were those staring out from the feline portraits.

Connolly, subject of the breaking story under discussion, represented something special to both of them: a common denominator that solidified their interests. In Emma's case, he was her lover – about as up-close and personal as it gets; as for Bob Crosby, he was a lifelong friend and confidant. That Connolly should have been taken into police custody the previous evening had come as a shock to both of them.

'I can't believe what's happened,' Emma was saying, the strain of events reflecting in her eyes. 'It's like some kind of elaborate practical joke.'

'Know what you mean,' Crosby empathized, spreading Kerrygold on his toast. 'I think the lunatics really have taken over the bloody asylum. I tried to talk to him last night ... didn't succeed.'

'I know; I tried to make contact myself got nowhere either.'

'I got stroppy, told this big red-neck inspector named Grennan who I was ... he couldn't give a monkey's. Later, I got one of my contacts in the force to fill me in.'

'What'd he say?'

Crosby put aside the marmalade he'd been heaping on his toast. 'It's a bit like those American detective series we used to watch in the 80s and 90s,' he said with a sardonic smile. 'Each week the main detective is falsely accused of involvement in a crime and his hard-arse boss demands his gun and badge. By the end of the episode he's reinstated, has his badge and gun returned and shakes hands with hard-arse as the credits roll. Following week, a variation on the theme happens all over again.'

'You saying Connolly's in a similar fix?' Emma asked. She called the man she loved *Connolly*, not *Jim*, when speaking to others, an affectation she'd picked up from his friends; it was, she discovered, an inverted term of affection that went back to his college days.

'Yeah,' Crosby said, 'except that the fix Connolly's in is not part of any Hollywood script. Superintendent Laz Rochford seems to believe – in spite of Connolly's exemplary record – he might be involved in what's happened.'

'What exactly *has* happened?'

Crosby waited while a waitress refilled their coffees before replying. 'Officially, no details have been released but I managed to get a brief outline from my contact. Nuala Buckley's body was found in the boiler shed at the rear of Iseult's house, still alive, but unconscious. Signs of a struggle were evident. They rushed her to hospital, put her on life-support … it's not good.'

Emma grimaced. 'Oh my God, that's terrible.'

'About as ugly as it gets.'

'How'd they know where to look?'

'Soon as word got out that Shane Buckley was Nuala's father the case took on a new urgency. In a search at Iseult Connolly's residence bloodstained sheets were found in the master bedroom. A bit later they discovered Nuala's unconscious body beneath a roll of tarpaulin.'

'And Iseult … what's the latest on Iseult?' Emma asked.

'Far as I know, the state pathologist has been called in.'

Emma stared at her boss. 'And Connolly … is suspected of what … murder … rape? Is that where this is going?'

Crosby's crestfallen expression spoke volumes. 'I don't know, Emma,' he said with a sigh, 'no charges have been preferred.'

'Is that a possibility?'

'What … that he'll be charged? God, I hope not. But with heavies like Edmund Smyth-O'Brien and Shane Buckley hovering in the background, the top-brass in Pearse St are determined to cover their collective arses.'

'This is bullshit,' Emma said, 'Connolly didn't *do* anything. The very idea that he'd rape … or attempt to kill someone is so … so ludicrous.'

'Couldn't agree with you more; Connolly wouldn't hurt a fly.'

'Yeah, except we're not dealing with a bloody fly …' Emma took a deep breath. 'I'm sorry, this whole thing is getting to me. I keep forgetting that you and Connolly go back a long way.'

A pained expression touched Crosby's face. 'You're right about that; we've been close since our teenage years.'

'Products of the Jesuits, right?'

'Right. I was senior to him but we got to know each other through sports. We were industrious lads back then, didn't neglect the books, got enough points to take our pick of university faculties. I hadn't the foggiest notion what career to pursue, plumped for English at Trinity in the end.'

'Should have brought him along with you.'

'Yes, maybe I should have, but, well, he was different, he knew exactly what he wanted. Against all advice, mine included, he followed the dictates of his heart, joined the police force, became a member of *An Garda Síochána.*'

'An odd choice for someone with such academic acumen.'

'That's one way of putting it. He told me it was a dream he'd cherished since boyhood. A bit like a priesthood vocation was how he put it, except in his case the calling came from the forces of law and order, not the Almighty. His parents were aghast; they did not, and would not, understand. I met them at the time, got the impression they were slightly ashamed of him. It was funny really; I overheard someone ask his mother what career her son had chosen. In answer, she uttered just the one word – *law*, and left it at that.'

'I presume their attitude softened when he rose through the ranks?'

'Nope! It never did. Even after he'd made detective inspector grade, they still behaved as though he'd failed them.'

'Just as well they're not alive today. Imagine what they'd say if they knew about this business with his wife ... or that he'd been accused of rape?'

'I doubt they'd be too impressed. The ironic thing is, marrying Iseult actually met with their approval. The fact that she was one of *the* Smyth-O'Briens compensated for his earlier transgressions.'

'You knew Iseult back then, yeah?'

'Sure, I did. Like a lot of other fellows, I was madly in lust with her.'

'You? You're serious? You fancied Iseult?'

'Don't look so shocked. I didn't always carry this bulk, didn't always have blood pressure, piles, ulcers and the compulsion to indulge in gastronomic extravaganzas. I'll have you know I was a handsome devil back then; it was said that I looked a lot like Timothy Bottoms.'

'*Whose* bottom?'

'Very funny, Emma; no, Timothy Bottoms is a fine actor; he's— Doesn't matter, fact is, I fancied Iseult Smyth-O'Brien something rotten. She was a real beaut, had all us young bucks striving to win the treasure she sat upon. A bit above my social standing admittedly, drank cocktails, went horse-riding, accompanied her parents on exotic holidays, wore the latest fashions and had her own car. I tried to chat her up once in Zoo's nightclub, plied her with drink and gave her my best lines.'

'And...?'

'Didn't work! Thought I'd pulled, but when I made my move she just smiled at me as though I was the village idiot.'

'So, how come Connolly managed to make it with her?'

'Good question. The answer to which remains a mystery ... even to this day. I've tried to analyse it, tried to figure how he managed to hook her. Connolly moved in some years after she'd given me the bum's rush. I'd no idea he fancied her, never thought of them as an item. Can't figure how he did it. I mean, OK, he had the looks and all that, but he was never what you might call a woman's man. Didn't have the moves ... if you know what I mean.'

'Like you had?'

'Now, now, Emma, you're mocking me,' Crosby said, wagging his finger at her and smiling. 'Anyway, for whatever reason, Iseult fell for him; they got married and the rest, as they say, is history.'

'Yes, a sad saga that has just taken a turn for the worse. Wait 'til our fellow hacks connect him to the case, they'll have a bloody field day. I'm going to find it difficult to report on this one.'

'That's not going to happen,' Crosby said, catching the attention of a waitress and miming a scribble in the air for the bill, 'I've given the assignment to Willie Thompson.'

'Oh?'

'You're too close to this one.'

'And I wouldn't be objective, that it?'

'In a nutshell, yes.'

Emma remained silent while Crosby settled the account. She was miffed but could see the merit in his decision. She was about to say as much, when he leaned across to her and whispered, 'Don't look now but do you see the three women sitting at the table to the left of the wine racks?'

Emma nodded. The women Crosby referred to appeared over-dressed for early breakfast, even in a posh restaurant like The Cat's Pyjamas.

'What about them?' she asked.

'The brunette in the centre with the power suit, know who she is?'

The woman looked familiar to Emma but she couldn't come up with a name. Like the female companions on either side of her, the woman appeared to be in her late thirties, or well-preserved forties. 'Should I know her?'

'No, not really,' Bob said, a smile hovering at the corners of his mouth, 'not unless you've attended one of her snooty charity bashes ... but there's a chance you'll get to know her in the near future.'

'How'd you figure that?'

'Name's Diana Elliott; ring any bells?'

'You don't mean—?'

'Yep, wife of Maurice Elliott, entrepreneur *extraordinaire*, philanderer of note, and leader of the Social Alliance Party; the man who's trying to woo you away from the *Post*.'

Emma knew of Diana Elliott; the woman had made her name as a top public relations consultant before marrying Elliott. More recently she'd become the 'brand leader' in the world of international fund raising. Her picture appeared regularly in the social columns, usually in the company of luminaries such as Bono and Bob Geldof. This was Emma's first time to see her 'in the flesh' so to speak.

'You want to guess what they're talking about?' Crosby asked.

'You're not going to tell me they're discussing my employment?'

Crosby smiled. 'Don't flatter yourself, Emma. No, they're probably discussing Iseult's death. I saw Iseult with them here a few times and remember thinking – Ireland's very own home-grown desperate housewives; rich bitches, all of them. There's something of the feline about them, don't you think, kind of predatory if you know what I mean?'

'Are you taking about females in general, or these three in particular?'

'I'm talking about Diana Elliott and her circle of well-heeled friends. You might get to know them if you decide to work for Maurice Elliott.'

'Is this your way of eliciting an answer from me ... about my plans?'

Crosby frowned. 'No, not really, but it would help me to know—'

'I'll let you know before the day is out,' Emma said, getting up from her chair, anxious to leave.

'Good,' Crosby said, slipping into his overcoat. 'The sooner it's settled the better.' He held the door open for her and moved to her side, walking with a lightness that belied his bulk.

Emma remained silent, her thoughts fixated on Connolly. She needed to talk to him. What Crosby had said about Iseult knowing Diana Elliott had made her feel uneasy. She had no explanation for this feeling of apprehension except an instinct that overlapping events were somehow working against Connolly. Making a decision about changing employment seemed almost frivolous compared to the predicament he was in.

CHAPTER 7

Connolly's career was in free fall. Being incarcerated in a cell represented something far worse than mere humiliation. Ironic really, in the past he'd locked up countless men and women in similar small ten by eight feet cells, he'd stripped them of their dignity, denied them freedom, interrogated them, and yes, on occasions, treated them like shit. And now, to use his late mother's oft repeated saying – the shoe was on the other foot.

Already, he'd endured what felt like a lifetime in captivity but was in fact only twenty-four hours. Most of that time had been spent doing what came under the heading – *helping the police with their enquiries*. His interrogators were colleagues, people he'd worked with on a daily basis. This represented a new perspective for him, an opportunity to see his fellow officers in an altogether different light.

Detective Inspector Seán Grennan headed up the investigation and appeared to relish the task of pushing him through the hoops. The fact that they were fellow cops cut little ice. Grennan's waistcoat seemed ready to pop its buttons as he straddled a back-to-front chair like some fat-arsed cowboy, his short legs splayed on either side, his chest pressing against the backrest. His inquisition technique, heavily laden with bluster and foul language, something he'd probably picked up from made-for-television movies, was difficult to stomach. Connolly had tried to reason with him. 'Hey, Seán, lighten up, it's *me*, Connolly ... remember? We're on the same side, we're the good guys—'

'We're *not* on the same side,' Grennan shot back, ''tis smug fuckers' – he pronounced it *fookers* – 'like you that gives the rest of us a bad name.'

Exchanges went steadily downhill after that, making Connolly wonder why Grennan should act in such a belligerent fashion. Did he hold a grudge from their time as recruits back in training college?

From day one there had been a competitive edge between them. They'd competed for the same position on the football team and more often than not Connolly had got the nod. The college debates represented another bone of contention. Grennan and he had spoken on different motions, the discussions sometimes becoming heated affairs, the free-flowing repartee descending to a personal invective that invariably saw Grennan come off second best.

Could Grennan still resent me for that?

Connolly tried to analyse his predicament. There was much he didn't understand. Had he not known Iseult so well he might have accepted her death as suicide. But, he did know her; he knew her better than most people – eleven years of marriage will do that – and every fibre of his being told him that she would never take her own life. So, why had she called and arranged for him to be present when the fatal act occurred? He'd racked his brains on that one and was still no closer to coming up with a satisfactory answer.

And what of Nuala Buckley, the young woman now on life support, the woman he was supposed to have raped? Iseult had hired her, ostensibly to tidy the house three mornings a week. In reality it was more an act of charity, a description from which both women would have recoiled. For the most part, Nuala's hours in the house had coincided with his time at work. He'd met her socially on a few occasions when she'd come back with Iseult after show-jumping events. He had never had any serious conversation with her, but from the few words that passed between them he thought her bright, wilful and intelligent. He'd once asked Iseult how come the daughter of a multimillionaire needed a part-time job; she'd replied that Nuala had been disowned by her father and needed money to provide for the children.

His thoughts returned to Emma. What must she be thinking? She was the only person apart from himself and Crosby who believed in his innocence.

Wait a sec, I'm being presumptuous.

As an investigative journalist, Emma questioned everything – part of her job description. Yes, they loved and respected each other, but – wasn't there always a *but* – was it possible she harboured doubts? Like St Thomas Aquinas, Emma insisted on tangible proof. She had an enquiring mind; that was her trademark. Far better that she set about unearthing the truth than leave him dependent on the mercy of the closed mind-set of Seán Grennan.

*

On Bob Crosby's advice, Emma had taken the day off. He'd made it clear that he wanted her out of the newsroom. She'd been given little choice but to comply. He wanted to protect her – and in turn protect his beloved newspaper – from becoming part of the story.

Photographic spreads in the latest edition of the *Post* showed Iseult Connolly and her father, Edmund Smyth-O'Brien. Nuala Buckley got similar treatment: her picture, along with that of her father, and an aerial shot of the Buckley stud farm, were given generous coverage. Other news items were consigned to inside pages. The press, like the police, tended to pay more attention to crime reports when the victim's address was aligned to the city's more affluent districts. This was the sort of double-standard nonsense that Emma despised. Experience had taught her that the crime of murder in better-off echelons of society caused alarm in establishment circles. It was viewed as a sign that the social disorder and moral decline of the proletariat threatened the whole 'fabric of society'.

Connolly's name had already made it into the media on account of his marriage to Iseult. So far, no one had alluded to the fact that he'd been hauled in for questioning. Emma was concerned that, sooner or later, her liaison with Connolly would get dragged into the mix. There were several journalists, some within the *Post*, who resented the fact that she had, on two occasions, scooped the award for best journalist of the year. Jealousy was the all pervasive malady that went hand-in-hand with journalism. She shuddered to think what might be coming down the line and decided to visit her parents' home in Slane.

Exiting the city, via Finglas, she had a one-hour drive ahead of her, time enough to think about what she would tell her mother and father. If her involvement in Connolly's life became public, the possibility existed that they might be door-stepped by reporters. A similar threat applied to her estranged husband, Vinny Bailey and his father. She would have to warn them.

She stopped in Tathony's of Ashbourne, halfway point on her journey, and bought a box of Lir, hand-made chocolates, for her mother before pressing onward. Lost in thought, thinking about the events buffeting her life, a song on the car radio caught her attention. The tune *Filthy/Gorgeous* brought memories of Vinny into sharp focus, not because of the weird title but because he insisted on playing air-guitar along with the funky bass-line every time the Scissor Sister's song was aired. Even when driving, his hands would temporary leave the steering wheel, his fingers plucking the four invisible strings.

It shocked her that she could still be so affected by an unexpected reminder of her time with Vinny. They'd been together for ten years so it shouldn't come as any surprise that episodes from the past should barge into her already overcrowded mind. There had been excitement at first, their lovemaking tender and heartfelt, but towards the end the spark of spontaneity dulled to lacklustre conjugal familiarity and self-conscious fumbling.

She'd been investigating the death of a powerful businessman when she first encountered Vinny. He had just turned his back on his involvement with the Irish Republican movement at the time. Their relationship, initially hostile, moved unexpectedly on to a romantic plain ... and all the way to the altar.

Emma expelled a sigh of relief as she pulled into the driveway of her parents' house, a two-storey period residence set in the heart of Meath's rich pastureland. The view from her old bedroom window offered a picture postcard vista of the River Boyne. As a teenager, living with her parents, she hadn't fully appreciated the comforts and security of home. Like many young people, anxious for independence, she'd taken her parents' love for granted. When she'd moved to Dublin, the city overwhelmed and delighted her but within a matter of months, returning home for weekends became something to look forward to. A poem by Francis Ledwidge that she hadn't appreciated in her schooldays had more recently taken on a resonance with which she now fully empathized. The poet, a native of Slane had been killed in France fighting in the Great War in 1917.

> *I walk the old frequented ways*
> *That wind around the tangled braes,*
> *I live again the sunny days*
> *Ere I the city knew.*

After she'd married Vinny and moved to their own apartment, she saw far less of the home place. Today though, her second visit since the split from Vinny, was a cause for concern. She hoped it would be less difficult than the last awkward meeting she'd had with her mother.

Hazel Boylan greeted her with the usual hugs and kisses. A good-looking sprightly woman with a short pageboy hairstyle, she looked too young to be Emma's mother. She'd been devastated by the marriage break-up, her compassionate eyes giving way, for once, to rebuke. Her disquiet had turned to something approaching anger when she'd discovered that Emma had a new man in her life. Yet paradoxically, the love Hazel had for her only daughter remained strong as ever. In time, Emma hoped, her mother would come to terms with the new arrangements.

Over a cup of tea, as Emma sought the right moment to talk about the current difficulties, Hazel surprised her by introducing the topic herself. 'I read that Iseult Connolly was found dead under suspicious circumstances.' Her voice retained its rich and lyrical softness. 'That's your detective friend's wife, if I'm not mistaken?'

'Ex-wife,' Emma corrected, sounding overly defensive. 'Yes, his *ex*-wife committed suicide.'

'Suicide? Oh, dear Lord. Please tell me it had nothing to do with you taking up with her husband?'

'No, Mum, nothing like that; it's just that he was the one to find her.' Emma had no wish to start defending Connolly. She'd done that before when she'd first told Hazel of the relationship. It hadn't made the slightest difference then, it wouldn't make a difference now.

'He was still seeing her?'

'No, Mum, he wasn't,' Emma said, masking a sigh of exaspera-tion. 'Apparently, Iseult phoned and asked him to come to the house. When he got there he found her in the garage.'

'And what about this other woman? They found another woman at the Connolly home. She's on life-support ... it's all over the papers ... on the radio and television. What do you suppose happened to her?'

In an effort to gather her thoughts, Emma persuaded her mother to move outside the house. She needed open space and fresh air to soften the story she had to tell. She loved to walk the pathway that ran from the house to the banks of the River Boyne. Linking arms with her mother, accompanied by Queeny the cat, Emma outlined everything she knew about the recent ugly events. Uncharacteristically, her mother remained silent. Only the soothing echo of running water filled the pauses in Emma's report. 'It's possible that the media could drag my name into this. It's even possible that they'll try to talk to you and Dad. It probably won't happen but, well ... I thought you should know.'

Hazel stopped walking, unlinked her arm from Emma's and looked out across the river. Queeny, in playful mood rubbed her back against Hazel's legs. Reflections from the sun bounced off the water's surface like a scattering of multifaceted diamonds as water ploughed through a stretch of rapids on its way towards the multi-arched stone bridge that allowed access to the village of Slane. Across the river from where they stood, newly planted woodlands formed a screen that hid all but the uppermost part of the eighteenth-century Slane Castle. The castle had become famous on account of its association with outdoor rock concerts. The Rolling Stones, U2, Bob Dylan, Queen and David Bowie had all performed in the vast riverside, natural amphitheatre. Emma had heard most of the acts without having to move from the front garden of her parents' house. On one occasion, back when she'd been an impressionable teenager, she'd gone to the castle, along with a bunch of friends, and mingled with the crowd. Bruce Springsteen, a particular favourite of hers at the time, had been the headline act. Even to this day, she still associated Springsteen with a fun time in her life.

Hazel's gaze returned to Emma. 'You've lost weight, I see. I hope you're looking after yourself. Please say you'll stay to dinner; I'd like you and your father to talk things over.'

'Mum, I wish I could but I have a meeting scheduled for this evening.'

'Oh, dear. I really think you ought to stay. Surely your meeting can't be more important than speaking to your father?'

'No Mum, of course not, but I've agreed to meet someone later and I can't get out of it.'

'Well, in that case,' Hazel said, every word laced with disappointment, 'I won't detain you any longer.' She turned on her heel and began walking back towards the house. Queeny followed at her heels, turning her head to glance back at Emma, the cat letting her know she'd upset Hazel. Emma struggled to find words that would ease the pain her mother was feeling. She didn't want to talk about the offer she'd had to work for a political party. Telling her mother that would only add further disillusionment. Besides, she still hadn't fully decided whether or not to quit the *Post*.

CHAPTER 8

Four women and a lone male occupied the swimming pool. Apart from them, the complex that housed the pool was empty. A huge digital clock, suspended from the arched roof, read 08.30, half an hour before official opening time. Two of the women, dressed in designer sports wear, wrap-round shades and tennis-court tans, watched from an elevated viewing gallery as their two companions splashed about in the pellucid water.

Brendan Edwards, the lone male, swam full lengths, back and forth, back and forth, ignoring the two female swimmers, never once altering his stroke. Edwards, manager of the complex, had accepted a substantial bribe to allow the women use the facilities before opening hours.

Margot Hillary, sitting in the viewing gallery, glanced surreptitiously around the pool's perimeter before nodding to the women in the water. They responded to her nod by swimming to the end of the pool and veering towards the lane occupied by Edwards. For Margot Hillary, this man had become an obsession. Even now, as her companions closed in on him, her mind sought to rationalize the circumstances that had contrived to intertwine their lives.

Edwards competed in the 2003 World Swimming Championships, winning two freestyle titles for his efforts, an achievement that proved to be the pinnacle of his career. One year later, after failing to qualify for the 2004 Olympic Games in Athens, his career stalled. At just thirty-one years of age prospects for meaningful employment seemed remote. Fate intervened. A bright young female producer with Zag-Wag, an independent television production company, had an inspired idea. Her concept involved showing off Edwards' fine physique while, at the same time, creating quality viewing.

Edwards was a natural in front of the camera. The show succeeded beyond expectations. Titled *Sports Coach*, the format concentrated on aspects of sports science with features on anatomy, growth and development, training principles, sports psychology, nutrition and related subjects. Assisted by two glamorous female assistants, Edwards catered for the learner as well as the top-flight competitive swimmer. The assistants' swimwear aped the *Baywatch* babes, a factor that boosted viewing figures and achieved for Edwards greater celebrity status than he'd earned as a competing athlete. He was particularly good with beginners, groups of boys and girls who'd never been in the water before. His patience, guidance and encouragement appealed to the viewers, making this segment the highpoint of the show.

Ratings reached unheard of levels for such a minority interest programme ensuring that a second series went into production. But Edwards was dropped after four weeks into the second run. No explanations were offered. Switchboards lit up, viewers demanding explanations. Parents, children and athletes alike were perplexed. Zag-Wag failed to offer a plausible reason for dropping Edwards. Rumours were rife, but only a few people on the inside knew the truth.

And truth was not pretty.

Two eleven year-old boys told their parents that Edwards had touched them improperly. Confronted with the accusation, Edwards was indignant. He used clips from the show to demonstrate the necessity of holding on to children during their initial attempts to stay afloat. The boys' parents were not satisfied; they persuaded their sons to repeat their story. Their words, punctuated by tears, left little room for doubt. The parents, reluctant to subject their boys to the ordeal of court proceedings, reached an agreement with the show's producers: Zag-Wag would drop Edwards from the show; the parents would not press charges.

That should have been the end of the matter. But the fuss had barely abated when a new chapter in the life of Brendan Edwards and his disreputable proclivities transpired. He secured a position as manager in one of the city's most exclusive leisure centres. Attached to the up-market Belhavel Hotel, the multimillion euro complex boasted a half-size Olympic swimming pool as well as the usual health and fitness facilities. Apart from taking responsibility for the running of the operation, Edwards' job description required that he involve himself in a daily session in the pool with the hotel's paying patrons.

Margot Hillary's mind snapped back to what was happening in the pool. She watched her two companions grab Brendan Edwards, saw him struggle to break free as the women ducked him beneath the water. Margot Hillary pushed the shades a little further down her nose, alarmed that the struggle had taken an unexpected turn. Her companions were expert swimmers, but it's doubtful that they had been prepared for the outcome that transpired.

Margot Hillary used the surface of her vanity mirror to form two lines of cocaine. The fine powder lines reflected on her face as her eyes, large and long-lashed, gazed down on the horizontal glass. For a woman of 44, she looked good. The snips 'n' tucks had been expensive, tedious and painful, but the results had been worth it. She had sultry looks, style and glamour, charisma and the money to support the maintenance requirements. The abundant flaming red hair that adorned her head in youth was now replaced with a shock of crimson and mahogany hair. It should look ridiculous on a woman her age – but it didn't. If anything, it had become her trademark.

She snorted the second line, felt the hit immediately. Self-doubts in regard to her role in the events at the pool earlier in the day seemed to vanish. She felt invigorated as she picked up the evening newspaper and read the top story for a second time.

SWIM CHAMP'S POOL DEATH.

The body of Brendan Edwards – former world champion swimmer and presenter of the recent Sports Coach television show – was recovered from the pool attached to Dublin's Belhavel Hotel this morning. A hotel spokesman claimed that no one other than Edwards had been present when the tragedy occurred. Edwards, it was learned, liked to exercise each morning before his official duties began. As a consequence, his workout was not recorded on closed-circuit camera. One explanation being put forward suggests that Edwards might have suffered a cardiac arrest.

Margot put the paper down. She had no wish to read the résumé of Edwards' achievements that followed. She lay back on her bed and tried not to dwell on the set of circumstances that tied her life to that of the swimmer. Her mind wandered back to the spoiled upbringing she'd had and the bright, glamorous career she'd enjoyed, the dysfunctional marriage she now endured and her partiality for drugs.

She'd grown up in the most unlikely Irish home imaginable. Her father, 'Ginger' Harris, a successful impresario, managed several rock groups in the 80s and 90s and amassed a fortune bringing international acts to Ireland. He married Gloria Whyte, lead singer with one of the groups he'd been promoting at the time. A talented vocalist in the Katie Melua mould, Gloria forsook her showbiz career for that of housewife. Margot was their only child.

As a teenager, Margot mingled with the glitzy people who hung with her parents. Many of them smoked dope, a factor that didn't bother her parents unduly. Their philosophy had it that drugs enhanced the creative drive and caused no damage when used intelligently. Their only admonition was that she never touch heroin on any account. Her interest back then centred mainly on equestrian pursuits. As a member of the Pony Club of Ireland she competed in gymkhanas across the country. She'd made lifelong friendships through her involvement with the horsy set; one of them, Iseult Smyth-O'Brien had been bridesmaid at her marriage to Norbert Hillary.

Norbert Hillary represented old money. His people had been wealthy landowners in County Meath dating back to the time of Cromwell. An astute businessman, he was tall and erect, his appearance striking rather than handsome. He increased the family's fortune tenfold by skilfully investing in stocks and shares and built a palatial home for his new bride on the outskirts of the city, complete with stable yard and paddocks, Within a year, Ronan, their only son was born. Margot had it all: wealth, beauty, intelligence and sophistication while Norbert, as a right of birth, held an elevated place in society. He epitomized the man who had everything, and that included a trophy wife. The reality alas, did not match the perception. Margot felt, wrongly as it happened, that the financial indices received more attention from him than his son and wife. He'd never shown any great aptitude for the kind of sex she needed and had, in recent years, given up altogether.

Margot busied her life bringing up Ronan, tending her beloved horses and visiting the beauty parlour. When sexual frustration overwhelmed her she sought refuge in the company of her female friends. With Ronan at school, she filled the void in her life by smoking dope, drinking cocktails and hanging out with these married women, women like herself who wanted more out of life than a sterile marriage. They were the ones who had rallied around her when Ronan found himself in trouble.

Ronan benefited from his parents' membership of the Belhavel Hotel's Leisure facilities. He'd learned to swim and had become a regular at the pool. Margot looked in on him from time to time to see how his skills were progressing, being careful not to let him see her. For an eleven-year-old, Ronan was gifted with above-average intelligence, something he'd inherited from his father. He was handsome and quite sensitive, attributes she liked to think came from her divide of the gene pool. One day he would possess the Hillary millions, become master of the manor and, more importantly as far as she was concerned, he'd be a lasting testimony to the fact that she had produced something of beauty and worth.

On one of her visits to the hotel's pool complex, something made her stop and delay a little longer. Taking her usual position in the viewing gallery, she'd been surprised to see Ronan in the company of an adult swimmer; usually the boy kept pretty much to himself. Her surprise was complete when she recognized the man by his side: it was Brendan Edwards. She'd seen Edwards on television and was familiar with the controversy that surrounded his sacking from the show. She watched Edwards and Ronan for some time, a measure of concern creeping into her mind. After several minutes, she saw Edwards exit the pool and head for the changing rooms. Before he disappeared through the doors he glanced back at Ronan and held up his hand to display three fingers. Margot then caught Ronan nodding his head in agreement with whatever Edwards' gesture signified.

She waited in the gallery, puzzled by what she'd witnessed. A few minutes elapsed before Ronan climbed out of the pool and headed to the changing rooms. Margot moved down to pool level and tracked her son, keeping a discreet distance. Two doors, one for gents, the other for ladies, led to the changing room area. She was about to enter through the gents' door when a man in swimming trunks emerged, making his way towards the pool. 'You got the wrong door, ma'am.' he said, pointing to the sign on the door.

'No, it's OK, I'm collecting my son,' Margot said, sounding more sure of herself than she felt. The man gave her a bogus smile and held the door open for her. Once inside, she surveyed the area to see if she could spot Ronan. The place seemed deserted and silent except for the sound of running water in one of the shower cubicles. She called out, 'Ronan, are you in there?' The sound of running water ceased. No one spoke. Margot felt her heart lurch. Was she making a fool of herself, jumping to the most unlikely conclusions? She reached for the shower's sliding door, grimaced, then jerked it to one side.

Margot stared open-mouthed. Ronan and Edwards stood before her, their naked bodies pressed against each other. Edwards' hands held on to Ronan's shoulders, his eyes stared back at her. In that suspended moment of horror she saw something perverse and malignant in those eyes. It was as though every quirk and warp in his psyche had been laid bare for her to see. Ronan's eyes reflected a mixture of fright, shame and bewilderment. For Margot, the scenes that followed were the stuff of nightmares.

As events in the changing rooms played out, Margot's brain shifted to overdrive, deciding what action to take. She should go to the authorities, have Edwards put away for life. That would be the proper course of action to take, but what effect would it have on Ronan? His life would be irrevocably damaged, his future as heir to the Hillary fortune put in jeopardy. Her dreams and aspirations for the boy would disappear like water down a plughole. All of this, she considered in the time it took to intake a breath. An alternative strategy was called for. She'd relied on her friends to concoct that strategy.

CHAPTER 9

After parking in the St Stephen's Green Shopping Centre car-park, Emma emerged on foot into daylight on South King Street, taking advantage of the plate glass shop fronts opposite the Gaiety Theatre to steal a quick glance at her reflection. Her white linen suit had gained extra creases but still looked elegant, complementing her hair and complexion to perfection. If only her inner turmoil matched the exterior façade, everything would be fine.

Anyone observing her walk through the crowds on Grafton Street would have said she was lost in her own world and they would've been right. She was deaf to the hustle and bustle, blind to the high-street stores, the shoppers, the flower sellers, the tourists, the beggars and the assorted street performers. Her offer of new employment should have been uppermost in her mind, but events from the previous days continued to seek ventilation with disturbing images of Connolly, Iseult and Nuala Buckley refusing to let go. It wasn't until she took a right turn into Nassau Street and passed by Trinity Library that she came to a decision with regard to her future employment.

Standing on the doorstep of the Social Alliance Party's office, a modest building adjacent to the Setanta Centre's courtyard, she pressed the intercom. She was still framing her words of acceptance when a disembodied voice bid her enter. Gloomy stairs led to a reception area on the first floor. From behind a grey steel reception desk, a stick-thin woman, early twenties, engrossed in conversation on the phone, used a finger flick to direct her towards a seat to one side of the reception desk.

Emma sat down, surprised that the Social Alliance Party, fronted by one of the country's top business moguls, should have such a spartan reception area. If there was logic to it, she'd missed it. Her first meeting with Maurice Elliott had taken place in the Michelin-starred restaurant L'Ecrivain on Baggott Street. Elliott had regaled her in the private room downstairs where he assured her some of the largest corporate deals in the country had been sealed. Over a culinary extravaganza, Elliott outlined his ambitions for his fledgling political party, his policies sounding vague, contradictory but definitely right of centre.

His master plan envisaged the use of his 132 country-wide estate agency offices as a network base for spreading his message. Several disaffected elected deputies from the main parties had signalled their interest in joining his grouping. Three ex-government ministers (shafted in recent reshuffles) were already on board and funding from the corporate sector was assured. His grandiose vision for Emma saw her as a latter-day John the Baptist, her mission to prepare the way and spread the gospel of the new political Messiah.

The receptionist put the phone down, looked at Emma with a smile that never reached her eyes. 'Can I help you?' she asked, her tone teetering on the edge of polite.

'I'm Emma Boylan. I've come to see Mr Elliott.'

'You have an appointment?'

'Yes, Mr Elliott asked me to call today.'

As the receptionist looked through the appointments, a young woman pushed through the entrance door and approached the desk. ''Scuse me,' she said in a strident tone. 'Let Maurice know I'm here.'

'Could you, like, take a seat, Miss Dunlop; be with you in a second,' the receptionist said coldly.

With a snort of derision, Miss Dunlop sat next to Emma. She had a wan complexion, a Cleopatra-style fringe, and eyes that were too heavily ringed in black eyeliner, metallic shadow and thick mascara. Her dress-sense suffered equally from an indiscriminate selection of designer labels. Emma couldn't help but notice that she was wearing a wig. At first, Emma, who put her age in the mid-thirties bracket, thought the wig represented some kind of fashion statement, but it then occurred to her that Miss Dunlop might possibly be ill, with cancer perhaps.

The receptionist beckoned to Emma. 'Don't see your name here,' she said, scepticism in her voice, 'You sure Mr Elliott said he'd see you?'

'Yes, I'm positive.'

'Well, looks like there's been, like, a breakdown in communications.'

'Could you let him know I'm here?' Emma suggested, her tone taking on a slight edge.

The receptionist shrugged her shoulders. 'Mr Elliott had to leave the office I'm afraid. If you wish I could, like, try contacting him on the phone?'

Emma interlocked her fingers, squeezed hard. 'Please do that,' she said, managing to restrain her impatience.

The receptionist made contact with Elliott, explained the situation to him, then thrust the phone at Emma. 'He'll have a word with you.'

Emma had to lean across the desk to take the phone. 'Ah, Mr Elliott,' she said, 'I was hoping to catch you here at the office.'

'Sorry, Emma, had to pop home. Any chance you'd make it out here?'

'Yeah, OK, no problem,' Emma lied smoothly. 'When?'

'Can you make it straight away? You know where I live?'

'Yes, I think I can find you. Be there within the hour.'

She was about to replace the receiver when Miss Dunlop pushed her aside and grabbed the telephone. 'Listen, Maurice,' she said angrily, 'I saw you sneak out of the office earlier. I will keep coming in here until—' She stopped talking and held the receiver away from her ear. 'You've cut the connection,' she said to the receptionist. 'You stupid cow, you've cut me off.'

'Yes, I did; Mr Elliott's instructions. He doesn't wish to speak to you.'

'Well, I wish to speak to him. Tell him that the next time he pokes his nose in here.' Miss Dunlop then stormed out of the reception area, the sound of her footsteps reverberating as she pounded down the stairs.

'Who on earth was that?' Emma asked.

'That's Lisa Dunlop; she was the receptionist here before I took over. Mr Elliott fired her because she was, like, useless. Now she's, like, threatening him with unfair dismissal or something. Good riddance if you ask me.'

Walking back to collect her car, Emma thought about Lisa Dunlop. One aspect of her behaviour exercised her curiosity. When the woman swung around to leave the reception area, the fringe of her wig had parted from her forehead. Beneath the fringe, Emma saw what she imagined was a portion of a tattoo. How very strange, she thought.

*

Connolly hoped Malcolm McAuley would help secure his release. McAuley, sitting opposite him was, he believed, the cleverest solicitor in the city. Apart from the initial interview, McAuley had been present at all the interrogation sessions. His voice resonated in a deep base sound that automatically conferred gravitas on his every utterance. He preferred to ration his advice to the confines of Connolly's holding cell, away from the ear of Connolly's accusers.

In his late forties, McAuley was tall, maybe six-three, with a broad chest and imposing figure. He had the self-assurance of a man confident of his abilities. His attire, like his manner, was meticulous. His bespoke tailoring was complemented by a head of precisely styled black hair, a handsome face and shrewd eyes, a good straight nose and the kind of flawless skin one associates with country curates who conform to teetotal and celibate lifestyles. Like Connolly, he was an 'old boy' from the Jesuits' Clongowes Wood College.

Right now, the solicitor used those shrewd eyes to survey Connolly. This was business. His friend was now a client in need of help. McAuley dismissed all familiarities, adapting instead a pragmatic professionalism. He used his fingers to tick off the main conclusions he'd reached. 'We both know you'll be charged at the hearing in the morning, right?'

'Right,' Connolly agreed.

'Grennan would like to charge you with the attempted murder of Nuala Buckley, but that's not going to happen. They've got nothing solid against you.'

'*Nothing solid*? They don't have anything at all! That's because I never went near the woman.'

'Agreed; what they've got is hundred per cent circumstantial ... but it's the kind of speculation that will sound plausible in front of a district judge.'

'You mean the fact that I had a key to the house.'

'There's that, yes, and the fact that your hairs were found on the bed. Your fingerprints were everywhere. You can't substantiate your whereabouts for the two hours leading up to your arrival at the house and you—'

'—Don't have an alibi ... yeah I know, I know, Jesus.'

'Surely someone saw you? Tell me again, what you were doing?'

'OK,' Connolly said grudgingly. 'Iseult called me before ten o'clock and insisted I show up on the dot of midday. I needed to get my head straight so I took some time out, went for a walk, thought about what she might want. I popped in to Tom Dunne, the barber, had a trim.'

'Does the barber remember you?'

'Nah! Tom Dunne's in his seventies, he's not sure of the time of day.'

'Too bad! He could have explained why hairs from your head were found in the bedroom. Pity. So, after visiting this barber...?'

'I headed up Grafton Street, passed through Fusiliers' Arch and sat beside the duck pond in St Stephen's Green. I gave full vent to my thoughts, trying to make sense of my time with Iseult. I was still no nearer to understanding anything when it was time to go back to the station, collect my car, drive to the house.'

'And you can't think of anyone, apart from the barber, who might have seen you during that period of time?'

'Hundreds saw me; but who's going to remember. Looks bad, right?'

'I won't lie to you, Jim, it's not good.'

'So, what are you going to do in the morning?'

'Try to get you out on bail.'

'What are my chances?'

'This is a high profile case, could go any way. So far, forensics have failed to come up with their findings on the death of Iseult. If foul play is established, we're in for a rough ride. Right now, our main concern is Nuala Buckley.' McAuley glanced at his notes. 'She's not expected to last much longer on life-support. The medical experts say she should have died after the attack. She suffered a fracture to the thyroid cartilage and had her central anterior post dislodged. Brute force was used to inflict that kind of damage.'

'But not enough to kill her outright?'

'That, we know,' McAuley said. 'But they're still trying to establish the extent to which she was sexually molested. There's evidence of vaginal abuse, indications of penetration but – and this is significant – no semen. My guess is, she was roughed up with some sort of object ... to make it look like rape.'

'Well, at least there's nothing to connect me to that, right?'

'Wrong! They can place you at the scene. The bloodstains in the bed match Nuala Buckley's blood type. Then, of course, there's your hair. You want me to go on?'

'No, I get the picture. That's why I need you to get me out of here fast; I need to find out who the real culprit is.'

'It doesn't work like that. If I succeed in having you released, you can have no part in the investigation.'

'Damn it, you're right; even with bail, I'll remain suspended, so not much chance of getting stuck in … at least not officially.'

'Officially or unofficially; I want you to stay clear. That's important. I don't want you to incriminate yourself or compromising your defence.'

'My defence? You think it'll go that far?'

'Pray it doesn't. But in that event, you'll need to think about employing a top-notch barrister.'

'Bloody hell!'

CHAPTER 10

mma had taken the coast road from Blackrock, through to Dun Laoghaire, hoping to make it to Elliott's house without getting snarled up in the evening commuter congestion. Bad idea. Her notion to opt for the more circuitous coast route had, it would appear, occurred to every other road user simultaneously. They were now all bumper to bumper, inhaling each other's exhaust fumes, moving at a snail's pace. A loud base sound throbbed from the speakers of the car behind her, its driver smoking what looked suspiciously like a joint, his head bobbing from side to side, his fingers rapping on the steering wheel, keeping time with the beat.

A forest of swaying sailboat masts peeped above the Dun Laoghaire West Pier wall, the tranquil scene mocking the landlocked motorists. A Jeep Cherokee, hauling a wide yacht on a trailer, barred Emma's efforts to overtake on the narrow traffic lanes leading to the harbour. After what seemed like an eternity, the offending driver swung left into the Royal St George Yacht Club, offering Emma a friendly wave of apology. She reciprocated with a brittle smile that didn't fool anyone.

The clock on the dashboard let her know she'd been on the road for three-quarters of an hour.

Christ, I'd fly to London in less time than this.

Thankfully, the traffic began to ease by the time she made Marine Parade. Most of the commuters had peeled off into the suburbs by the time she reached the shore-side drive overlooking Scotsman's Bay. This neighbourhood had a settled air of respectability about it with large, well-maintained houses and perfectly landscaped gardens. The cars in the driveways – Mercedes, BMWs and gleaming Jaguar XJRs – suggested a well-heeled, middle-aged, middle-class population.

Past the 'Forty-Foot Bathing Place' with its ambiguous sign –

K.T. McCaffrey

FORTY FOOT GENTLEMEN ONLY – she came to the Martello Tower, a landmark she'd once visited with her parents back when she'd been studying for her Leaving Cert. The forty-foot high edifice, she'd learned then, had been built in the early nineteenth century as a deterrent against the threat of invasion by Napoleon. The invasion never materialized but a century later the tower had provided James Joyce with the setting for the opening chapter of his masterpiece, *Ulysses*. Today, with the passage of another century, the tower operated as a museum dedicated to the memory of the enigmatic writer. To the east, Emma could see the full panorama of Dublin Bay, a vista Joyce referred to as the *snotgreen sea*.

On the approach to Bullock Harbour, Elliott's house came into view. She pulled into the steep upward sloped driveway of the Victorian pile, impressed by the uncluttered sea view it offered. Free from the car and traffic fumes, she stood in front of the house and filled her lungs with fresh air. Elliott greeted her effusively, holding her hand for longer than was necessary.

'Wow!' she exclaimed. 'This place is truly breathtaking.'

'Indeed it is, even if I say so myself,' he enthused, finally releasing her hand. 'Bought it twenty years ago for seven hundred thousand; I'd probably get the guts of five million if I put it on the market today.'

'True, but would you want to part with it?'

'Probably not, but then everything has its price. Still, you're right; I've put too much work into the garden to think about leaving.'

'You do the gardening yourself?' Emma asked, impressed.

'Yes. Well, no, no, not really. I get a little help from a professional but the vision is mine. Since moving here I've planted eighty varieties of rhododendrons as well as the azaleas, camellias and roses.'

'It's wonderful,' Emma agreed, feeling the scent-laden breeze flap the flares of her linen suit against her legs.

'Yes, it is,' Elliott agreed, slipping into estate-agent mode. 'This area has a microclimate that allows rare and tender plants to flourish. Mind you, I have to ensure they're adequately sheltered with shrubbery; that's essential. As you can see I've managed to find a few unusual and exotic plants; picked them up on my travels abroad.'

Horticultural delights acknowledged, Emma was ushered into a brightly lit hallway and guided towards a spacious drawing-room. The brightness allowed her to see Elliott in a less flattering environment than that which prevailed in restaurant L'Ecrivain. At 46, he had taken, what Emma considered, the first downward steps on the male midlife escalator, a journey that would eventually take him all the way from desirable man-about-town to middle-aged, frisky old rake, and on to the inevitable expanding stomach and fading looks. She had difficulty picturing him as the all conquering 'ladies man' depicted by Bob Crosby, but she could detect a mischievous twinkle in his eye, a glint that held out the promise (or threat) of freewheeling sexuality. He offered to fix her a drink. She declined, settling for coffee instead.

While Elliott was in the kitchen, acceding to her request, Emma heard the sound of conversation in the background. There were two distinct voices, both female, but she failed to get the gist of what was being said. Elliott returned with the coffee and she gave up on the eavesdropping.

'Let's sit by the window,' he suggested. 'We can enjoy the scenery while we talk, watch the seals on the rocks down by the harbour.' He sat beside her on a three-seater couch, his hip brushing hers, while balancing a gin and tonic in his right hand. 'Sorry to drag you out here, but it's been a bitch of a day,' he said, launching into a description of said day, allowing Emma to interject occasionally or shake her head at appropriate junctures. He had just about finished his commentary when the telephone interrupted his flow. 'Will you excuse me a minute,' he said, 'got to take this in the study?'

Emma nodded compliantly, glad of the opportunity to have a look around the room on her own. Original oil paintings, most of them embodying nautical themes, graced the walls. One particular painting, depicting a magnificent house in the Olivia Valeres district of Marbella, took pride of place. This property, Emma knew from her research into Elliott's lifestyle, was his holiday residence in Spain's Costa del Sol. While examining the *objets d'art*, she could hear the two women talking in the background. If curiosity really did kill cats, she'd be dead years ago. She moved to the hallway, ostensibly to admire the artefacts but in reality, to get a fix on the talkers. Elliott had veered to the right, she turned left.

She peered into a large reception room that opened on to an even larger conservatory. It was now possible to see the talkers. Diana Elliott was instantly recognizable as the woman Bob Crosby had pointed out in The Cat's Pyjamas. She had that exotic allure and charismatic appeal that set some women apart. Her stylish outfit, a winter-white suit, complimented her tanned complexion to perfection, her skin appearing to glow in the sunlight shafting through the overhead glass.

The face of the woman sitting next to Diana Elliott was turned away from Emma, showing just an abundance of flaming copper-coloured hair. A plume of smoke indicated that she was smoking. When she pivoted around to full-face view, traces of cosmetic surgery were visible under her eyes, both rims showing faint outlines of stitches. More significantly, it was apparent that the woman was smoking a joint. Emma watched her pass it to Diana Elliott. And then, as though aware of scrutiny, the woman slipped on a pair of outsize sunglasses. Like Elliott's wife, she wore expensive clothes. What Emma could hear of the conversation intrigued her; they were discussing anal bleaching and colonic irrigation, evaluating its contribution to a greater feeling of lightness and wellbeing.

They're discussing arseholes?

A sound from within the house warned Emma that Maurice Elliott had finished his call and was on his way back. She retraced her footsteps hurriedly but failed to make it in time. Elliott stopped short when he saw her. She attempted to cover up by affecting a pose in front of a meticulously crafted model of Elliott's pleasure cruiser. 'What a beautiful vessel,' she said, trying to sound nonchalant.

'Oh, *that*?' Elliott said curtly, indicating with a shepherding hand that she should proceed him into the drawing-room. His dour expression made it clear that a mood change had taken place. At first, Emma wondered if her extracurricular exploration could be to blame but quickly dismissed that notion. It seemed more likely that the telephone call had triggered the mood swing. Elliott stood for a moment looking out the bay window, his back to her. 'I've had some rather disturbing news,' he said, without turning to face her.

'Sorry to hear that,' Emma said, thinking that perhaps a death in the family had occurred. 'Maybe you'd like to postpone our talk … I could get around to your office in the morning. We could—'

'This can't wait,' he interrupted, turning to face her with a sullen stare, 'this concerns you.'

'What … the disturbing news? Concerns me?'

'Yes. I've just heard something that alters everything. It concerns the death of Iseult Connolly and … the attack on Nuala Buckley. It's come to my attention that Iseult's ex-husband is the prime suspect. None of this would bother me … except that it ties you into the story.'

'What?' Emma said, with a sinking feeling. 'What do you mean?'

'I'm told you are Connolly's fancy woman, that he dumped Iseult for you, and that you were present at the scene of the crime.'

Emma groped for words. 'But … but that's a total distortion … I didn't, I mean … he didn't leave her for—'

'Let's cut the crap,' Elliott snapped, 'I need straight answers. Are you living with Detective Inspector Connolly?'

'Yes, but—'

'Did you see Iseult Connolly's body in the garage?'

'Yes, I went there because—'

'You *were* with Detective Connolly when he discovered the body?'

'No, I wasn't. Look, you're making this sound as though—'

'I'm not making it sound like anything,' Elliott said testily. 'I'm merely voicing the accusations that will be levelled at you when the press find out.'

'Yes, but—'

'You might well have a legitimate rationale, I don't know, but the media will run the story come what may. You and the detective are about to become the focus of a very hostile press.'

'That's crazy,' Emma said, her voice an indignant croak. 'Detective Inspector Connolly and me … we're not responsible for what's happened. We just happened to be in the wrong place at the wrong—'

'That's as maybe, but it leaves you with a major credibility deficit. In short, Ms Boylan, you're not the person to head up my media management.'

Emma wanted to decry the injustice of it all but desisted. Her ability to think on her feet came into play. 'The question of my employment is not at issue,' she said, masking the turmoil churning inside her. 'I've come here to let you know I've decided against taking up the position with your organization.'

It was a lie, but she hoped the look on his face meant he believed her. Just as well Elliott could not hear the sound of her heart thumping in her chest. He remained silent for a moment, clearly wrong-footed by the unexpected revelation. 'Well, in that case,' he said, his tone intended to terminate the conversation, 'we've got nothing else to discuss.'

Without a further word being spoken, he escorted her to the front door.

CHAPTER 11

The hearing into Connolly's involvement in Nuala Buckley's near-fatal attack appeared all very civilized and low-key to Emma. Sitting next to Bob Crosby in Dun Laoghaire's District Court building, she listened intently as the law practitioners made legalistic sounding statements. Though not fully *au fait* with the finer points of law, she followed proceedings with relative ease.

Connolly, sitting next to his solicitor, acknowledged her presence with a quick nod before returning his attention to the business in hand. Were it not for the presence of two uniformed officers and half-a-dozen other observers, one might be forgiven for thinking that a county council, or residents' association, meeting was in progress. Emma recognized Detective Inspector Seán Grennan from his visit to their apartment. District Judge Tom English, a slack-faced, over-weight man in his sixties took charge of proceedings.

Grennan detailed the events leading up to the discovery of Nuala Buckley's unconscious body. Reading from his charge sheet, using a liberal sprinkling of technical jargon, he gave a step-by-step account of the procedures he'd employed in the arrest, caution and detention of the accused.

Bob Crosby, his face flushed from the effects of blood pressure, exchanged brief whispers with Emma while continuing to follow proceedings. Earlier that morning, before Emma had left for the hearing, he had telephoned to discuss, among other things, her encounter with Maurice Elliott. If Crosby derived satisfaction from her failed career move, then she'd missed it, but gauging reaction over a telephone line was never easy. Before hanging up, she'd steered the conversation to the question of her employment. After an ominous silence, Crosby promised to discuss it after the court sitting.

Right now, there was a brief hiatus in proceedings. The courtroom filled with the heavy air of expectancy as Judge English, with a world-weary expression, shuffled his papers, examined his notes and underlined sections with his pen. Emma watched as Jim Connolly and his solicitor whispered earnestly to each other, their expressions grim. Grennan had moved to a corner of the room and was speaking quietly into his mobile phone.

Emma nudged Crosby. 'Will they hold Connolly in custody?'

'Hard to say. McAuley will try to have him released. I've got surety in readiness should it be needed – it's personal, nothing to do with the *Post*.'

'What if he doesn't get bail?'

'Let's just wait and see,' Crosby suggested.

Judge English cleared his throat, looked at the assembled personnel then back to his notes. He made a short summary of the facts before confirming that the accused would be remanded in custody until a trial date was fixed.

McAuley shot to his feet. He sought leave to have his client released on bail, sighting Connolly's exemplary record and good character as justifiable reasons. Judge English acceded to the request, ruling that Connolly could be freed on bail once an independent surety was provided. McAuley agreed. Further conditions were imposed: Connolly must reside at all times at his current address, surrender his passport and have no duplicate passport issued in the interim. Proceedings were drawing to a conclusion when, unexpectedly, a young woman who'd been sitting to one side of Emma stood up. 'What about Nuala's children,' she asked the judge. 'What's to become of them while their mother lies in a coma?'

Judge English leaned his head a little sideways and appeared to squint in her direction. 'Who, may we enquire, are you madam?'

'I'm Ann Buckley … Nuala's sister,' the woman said, self-consciously squeezing her fingers into her palms, 'I've been looking after Chris and Katie ever since' – she stopped and glanced at Connolly – 'ever since their mother's been on life-support.'

A collective intake of breath crackled like static in the room. Emma had half expected Nuala's father, Shane Buckley, to make an appearance, but if he was in the courtroom, she didn't see him. It hadn't occurred to her that Nuala's younger sister would attend. Like those around her, Emma turned to observe the woman. She looked 28 or 29, maybe a tad older, had tousled toffee-gold hair, an even tan and bright eyes. She wore stone-washed denim slacks, a denim wool-trimmed fleece, and a tight-fitting holly-green top. Her tan seemed strangely out of kilter with the colourless surroundings.

Judge English, who'd been momentarily flustered, quickly regained his composure. As one who was known to mix in the same rarefied circle as Shane Buckley, he was keen to show due deference to the bloodstock magnate's daughter. 'I appreciate the stress you are suffering Ms Buckley,' he offered, 'but this is not an appropriate forum to air such grievances. I suggest you talk to the social services people.'

'They've been around already,' Ann Buckley said, swallowing her breath, 'threatened to give Chris and Katie to Nuala's ex partner. That can't be allowed to happen—'

'I must stop you there,' the judge said. 'The matter you speak of is outside the remit of these proceedings. I'm sorry Ms Buckley but I have no jurisdiction in regard to domestic arrangements.'

The young woman looked around her, glancing anxiously from face to face as though seeking support, her fingers fidgeting with the borders on her fleece. 'This needs to be sorted out before something bad happens.'

The judge beckoned a court official to his side, whispered something in his ear before returning his attention to Ann Buckley. 'This official will take you to a social welfare person who'll advise you on the most appropriate action to take. That's the best I can do.'

'Thank you, I appreciate your help.'

An awkward silence prevailed as the woman was escorted from the room. As soon as she'd gone, Judge English wrapped up proceedings and left the bench. Connolly, McAuley and Crosby made their way to the clerk's office to sort out bail bonds. For five minutes, Emma sat alone pondering the significance of the events that had just taken place, wondering what difference it might bring to the relationship she enjoyed with Connolly. She was still deep in contemplation when she saw him emerge from the clerk's office, followed by Crosby and McAuley. She kissed Connolly's cheek and hugged him in a prolonged embrace. McAuley interrupted to say he had to dash away but Crosby seemed anxious to remain.

'Let's get out of here,' Connolly said, the strain of the previous days all too evident in his voice.

They were about to leave the building when they heard what sounded like a commotion taking place outside the exit door. Connolly halted abruptly. 'Damn!' he said, taking Emma by the arm.

'Someone's tipped off the press. If they see us together we'll be plastered across every blasted paper by the afternoon. I'll go out first, try to mollify them. You got your car nearby?'

'Yeah, it's parked on Harbour Road, opposite the Royal Irish Yacht Club; you can't miss it. Here, take my keys.'

'Thanks. You'd better get a taxi back to the apartment later … when the coast is clear.'

'No need for that,' Crosby said, 'I'll drive Emma home; I need to sort out a few details with her anyway.'

'Good, that's fine,' Connolly said, pushing through the swing doors and into the midst of the waiting reporters. The flashbulbs and wail of questions that followed were cut off from Emma's hearing as soon as the doors closed. For her, the realization that this was the sort of reception she could expect from here on depressed her. She was all too aware of how the media took special delight in demolishing one of their own. The outlook for Connolly, she realized, looked even more bleak; he hadn't a prayer: it was always open season when it came to roasting cops.

Crosby sighed. 'Thought that would happen … just didn't think it would happen so soon. I'd still like us to have our little chat if that's OK with you?'

'Yeah sure, why not; we can't put off the inevitable.'

'Right then, there's a pub up the street, The Old Mariner, we'll have a drink there … sort out what needs sorting.'

Reporters swarmed around Connolly like crazed killer bees, chasing him down Harbour Road, pestering him every step of the way until he reached Emma's car. They clung to the bonnet as he pulled away from the kerb, pressing lenses and microphones against the windows.

While the rabid hacks pursued Connolly, Emma and Crosby slipped quietly away from the courthouse. Once inside The Old Mariner, Crosby gave her the news she'd been dreading: her job was gone, at least on a temporary basis. She wasn't wanted back at the *Post* until the storm passed over. Her presence, according to Crosby, would be disruptive to the smooth running of the paper. Besides, his chairman, who had to answer to a board of directors who, in turn, had to answer to investors, insisted she take indefinite leave. So, in the space of a few days she'd blown her chance of working for Elliott's political party and been given the old heave-ho from the *Post*.

Over a pint of beer, Crosby came up with a suggestion that went someway towards ameliorating the impact. She could work freelance provided her by-line didn't appear, and provided she didn't show her face in the building. 'We could call you a special correspondent,' he suggested. 'You come up with any newsworthy articles, we'll pay top dollar, can't play fairer than that.'

Oh yes you can.

Emma wanted to argue the toss but decided to button it; she was in no position to expect any better, after all, she'd been prepared to walk away from the job, a factor Crosby had been quick to remind her.

She got back to the apartment by lunchtime. As she entered, a television news flash announced the death of Nuala Buckley. The life-support machine had been switched off. The newsreader stated that Connolly – the detective charged with causing grievous bodily harm to Nuala – had been released on bail. This was followed by footage of Connolly being chased by the rabble of reporters, the whole ignominious episode making him look like some kind of hunted fugitive. 'Bloody hell, they've found me guilty already,' he said dejectedly, 'all we need now is the lynching party.'

Emma switched the television off, put her arms around Connolly and hugged him until the tension in his body eased. They kissed, held one another, and hurriedly removed items of clothing from each other as they proceeded in faltering stages towards the bedroom. They made love with an urgency that overwhelmed both of them. Later, much later, feeling exhausted and hungry they decided to go out for something to eat.

They strolled along Ormond Quay, took the Liffey boardwalk at Grattan Bridge and sauntered above the river's flow until they reached the Ha'penny Bridge. Halfway across the slim arched span, a young Dutch couple handed Emma a camera and asked if she would take their picture. They wanted to be photographed against the backdrop of O'Connell's Bridge, Liberty Hall and the Custom House. Emma obliged willingly, warmed by the infectious glow of happiness in the couple's smiles. A seagull wheeled into camera frame as Emma clicked the picture. April seemed to bring out the best in the city. Receding afternoon sunshine played softly on the water's rippled surface; a light breeze blew upstream and a team of rowers skimmed through the currents, their synchronized oars catching the light as they sliced the water. After handing back the camera, Emma and Connolly jostled their way through the throng of weekend shoppers and visitors as they crossed to the south side of the river. They were about to enter the Merchants Arch when they spotted the first poster.

RAPE VICTIM DIES – COP SUSPECT GETS BAIL

'Good fuck,' Connolly cursed.

Emma stared in disbelief. The evening paper's poster, secured to a lamppost, stopped her in her tracks. Fearing the worst, she glanced left to Aston Quay, then right to Wellington Quay. Every other lamp-post displayed similar posters. Connolly approached a newspaper vendor beneath the arch and bought a paper. Its banner headline echoed the poster's message. His photograph, alongside those of Iseult and Nuala, accompanied the text. A second article, featuring 'grieving father' Shane Buckley, dealt with his prominence in the bloodstock industry and hinted strongly at the strained relationship that existed between father and daughter.

Emma remained silent as they merged with the throng in Crown Alley. Children, resisting their parents' restraints, laughed and played in the crisp evening air; young men linked arms with their girlfriends, chatting happily, oblivious to all but each other; shoppers with branded carrier bags headed for car-parks or buses. Amid this moving mass of humanity, Emma felt alone and lost, out of sync with her own body, divorced from those around her and fearful for the man by her side. Maybe a little fearful for herself too. She watched him fold the newspaper and throw it into a dustbin.

In Luigi Malone's, a restaurant with a cheerful ambience and an eclectic mix of diners, they had two leisurely drinks before ordering food. By the time they sat down to their starters, they had partially dispelled the dark gloom oppressing them. The main course was good and the house wine helped mellow their mood even further. Awaiting their desserts, Connolly raised his wineglass. 'To those who've gone,' he proposed.

Emma clinked glasses. 'And to you, Jim, an innocent man—'

A camera flash went off in their faces, the white brilliant illumination blinding them momentarily. In the seconds it took to realize what had happened, the photographer had sprinted from the restaurant. Connolly leaped to his feet, knocking his chair over in the process, ready to give chase. Emma grabbed his arm, 'No, Jim, that'll only make things worse.'

Connolly heeded her advice, righted his fallen chair and glanced sheepishly at nearby diners. He gave them a feeble wave and a forced smile before resuming his seat. Emma waited until the other diners lost interest in them before speaking. 'Well, we both know what'll be on the front pages of Sunday's papers.'

'I know, I know,' Connolly said resignedly, 'I'm just sorry you had to get dragged into it.'

'There's not a whole lot we can do about that now.'

Connolly ordered a second bottle of wine. And when that bottle was consumed he called for another. Later, as evening melted into night, they indulged in a pub crawl. The second pub they visited had a television showing the nine o'clock news. Top item featured the death of Nuala Buckley and the footage of Connolly's courthouse scramble. None of the revellers paid the slightest attention to the screen. Emma and Connolly had by now progressed to a stage beyond 'merry' and were well on the way to becoming smashed.

The build up of tension that had accumulated over recent days, eased by the intake of alcohol, had vanished. They began to giggle like schoolchildren. When a barman refused to serve them, Connolly bowed theatrically and left. They visited several more pubs on their way home and found two that served them. It was after midnight by the time they stumbled back towards the apartment, serenading each other with the most out-of-tune version of 'Molly Malone' ever to ring out across the River Liffey.

Connolly had already been to the shops by the time Emma awoke. Her head hurt. Her mouth tasted like the bottom of an ashtray. Only a hazy recollection of the previous night's escapades remained. They'd laughed and clung to each other as they staggered home by the Liffey side. And then, afterwards in bed they'd tried to make love. That was when the giggling began in earnest. Connolly, suffering from brewer's droop, had needed more than a little encouragement to coax his hydraulics into action. After prolonged fits of laughter, fumbling, farting and belching their appetite for sex had finally given way to exhaustion. At some point during the night, Emma had gone to the bathroom to empty her bladder. She'd felt nauseous from the excess intake of food and alcohol and imagined her stomach to be bloated to twice its normal size. She decided to induce vomiting to get rid of the noxious concoction. It was an unpleasant exercise, but as soon as it was over, and she'd washed her mouth, she felt marginally better.

In the morning, Connolly, who appeared to have weathered the alcohol damage better than she had, went out and bought a selection of Sunday papers. Emma hauled herself up by her elbows, sat back against the pillows and propped the paper against her raised knees. It took a moment before her eyes fully focused. As expected, the photograph from the restaurant featured prominently on the front page. The headline read:

ON BAIL AND ON THE TOWN!

Beneath the picture, a caption read:

Detective Inspector Jim Connolly, on bail, awaiting trial for his suspected involvement in the death of Nuala Buckley, dining with

Post investigative journalist, Emma Boylan, last evening in Dublin's Temple Bar district.

Introducing Emma's name in the accompanying text represented a new development. After referring to her two *'Journalist of the Year'* awards, they proceeded to do a hatchet job, portraying her as a *femme fatale*, a woman who'd left her husband and beguiled Connolly into leaving his wife.

Emma put the paper down, looked at Connolly with fury in her eyes, 'The bastards!' she hissed, 'how can they say such horrible things?'

'Well, you work for a rival newspaper. They're loving this.'

'Yeah, I can just imagine. I'd love to sue their arses.'

'Why don't you?'

'Fat chance of that. No, I can't sue.'

'Why ever not? They've suggested that you—'

'That's just it, they've *suggested*, but they haven't actually stated it as fact. They've couched their words in a way that gives them an "out" should I wish to challenge them.'

'So, what do we do about it?'

'What do we do about it?' she repeated, as she swung her legs out of the bed. 'I'll tell you what we'll bloody-well do, we'll go find the truth about Iseult's death, we'll discover who really killed Nuala; we'll find out who's trying to railroad you for the crime … and we'll find the bastard who's orchestrating this vendetta against us.'

CHAPTER 13

mma parked beside a florist's stall to one side of the main entrance to Mount Jerome Cemetery. Not a legal parking spot, but she hoped the authorities would have enough on their hands coping with the increased traffic to bother about her minor infringement. She joined the throng making its way up the long narrow pathway that led to Nuala Buckley's final resting-place. A steady drizzle began to fall, prompting mourners to unfurl their umbrellas as they grouped around the freshly dug grave.

The deaths of Iseult Connolly and Nuala Buckley had captured the public's imagination. That two decent, law-abiding citizens, belonging to highly respectable families, should meet with such unnatural deaths heightened interest and ensured saturation coverage in the media. The procession of cars following Nuala's hearse backed all the way to Harold's Cross, causing traffic delays along the Grand Canal Way and Grove Road.

The Coroner's office needed to hold on to Iseult Connolly's body for further examination, but her funeral, when it took place, would keep the story of the women's deaths on the front pages and rein-force the clamour for justice. Emma too, wanted justice but she was painfully aware that to date the only suspect on the horizon was Connolly.

An elderly priest intoned prayers into a crackling microphone as the coffin was lowered. Audible sobs came from those who had come to pay their respects. Black-grey clouds opened as the undertakers covered the grave with a mock grass board. Floral wreaths of all shapes, sizes and colours were flattened in the downpour. Ann Buckley stood next to her father, her tears merging with the rain as friends tried to console her, shaking her hand, mouthed hushed, sibi-lant words – *sorry for your troubles*. In response, her lips barely moved, her replies inaudible.

Emma had been struck by the concern Ann had displayed at Connolly's court hearing; Ann's fear that Nuala's estranged partner might get custody of the two children had sounded heartfelt and desperate. It provoked several questions in Emma's mind; questions like, for instance, who was this mysterious partner? Why was Ann fearful that he might be reunited with Nuala's children? Was he a threat to them? Was he present at their mother's burial? Had the police questioned him? Had he an alibi for her time of death?

Emma searched the faces of the bereaved family group. She recognized Ann's father Shane from the many pictures of him that had appeared on the racing pages. He stood next to Edmund Smyth-O'Brien. It was hard not to be touched by the sight of two grieving fathers, both wealthy, both powerful, here reduced to impotent figures, their combined influence in the material world powerless to alter the tragic event unfolding before their eyes.

Emma spotted Diana Elliott alongside one of the women who'd been with her in The Cat's Pyjamas. Both women were attired in what Emma liked to term 'designer sombre'. These women, it seemed, liked to dress the part no matter what the occasion. Emma noticed another face in the crowd; could the person standing to the left of Shane Buckley be Nuala's ex-partner? Could he be the tall, dark-haired young man accepting condolences from those around him? A forlorn expression marred what would, in different circumstances, be regarded as a handsome face.

The rain stopped as a decade of the rosary brought the graveside ceremony to a conclusion. Slowly, the mourners began making their way out of the cemetery. It seemed odd to Emma that Ann did not accompany her father Shane. He drove away on his own as Ann made her way to another car. It was only when Ann's car pulled on to the road and headed between the cemetery gates that Emma noticed Maurice Elliott behind the wheel. That gave her pause for thought. What connection had Elliott with Ann Buckley or, for that matter, Nuala Buckley? Thinking about this, she noticed Diana Elliott making her way from the graveside on foot. Diana stared intently at her husband's departing car. There was no mistaking the expression in her eyes; if looks could kill, then Maurice Elliott was a dead man. Or, could the hostility be reserved for Ann Buckley?

CHAPTER 14

The four women looked pleased with themselves as they drank their champagne toast. They'd met for breakfast in The Cat's Pyjamas to celebrate the successful completion of their latest project. Weeks of careful planning had gone into the venture. Meetings had taken place on a regular basis. With the help of three conspirators Elizabeth Telford had brought closure to a scheme she'd devised to redress a grievous wrong inflicted on her.

Fourteen years had elapsed since Elizabeth Telford worked for Thackaberry Securities, a leading commercial bank. The experience had profoundly affected her. She'd given four years to the bank but, in physical and mental terms, they had extracted double that toll from her. She'd been 28 at the time. The panel interviewing her – three male executives – had asked the usual questions but their main preoccupation, it seemed to her, had been her appearance. That didn't bother her; she'd taken a lot of trouble to ensure she was presentable. She was aware of people's reaction to her well-proportioned figure and shapely legs, but whether it was her CV or her vital statistics that got her the job mattered little. The salary had been what counted, that and the opportunity to enhance her career prospects.

Initially, she toiled in the back office. A tough grind. Her immediate boss, Avril Coyle, had been a hard taskmaster. The same age as herself, Avril possessed striking looks, purposeful poise, and something of a Jekyll and Hyde personality. To the bosses, Avril was sugar and spice; to those working alongside her, she could be difficult, demanding and downright nasty. When something went wrong, as it did most days, Avril invariably shifted the blame on to Elizabeth. On those occasions, Elizabeth quietly provided evidence to the contrary, showing where the real fault lay. She'd kept her head down, worked hard, avoided rows, and generally impressed the bank's bosses.

Four purgatorial years later, she applied for a job advertised in the financial press. Anglo Celtic Securities (A.C.S.), an old established corporate bank on the corner of Harcourt Street, was impressed by her interview. After two call-backs, she convinced them that she was the right person for the post. Doubts were raised about her lack of experience in dealing with the corporate sector but she still landed the job. All would have been well except that, unknown to her, Avril Coyle had also replied to the ad. In a cruel twist of fate she too had been successful. To make matters worse, they were slotted together, each having equal status. Hostilities between them ceased. Outwardly they were pleasant to each other, their smiles false as a losing actor's beam on Oscar night.

Both had responsibility for securing new clients, their prospects for advancement depending on new business generated. Elizabeth had a talent for attracting first-time customers, ensuring extra bonuses and approval from her bosses. Socially, things were on the up and up. She rubbed shoulders with the city's most eligible bachelors. One of them, Gordon Dankar, asked her out after he'd concluded a large investment deal with the bank. The dinner date that followed went well. Within days, Gordon asked her out again. She was smitten. Only a few years older than her, he was handsome, single, and had amassed a sizeable fortune trading in stocks and shares.

Elizabeth's bosses discovered that Dankar had connections with several cash-rich consortiums and suggested that she 'use her feminine charm' to lure that business their way. They were unaware that she and Dankar had by then become lovers. Dankar liked to boast to her about his high-roller friends and the lucrative share deals he conducted. She'd got used to hearing him make protracted phone calls to discuss the purchase or sale of securities and such likes with business acquaintances. Having knowledge of his wheeling and dealing gave her the perfect opportunity to generate new investments, but she resisted such temptation, feeling loath to debase their relationship or take advantage of her position.

She was in love and it was the most wonderful feeling in the world. They had fun together; they laughed a lot and teased each other while playing naughty bedroom games. Gordon Dankar sometimes called her Betty-the-banker as a pet name, something she hated. In school, because of her slim build, she had been called *Thin Lizzy* by a rival group of girls. Ever since, she'd insisted on being called Elizabeth, not *Liz, Lizzy, Beth,* or *Betty.* In a none-too-subtle effort to stop Gordon using the hated moniker, she would call him Dankar-the-wanker. This, he confessed had been his nickname at school; it was also something he loathed. A truce was called; there would be no more name calling.

The affair had entered its third year when she invited him to meet her parents. She'd wanted to suggest this for quite a while but had waited for an opportune moment to present itself. They had just made love, and were in a state of post-coital bliss when she'd finally asked him. His answer, when it came, stunned her. 'No, I don't think so,' he said, opening his eyes and sitting up against the pillows.

'Oh? I thought it would—'

'No, no, the thing is … well, there's something I ought to tell you. I'm sorry about this … should've told you ages ago … oh, damn—'

'What? For God's sake, what haven't you told me?'

'This weekend I plan to announce my engagement.'

Elizabeth stared at him, uncomprehending. 'But … but, what are you saying? We've been going out together for … Jesus Christ, we've just made love … tell me this is a wind-up?'

Dankar got out of the bed, grabbed his clothes and began to dress. 'Look, I'm sorry. I thought what we had was just for … well, sort of fun and frolics, I never saw us as a serious—'

A blast from a shotgun could not have been more devastating. The self-imposed restraint she'd maintained for years shattered like a dam giving way under a billion tons of pressure. She leaped from the bed, screaming profanities, raining punches, tearing at his face, pushing, shoving, and gouging at him. Dankar backed away, deflecting her flaying hands as he reversed out of the room and down the stairs. At the bottom of the stairs he turned and fled for his car. She would have followed except she was partially naked. As it was, her screams had aroused the interest of fellow flat dwellers. Feeling humiliated, she returned to her room, threw herself on the bed and sobbed.

A second devastating blow followed two days later: Dankar named Avril Coyle as his new fiancée.

The following month Avril succeeded in getting Dankar to persuade his business partners to bank with A.C.S. She was promptly promoted to head of Elizabeth's division.

Elizabeth handed in her notice. A week later, with the aid of an impressive CV, she secured employment in the Shannon & Dockrell

Bank. Her talents were appreciated there and exploited in full measure. A little older and a whole lot wiser, she seduced one of her richest clients (though she'd made him believe he'd been the one to instigate it) and walked down the aisle six months later. He turned out to be a good man, a generous provider, and an easy person to live with. Love? No, she didn't love him in that dreamy, romantic sort of way. Christ, no; that degree of emotional involvement had fused and burned out of her psyche forever, thanks to Gordon Dankar.

She lived in a sumptuous home and had a husband willing to pamper her with baubles, bangles and all the material possessions one could possibly desire. Through the cocktail circuit, and what passed for high society in Dublin, she formed firm friendships with a small group of like-minded women. Like her, these kindred spirits had too much leisure time on their hands but no real direction, boundless energy but no channels to adequately absorb it. Because of their marital status, wed to pillars of the community, social conventions imposed unwritten limits on their activities. To combat this sense of purposelessness, they banded together to create activities that would stimulate their lives.

Elizabeth Telford had kept tabs on Gordon Dankar's career. Articles in the press were cut out and pasted in her scrapbooks. Through friends, who moved in similar circles to that of the Dankars, she'd learned some unsavoury facts. Dankar lived with Avril and their two children in a luxurious house on Howth Head. He also owned an apartment on Clarion Quay, a luxury penthouse pad within walking distance of his office in the International Financial Services Centre (IFSC). Whenever some major deal neared completion, and all-night brain-storming sessions were called for, he used the penthouse to grab a few hours' sleep and a change of wardrobe. Elizabeth learned that Dankar had other uses for his Clarion Quay pad.

In recent times there had been a mushrooming of prostitution in and around the IFSC. Stockbrokers, bankers and financiers working in this area sometimes mixed with the underbelly of the city's vice trade. Gordon Dankar availed of those services on occasions and brought the objects of his lustful needs back to the penthouse.

With the connivance of her friends, Elizabeth secured the services of an escort lady to inveigle her way into Dankar's affections. She offered the woman three times what Dankar had paid her to perform a number of tasks while in his penthouse. The escort, a resourceful woman in her twenties had learned her trade well. In the space of three weeks she uncovered the user name and password to Dankar's computer system. This information had been passed to specially selected 'cleaning personnel', a team of IT specialists who were adept at manipulating computer files. In tandem with this scheme, Elizabeth's friends arranged a break-in at Dankar's home. Nothing was taken but a number of computer files were carefully secreted among the household contents.

And now the results of Elizabeth's schemes had come to fruition. She passed out copies of the morning papers to her three friends in The Cat's Pyjamas. Sipping golden bubbly, they read the front-page article.

TOP FINANCIER PROSECUTED FOR INSIDER TRADING

Senior Garda officers from the fraud squad, acting on an anonymous tip-off, raided the penthouse apartment of high-flying financier Gordon Dankar in the early hours of yesterday morning. Investigating officers removed computers and disks containing details of dealings in shares and options. The records, mostly dating back to transactions conducted a decade earlier, clearly show that Dankar violated a fiduciary by virtue of his insider knowledge. Dankar invested heavily in a number of the country's best known corporations mere days before they informed the Stock Exchange of take-over plans.

In a simultaneous raid, further disks were discovered at Dankar's home. Insp. Joe Davis, in charge of the investigation is carrying out on-going searches. Dankar's solicitor claims the files were planted, insisting that his client has been framed. However, an informed source from the IFSC claims that the information contained in the files is an accurate record of Dankar's share dealing at the time. If this proves to be the case then Dankar will be barred from trading on the Stock Exchange and faces the possibility of a custodial sentence.

'Cheers,' Elizabeth said, as all four women clinked glasses.

CHAPTER 15

'**P**lease go away,' Ann Buckley said, closing the door in Emma's face, 'I don't wish to talk to the press, OK?'

Emma stood her ground. 'Look Ann, please, I know how you feel ... all I want to do is have a word—'

'No, you *don't* know how I feel. I've nothing to say to you.'

'You're wrong! You and I both want answers: we need to know who killed your sister.'

Ann Buckley blinked. She appeared more composed than when she'd interrupted proceedings at the district court. Today, it was possible to spot paleness behind the tan. Her grey-green eyes looked drained, as though they'd been subjected to too much grief, exposed to too much stress. Yet, when she spoke, a contradictory, self-assured timbre underlined each word. 'I understood they *had* the killer,' she said. 'He's a detective and he's what ... your partner? I'm not a bloody fool; I read the papers; I've seen pictures of you together. Now you're here, I have to wonder why.'

'I want to talk to you. Like I say, I want what you want—'

'To get at the truth, yeah? Discover who *really* killed Nuala?'

Emma ignored the sarcasm, said, 'Right.'

Ann Buckley opened the door, beckoned Emma inside. This had been Nuala's house, a terraced redbrick off Mountpleasant Avenue. It consisted of a living-room and kitchen on the ground floor and two bedrooms and a bathroom upstairs. Cardboard boxes were piled haphazardly in the hallway. 'Nuala's stuff,' Ann explained, as she threaded her way to a small untidy kitchen. 'I'm moving it to my father's place.' She shifted a Barbie doll and a child's paint set from a chair to allow Emma sit, 'So, how can I help you? I'm a bit busy right now, what with Nuala's kids and—'

'Where are the children?' Emma interrupted.

Before Ann could answer, a noise came from upstairs. 'Blast!' a man's voice yelled out. 'The stupid refuse sack's just split down the middle. I told you we'd put too much into it.' The person behind the voice appeared, a jumble of clothes balanced precariously on his outstretched arms, his chin securing the pile in place. He stopped when he saw Emma. 'Didn't know we had company,' he said, looking over the bundle of clothes.

Ann made the introductions. 'This is Sam … Sam Cline. He's helping me pack. Sam, this is Emma Boylan, she's with the *Post*.'

Cline let the clothes fall to the floor and moved to Ann's side. He was a good-looking young man with long, luxuriant fair hair, spiky on top, something akin to Jon Bon Jovi's mop circa 1997. With well-defined cheekbones and designer stubble, he wore a gold stud in his left earlobe that looked to Emma like a miniature tuning fork. Sensing Emma's assessment, Cline placed his hands on Ann's shoulder, his long slender fingers gently kneading the base of her neck. 'You agreed not to talk to the press,' he said to her, 'you know how they quote out of context.'

'It's all right, Sam,' Ann said, his interjection appearing to annoy her. 'It's OK, I'm fine.'

Cline stood his ground, fixing Emma with his stare.

'I'm fine,' Ann repeated, 'There's a few more plastic sacks in the main bedroom; use one inside the other … stops them splitting.'

Cline picked up the scattered clothes and headed upstairs, the scowl on his face affirming his resentment. As soon as he'd gone Ann plugged in the coffee-maker. 'Want some?' she asked.

'Love a cup,' Emma said. 'Sorry if I upset your boyfriend. I—'

'No, no, Sam's not my boyfriend, God no! He was close to Nuala. Her death, well, it really shook him up. He's a sensitive soul … a musician, a classical musician. He's feeling a bit raw and emotional right now. We all are.'

'Yes, I can understand that.'

'Thanks. So, how can I help you?'

'I admire your attitude; you were brave to tackle the judge about Nuala's children. Did you get it sorted?'

Ann hesitated. The plop-plop-plop sound of coffee percolating filled the awkward pause 'Chris and Katie,' she said at length, 'are with my father. He didn't want them at first … he can be so pig-headed … refused to acknowledge their existence until this happened. I persuaded him to take them, at least on a temporary basis. He's agreed to pay a child-minder until things are sorted. Not sure what'll happen long term.'

'You told Judge English you didn't want Nuala's ex-partner to get custody. Why was that?'

Ann busied herself pouring the coffee before answering. 'That's all in the past; I really don't want to go there.'

'Look, you can talk to me off the record – what you say is just between the two of us – is that OK?'

'I don't know ... yeah, I suppose so.'

'Can you tell me what the children's father has done to upset you?'

'You promise not to put anything I say in your paper?'

'That's what I said. As it happens I no longer work for the *Post*.'

'What, they fired you?'

'Well, suspended more like ... until I can prove Connolly had nothing to do with your sister's death. I need to find out what actually happened and I'm hoping that you can help me.'

Ann remained silent as she added milk and sugar to her coffee. She began to stir it, almost as though Emma weren't there, her eyes staring into the mid-distance. Emma wanted to decipher what lay behind the vacant stare. 'I was asking about the children's father. Why do you want to keep him away?'

'Because he's ... because he's a nasty piece of work.'

'What makes you say that?'

'He's a rapist. His name's Darren Dempsey; he was charged.'

'Oh! Did he do time for it?'

'Not Dempsey,' she said angrily, 'he got away with it. The police screwed up; got the wrong date on the warrant, something stupid like that.'

'So this man, this Darren Dempsey got off on a technicality?'

'Doesn't alter the fact that he's a rapist; the bastard tried it on me.'

'What? But ... but surely you reported it?'

'Wasn't that simple. Nuala was in Holles St hospital giving birth to Katie at the time. I took time off work to baby-sit Chris. Back then, Nuala and Dempsey were living together in a rented house in Drumcondra. My father washed his hands of Nuala.'

'What about your mother?'

'Our mother's dead.'

'Sorry to hear that.'

'It's all right, we were kids when she died. Without her, Dad became over protective. He's a very proud man. As you probably know, he owns the Carrigmore Stud in Wicklow. He had plans for Nuala and I to take over the running of the place when he retired.

Nuala was his favourite. Trouble was, he tried to control her life, vet her friends, tell her how to dress and behave. Nuala was feisty, head-strong, and Dad was stubborn as a mule. They fought every day, one row after another. Finally, Nuala snapped; she'd had enough. She loved the horses but she couldn't take Dad's domineering ways. She moved to the city, hung with a wild crowd, went a bit mental, you know – sex, drugs, rock 'n' roll the lot. Screwed around with anyone and everyone. And then she became pregnant.'

'She told you about it?'

'Yes, she begged me not to tell Father but somehow or other he found out. He insisted that she terminate the pregnancy and offered to pay for everything. He was prepared to take her back to Carrigmore and find her a man "with the right pedigree". Nuala was having none of it. A vicious slanging match ensued. Terrible things were said: he called her a common whore, said she'd besmirched the Buckley name. He threatened to cut off her annual allowance, remove her from his will and disinherit her.'

'How did she react to that?'

'Can't you just imagine? She told him where he could stick his will and went ahead and had the baby. I continued to work at home with the horses but I kept in touch with Nuala. She was my only sister and we were very close. I finally got to meet the father of her child, Darren Dempsey, and what a let-down that turned out to be.'

'Why do you say that?'

'From day one I could tell that Dempsey wasn't up to much. For sure, he had the looks; I could understand how he might appeal to women, but I was disappointed, thinking Nuala should have been more discerning.'

'Did Nuala know how you felt?'

'No, I didn't see much point in telling her.'

'You were going to tell me what happened when Nuala was having her second baby.'

'Yes, sorry. Like I was saying, Nuala was in the hospital giving birth to Katie. Dempsey came home after visiting her; had a skinful taken, could hardly stand. He put his arms around me to steady himself ... and that was OK, but then he tried to kiss me. I pushed him back, told him to go sober up. After that, I fed Chris, changed his nappy, put him to bed for the night and went to bed myself. Later, Dempsey came to my room, woke me up and said he wanted to sort things out. The look I saw in his eyes was enough for me. I screamed and tried to push him out. The noise woke Chris. Dempsey hung on to me and knocked me back in the bed but I managed to get away from him. I grabbed baby Chris and held him in front of me like a shield as I backed out of the room. That seemed to sober Dempsey. He left me alone after that.'

'You told Nuala about this, surely?'

'Well, no, not straight away. Didn't want to upset her, what with the new baby and all. I held my tongue until the day Dempsey was taken in on a charge of rape. A woman claimed he'd spiked her drink before luring her to his car. She reported it to the police. Two days later they brought him in. The victim picked him from a line-up.'

'Did you know the girl who accused him?'

'No, I didn't – she gave evidence in camera.'

'So you told Nuala what happened?'

'Couldn't stay quiet any longer. The court case took place three months after Katie was born. I had to tell Nuala. They split after that.'

Emma had more questions but she was aware of sounds coming from upstairs. Ann got up from the table and brought her coffee mug to the sink and glanced at her watch. Emma knew her time was up. 'I'll let you get on with your packing,' she said. 'Tell me one more thing before I go: did I see Darren Dempsey standing by the grave-side at Nuala's burial?'

'You probably did. I can't believe he had the audacity to turn up. I was flabbergasted when I saw him accepting condolences.'

'Was he the good-looking, tallish man standing to the left of Edmund Smyth-O'Brien?'

'Yes, what a hypocrite!'

'He looked pretty broken up to me.'

'Crocodile tears, I assure you.'

'And Maurice Elliott? I saw you get into his car after the funeral. You and he are friends?'

'You know Maurice?'

'Yes, I do,' Emma said, making it sound as though they were on the best of terms. 'I went to his house in Sandycove recently to discuss his new political party. Nice place he's got. You been there?'

'No, I haven't. Maurice was Nuala's friend.'

'Really?' Emma said, remembering the hostile expression in Diana's eyes as she stared at Maurice's car leaving the graveyard.

'Yes, I think Nuala thought Maurice would split from Diana ... move in with her, something like that.'

'But, I thought Nuala and Diana were friends?

'True! But Nuala was a past master at messing up all her relationships. When it came to men, she had a talent for picking pricks.' Ann paused and looked directly into Emma's eyes. 'Funny how the wrong kind of men seem to gravitate to certain women.'

'Sorry, I'm not sure I follow you?' Emma said.

'Your detective friend Connolly, he too, had an eye for Nuala.'

'What?' Emma said, visibly shaken. 'That's not true.'

'Oh? You didn't know?'

'No, I don't know ... and, sorry, but I don't believe—'

'Well, maybe I'm speaking out of turn. A friend of mine said something about Iseult Connolly's *old man* sniffing around Nuala.'

Emma shook her head, confused. 'Surely the term "old man" referred to Iseult's father.'

'No, not in this instance.'

'Why do you say that?'

'Family history! My father and Iseult's father have been friends for as long as I can remember.' A far-away look crept into Ann's eyes. 'I was eight years old the first time I met Iseult. Our families had got together for an Easter dinner. Nuala and Iseult were teenagers and were best friends. I looked up to both of them and couldn't wait to grow up and be like them. They went to parties together and were members of the same pony club. And then, years later, you can imagine my father's wrath when he discovered that Nuala was working as a "domestic" for Iseult. He felt belittled, claimed Nuala was purposely wiping his nose in it. So, you see, the idea that Smyth-O'Brien would be the one to show an interest in Nuala is just plain daft.'

Emma didn't quite follow the logic of Ann's argument but let it go. 'Tell me something, Ann, this friend of yours who mentioned Iseult's *old man*, could you give me her name?'

'I'd prefer not to say.'

'It's important to me. I need to know the truth.'

Ann shrugged her shoulders. 'Yes, I can see that. Too many good women are fooled by false lovers. You promise not to mention my name?'

'Promise!'

'OK. My friend's name is Margot Hillary.'

Emma wanted to continue but Cline returned. He dumped a handful of photographs on to the seat of a chair, accidentally knocking one of them to the ground. Emma picked it up, saw that it was a picture of two smiling children. 'Are these Nuala's?' she asked.

'Yes,' Ann said, taking it from Emma and pointing to a baby girl. 'That's little Katie, a proper little madam, and that's Chris beside her – he's eighteen months older but she's the domineering one. This photo was taken about a year ago.'

'They're beautiful,' Emma said, captivated by the two smiling faces. 'How have they reacted to the death of their mother?'

'Well, poor little Katie is too young to properly understand what's happened. With Chris it's different; he's five. He knows something bad has happened but he's so occupied by all the fuss in moving to his grandfather's big house in Wicklow that he's saying little.'

'Poor things,' Emma said.

Cline took the photograph from Ann and put it back with the rest of the stuff. 'Look, it's time we got a move on,' he said to Ann, this time making no attempt to disguise the fact that he wanted Emma out of the way.

'It's OK, I'm off,' Emma said. 'I can see how busy you are. Thanks for talking to me. Best of luck with the children; they're absolutely adorable.'

CHAPTER 16

It had been an hour since Margot inhaled but the buzz remained. She felt good, strong, ready to take on the world. Well, not the world perhaps, but ready to lock horns with the journalist sitting opposite her. Margot Hillary had been expecting Emma Boylan and had prepared for the encounter. Cocaine would make the exchange that bit more agreeable. She embraced the recreational drug culture and welcomed the Utopian flights of disengagement it provided. It never failed to dispel the despair that threatened to overwhelm her.

Ever since the events that led to the death of the pervert who'd abused her son, her daily existence had evolved into a state of dream-like illusion. The big house she lived in with Norbert had, for her at least, become a mausoleum for the un-dead, a horror of primeval proportions. Her son, Ronan, who would one day inherit the Hillary estate and fortune was at boarding-school. In the year since the pool incident, her fears that Ronan might be gay had solidified. As far as she could ascertain, Norbert had no idea; such a notion would never occur to him. For him, it was enough to know he had a son and heir, a direct bloodline in readiness to promulgate the Hillary dynasty. If Ronan's sexual proclivities were as she suspected, then the Hillary bloodline might not reign as long as her husband envisaged, but Margot had long since given up worrying about such matters.

The after-burn still glowed as Margot studied Emma Boylan from behind her shades. She knew quite a lot about the investigative journalist. Her long-time friend Iseult Connolly had mentioned *that Boylan bitch* many times in the lead up to her acrimonious split from her detective husband. It's doubtful if Iseult ever loved Connolly – she positively loathed him in the end – and had several affairs before, during, and after, the split. Margot could not understand why Iseult felt so aggrieved that her ex had taken up with Emma in, what she termed, his *shitty little policeman's existence.* And now *that Boylan bitch* was here asking questions.

Margot could see Emma Boylan trying to get a fix on her, endeavouring to peek behind the shades, look into her eyes, probe inside her head. Well, she could piss up a gum tree on that score. The surgical scars had all but vanished but removing the shades would expose her dilated pupils. She would not give the journalist that satisfaction. Instead, she draped her body – a little on the tall side but well proportioned – gracefully on the chair opposite the journalist and decorously crossed her legs. Wearing a calf-length skirt, split to mid-thigh, and a loose white blouse with top buttons undone, she felt deliciously salacious. 'Yes,' she said, her voice ever so lightly slurred in reply to an earlier question from Emma, 'I was a close friend of Iseult Connolly. Through her I got to know Nuala Buckley.'

Emma couldn't penetrate Margot's dark shades or decipher what expression the hidden eyes held but even so, the woman managed to evoke an unmistakable aura of sexuality, a factor that somewhat unsettled Emma.

Christ, I think she's coming on to me.

There was something about Margot's mouth that seemed particularly sensual; the way her lips remained slightly parted while her tongue delicately caressed her front teeth. Emma forced herself to concentrate on the matter in hand. 'I've explained why I'm here,' she said, referring to their earlier conversation. 'I'd like you to tell me what you know about Nuala's men friends.'

'By that, I take it you mean *your* friend – the detective?' Margot said, her elongated fingernails fiddling with crimson tresses of hair that owed little to the colour nature had intended.

'I'm not aware that Connolly had a relationship with Nuala Buckley.'

'Hmmm? Well, I can only tell you what I know. I called to see Iseult on the morning she died. I spoke to Nuala Buckley at the door. She told me Iseult had gone out on Ragtime – that's her horse – and wouldn't be back till noon. Your policeman friend was there at the time.'

'You're mistaken,' Emma said defiantly, 'he couldn't have been.'

'His car was in the driveway.'

'Who says it was his car?'

'I do! I *actually* saw him as I stood talking to Nuala.'

'You saw Detective Inspector Connolly in Iseult's house?'

'That's what I just said.'

'What time did you get there?'

'Eleven-fifteen.'

'Really? Why didn't you go to the police with this information?'

'I assumed they already knew. Wasn't until last night that I realized I ought to talk to the authorities.'

'Why, what happened last night?'

'I was dining with a friend and happened to hear something that made me realize I should have gone forward with what I knew.'

'What exactly did you hear?'

'I don't want you to feel bad about this, Ms Boylan, but you're not the only woman in Connolly's life. He also had the hots for Nuala Buckley.'

Emma was finding it hard to stifle the fury uncoiling inside her. 'You are wrong, very wrong! I do not believe—'

'I'm not wrong, I assure you. Nuala confided in a good friend of mine, who told me in turn that Connolly pestered Nuala to go out with him.'

'Why would Nuala Buckley discuss this with your friend?'

'Nuala didn't know whether or not to tell Iseult about Connolly's approaches so she sounded out my friend.'

'And what did this *friend* advise Nuala to do?'

'She suggested that Iseult be told. I mean, it wasn't as if Iseult and Connolly were still husband and wife.'

'Did Nuala actually tell Iseult?'

'That, I don't know. Nuala's dead. Iseult's dead. We'll never know.'

'This friend of yours, may I have her name?'

'I think she'd prefer to stay out of this if it's all the same to you.'

Emma's frustration spilled over. 'No, it's not all the same to me,' she blurted. 'Like you say, two women are dead.'

'You're a journalist, right? Shouldn't you bring a little objectivity to this, remove the blinkers?'

'Meaning...?'

Margot sighed theatrically. 'Iseult knew what Connolly was like; gave him his marching orders, but he still came back. You tell me what Connolly was doing in that house when the women met their deaths?'

'You've got it wrong!' Emma said, taking a deep breath. 'Connolly is a *good* man. I aim to prove it ... with or without your help.'

'Oh, very well then. I'll give you the name of my friend, but I might as well warn you it will just confirm what I've already told you.'

'The name, *please?*'

'Diana Elliott.'

'Maurice Elliott's wife, yes?'

'None other.'

Emma was about to probe further but stopped when a man entered the room. 'Oh, sorry, Margot,' he said in a deep sonorous voice, 'didn't realize you had company.'

A look of irritation crossed Margot's face, the expression quickly masked by a smile. 'This is my husband Norbert,' she said, using splayed fingers to indicate the patrician figure standing before them. 'Norbert, this is Ms Emma Boylan. She's a journalist with the *Post*. She's enquiring about ... poor Iseult.'

Emma shook his hand. 'Pleased to meet you, Mr Hillary,'

'Name's Norbert,' he said, holding her hand in a firm grip. 'A terrible business. Poor Iseult, a wilful person all her life, but dear God, I never thought she would ... well, you know. And Shane Buckley's daughter; what's the world coming to?'

Emma nodded in agreement, retrieved her hand from his grip. Norbert Hillary's face put her in mind of the old-fashioned portraiture from the Victorian age. He had a longish face, large nose, good eyes, silver hair, split down the centre, and a silver moustache. His manner and appearance were in marked contrast to that of his wife.

'So, tell me, Emma,' he asked, 'what's your interest in this tragedy?'

Emma felt awkward, not knowing how best to explain her involvement. Before she could reply, Margot cut in. 'Iseult's ex-husband, Detective Connolly, is living with this young lady.' she said to her husband. 'He was the one who found the body; right now he's helping the police with their enquiries.' Margot's face, so perfectly made-up, took on the look of bored detachment when speaking to Norbert.

'Oh dear, I see,' Norbert said, studying Emma with renewed interest. 'And what makes you think my wife can help?'

'I'm talking to all those who knew Iseult; I'm hoping to discover what really happened.'

'Most commendable,' he said, 'but just remember this: when one seeks the truth, the answer, when it comes, might not be to the seeker's liking.'

onnolly paced the apartment, his size nines covering the entire floor area several times over, his mind shooting off in multiple tangents: so many thoughts, so many *what ifs* and *buts*. Emma, gone for the day, had left him with nothing but the four walls for companionship, a solitude that conspired to crush his spirits. Self-imposed solitary confinement felt alien, but what choice did he have? His solicitor's advice had been unequivocal – *under no circumstances involve yourself in the investigation*. On top of that, the chief super had given him some so-called friendly advice – *keep a low profile while investigations remained on-going*. And, as though that weren't enough, Bob Crosby had thrown in his tuppence-ha'penny worth – *don't poke your nose above the parapet*.

Twice he'd opened the drinks cabinet. A tempting prospect but he knew what drink did to him. Cigarettes? Neither he nor Emma smoked, but if there had been a packet lying about he'd have had a go. He needed something, anything, to occupy himself. Since this whole crazy business erupted he had theorized on every possible aspect of the deaths of the two women. At night, he lay awake extrapolating fanciful scenarios, all of them amounting to nothing more than a great fat zero.

Unconsciously, he ran his fingers through the fine strands of silver hair that swept above his ears.

Music, that's what I need, music, noise, a racket.

He flicked through the CD rack, selected Amy Winehouse's *Back to Black*, one of Emma's favourites. The blast of music ended the God-awful silence, blunted the echoes but failed to deliver escapism. Like a caged lion, he prowled the confined space, his every instinct urging him to get out and do the job he'd been trained to do: *detection*.

Emma and he had discussed the situation *ad nauseam*. He'd wanted to enlist her in the role of proxy detective, have her follow up on a series of leads he considered useful but she would have none of it. He should have known better. Emma insisted, as always, on doing her own investigation. And that meant doing it her way.

Can't take any more Amy Winehouse.

Not today.

The soulful track, *Tears Dry on their Own* was tearing him apart. Back to empty solitude. He stopped pacing, stood beside the large picture window overlooking the Liffey quays, and observed the world as it went about its everyday business. He pushed open a section of window and stepped on to the small crescent-shaped wrought-iron balcony. From this lofty position, he subjected his lungs to an intake of the biting air blowing up from the river. A combination of recent heavy rains and high tides had swollen the river several feet above its normal waterline. The blustery April afternoon carried a whiff of barley and hops on the breeze, a residue from the huge Guinness brewery further upstream, the distinctive smell, augmented by the ever-present rich aroma of the river itself, an integral part of the city's character. Wasn't always like that of course. Until quite recent times the river carried most of Dublin's sewage to the sea, leaving a pungent aroma in its wake which, if harnessed, would surely have driven a large turbine. Legend had it that Dublin wit, Oliver St John Gogarty, once swam across the river to avoid loan-sharks in pursuit. When his friend James Joyce said to him, 'I believe you swam the Liffey,' Gogarty replied, 'No, I was just going through the motions.'

The sky promised rain. More rain. Earlier downpours meant that the masonry of the buildings reflected his mood: dark and oppressive. Below him, a segment of Dublin's million citizens moved about without any discernible pattern or purpose. Traffic crept sluggishly along the quays, criss-crossing the bridges that linked the capital's north and south sides. The wide swell of water, hemmed in by steep granite walls, moved seaward as squawking seagulls indulged in a wild, erratic, gymnastic ballet above the flow. Connolly just stood there, seeing everything and seeing nothing, freezing his arse off, his body statue-like in its stillness.

He had no idea how long he stood like that, a forlorn, solitary figure framed in a big window and dwarfed by the city's vastness. Somewhere, a bell rang, its sound lost in the abstract thoughts swirling through his brain. The sound persisted, forcing him to take cognisance of its insistent peal. Someone was buzzing the intercom. He hoped it might be Emma but remembered she had a key.

Damn!

He spoke into the intercom. 'Who is it?'

'Is Emma there?' a male voice asked.

Connolly thought he recognized the speaker. 'Who wants to know?'

There was a pause, then the voice again. 'It's Vinny Bailey.'

'Come on up,' he said, wondering if he should have encouraged him to go away. What he didn't need right now was a confrontation with Emma's ex. Too late. The man stood outside his door.

'Hello, Vinny,' Connolly said, 'come on in.'

Vinny looked around somewhat sheepishly, hoping to see Emma. 'She here?' he asked, his delivery, like his countenance, icy as an Arctic blast.

'No, she's out,' he replied awkwardly.

Both men faced each other, making direct eye contact. 'I thought you ought to come up,' Connolly offered, 'leave a message or ... whatever. If Emma knew you called and thought I turned you away, well ... you can imagine the fuss.' Connolly's attempt at a smile failed. 'You know what she's like – always wanting to do the right thing, always—'

'Yeah, I *do* know. I was married to her for ten years.'

'Yes, Vinny, of course you were. Look, was there something in particular you wanted to see her about? I can pass on a message, or—?'

'Give me her new mobile number. I've tried to call her but it looks like you've got her to change her number.'

'You're wrong! I didn't make her do anything,' Connolly said with growing irritation. 'Emma changed the number herself.'

'Yeah right, whatever. Can I have it?'

'No, sorry, Emma decides who gets her number; it's got nothing to do with me.'

Vinny swayed a little, a disagreeable smirk distorting his lips. He was as tall as Connolly and had a similar strong build but that was the extent of their similarity. Connolly was a city person through and through whereas Vinny fell into the tweed and cords category, a bohemian at heart, though living with Emma had smoothed some of the rougher edges. Yet, something of the outsider remained part of his persona. He would never feel at ease with the establishment, never lend support to 'the natural party of government', and never fully trust in the country's forces of law and order.

'You've gone to great lengths to stop Emma contacting me,' Vinny said, undisguised resentment rolling off his tongue. 'Problem is, I need to *see* her, hear first hand what sort of mess you've got her into.'

'Look,' Connolly said, adopting a cut-the-bullshit inflection, 'Emma Boylan is an adult, and a very capable one at that; you being married to her all those years should know she's big on independence, makes all her own decisions. I wouldn't want to change that, or make her do anything she didn't want to do. But look, look ... I don't think this is the place or the—'

Vinny held up a hand, forestalling Connolly's protestations. 'I see pictures of Emma plastered over the newspapers; she looks terrible, way too thin ... sick from all the grief you're giving her. I read stories suggesting that she's become – what? – a scarlet woman, a *femme fatale*, a slapper on the town, a wrecker of marriages. I just want to ask her how she could let you do that to her. I thought that maybe, just maybe, she could do with a genuine friend right about now, someone with her best interest at heart, someone who knows the meaning of true friendship, someone who respects her and can take her away from the madness you've involved her in.'

'I think you've said enough—'

'Said enough? Jesus, I haven't even started. I rang the *Post* and they told me she no longer works there. What the hell's going on? I rang her parents, talked to her mother; the poor woman was too upset to speak. So, I took it upon myself to come here, to let her know I haven't abandoned her.'

'Might be best if you left now,' Connolly said, indicating the door.

'Don't like hearing some home truths, that it?'

'Look, Vinny, I've no intention of arguing with you. When Emma comes home I'll pass on your concerns.'

Vinny's eyes filled with accusation, resentment, confusion, and fury; his fists twitched, itching to have a pop at Connolly. 'I'm going,' he snapped, looking as though he wanted to say more but unable to find the appropriate stinging rebuke to mark his exit.

Connolly returned to the drinks cabinet. The confrontation had got to him. He picked up a glass and the Jameson bottle and was about to pour a measure when he stopped, thought better of it. The urge to smash the glass against the wall, see it explode into smithereens, took hold of his consciousness for a fleeting moment, but he checked himself, put the glass back where it belonged. Years of continuous marital trouble and strife with Iseult had forced him to curb his temper and weather bouts of frustration.

Need to clear my head.

He moved to the kitchen, sat down, drummed his fingers on the worktop till they ached. It was the first time he'd been forced to give serious consideration to the collateral damage his problems were inflicting on Emma. One thing that Vinny said had struck a chord: Emma had lost too much weight of late, something that didn't suit her. When all this trouble was sorted and the dust settled, he would talk to her about it, see if there was an underlying problem, find out if he was, as Vinny suggested, responsible. He was still pondering this dilemma when the intercom rang again. Reluctantly he answered it. 'Who is it?' he asked.

'Grennan and DS Lidden. May we come in?'

'Sure, come on up,' Connolly answered, puzzled by their arrival. As soon as they entered he spotted an ominous expression on Grennan's face. 'What can I do for you gentlemen?' he asked.

'I'm placing you under arrest for the murders of Iseult Connolly and Nuala Buckley,' Grennan said, sounding far too pleased with himself.

'Now, just a bloody minute,' Connolly said, feeling as though he'd been on the end of a sucker-punch to the gut, 'I haven't killed anybody and damn-well you know it; not Nuala Buckley, not Iseult, not anybody, period.'

'We don't have to tell you a fooken thing,' Grennan said, with a smirk. 'But seeing as how you once wore the uniform, here's the score: we now have a statement from a witness who puts you at the scene of the crime almost an hour before the time you've admitted to. Furthermore, this witness will swear you were in the house with Nuala Buckley before Iseult Connolly returned. We have yet another witness who will confirm that you were trying to get your leg over Nuala Buckley for quite a while before finally killing her. As regards your poor dead missus, we now have confirmation that she too was murdered. Our friends in pathology discovered a tiny incision mark on the nape of her neck where a hypodermic needle was used. The pin-prick mark was well hidden by her hair, but we now can say for certain that she was unconscious before she was exposed to the car's exhaust fumes. So, you see, clever and all as you think you are, that whole suicide codology you set up is not going to wash. In a word, Mr Smart-arse, you're fooked.'

T raffic lights brought Emma to a halt on the north-west corner of Merrion Square, directly opposite the Oscar Wilde statue. The great dramatist and poet, in a typical pose of cheeky insouciance, stared through the park's railings as though observing the driver picking his nose in the lane next to Emma or, more likely, keeping watch on his boyhood home on the opposite corner of the street. It was there, in No.1, that Sir William and Lady Jane Francesca immersed their son in the bohemian atmosphere prevalent for many of the leading artists, lawyers, and scientists of their day.

Waiting on the lights to change, Emma's mobile bleeped, its sound an affirmation of the technological developments that had taken place since the 1770s when the surrounding Georgian architecture had been laid out. No need for traffic lights back then; no fear of road rage among the horse and buggy fraternity. The nose excavator in the car next to Emma was about to engage in some unspeakable action with his find when, mercifully, the lights changed. Emma took a left turn, pulled to a stop opposite the National Gallery and hit the answer button.

'Bad news,' Bob Crosby said. 'They've hauled him in again.'

'What? Who's hauled who in? What're you talking about?'

'Connolly's been arrested. This time the charge is murder.'

'But he's already out on bail. What the hell—?'

'Apparently, they've got new evidence.'

'He hasn't contacted me,' Emma said, annoyed to be hearing the news second-hand, cross with the messenger.

'He hasn't had a chance to contact anyone except his solicitor,' Crosby explained. 'It was McAuley who filled me in.'

'What? Are you saying I can't see him ... or talk to him?'

'Not for the moment, Emma. According to McAuley the police are gung-ho, convinced he's their man.'

'Well, that's just bloody great ... bunch of stupid gobshites.'

'Have you come up with anything?'

Emma sighed deeply. 'Not really; I'm getting nowhere fast I'm afraid.'

'Hang in there, Emma. Remember, we have one great advantage over our friends on the force.'

'We have?'

'Yes! We *know* Connolly's innocent ... that's the difference.'

'Yeah, right,' Emma said, with little enthusiasm. 'I'll carry on with what I'm doing. Something's got to turn up.'

'Good, that's the attitude. One more thing, Emma, almost forgot, a number of messages came in for you, stuff that can wait for the most part, but two of the calls were referred to me.'

'Oh, yeah? What were they?'

'One was from Vinny. He says he's being prevented from contacting you. He called to your apartment, wanted your mobile number but Connolly refused to give it. Vinny took umbrage, got in touch with your parents.'

'Damn it! That's all I need. It's my fault, I should have called him, should have called my father too. Did you say there was another message?'

'Yes. Bit strange, this one. Do you know a woman named Lisa Dunlop?'

Emma had to think for a second. 'Yes, Bob, I met her briefly in the Social Alliance Party building.'

'You don't say! Works for Maurice Elliott, does she?'

'No. She *used* to work for him but he fired her.'

'She wants to talk to you; says it's urgent. She got through to Willie Thompson, claimed to have something important to tell *you* ... nobody else.'

'When was this?'

'Yesterday. I only heard about it this morning.'

'How do I make contact?'

'She left her mobile number. You got a pen?'

Emma took her notebook from her bag, scribbled down the number. 'She give you an address?'

''Fraid not. You'll have to call her. Thompson says she sounded flaky.'

'Just what I need! Anything else?'

'No, That's about it. Just remember what I told you: our man is innocent. Bear that in mind and we'll all come through this. OK?'

'Sure, Bob. See you anon.'

Emma felt a stab of guilt. Crosby's remark about *knowing* Connolly was innocent sent shudders up her spine. Who was he trying to assure? Himself? Her? Both of them? For the first time, she allowed the faintest glimmer of doubt to surface. Feeling ashamed, she brushed the thought aside. She needed to sort out a few minor details, like having a word with Vinny. Not contacting her ex had been a mistake. She resolved to call him and her father before the day ended. But right now, there was something more urgent to attend to. She looked at the number Crosby had given her for Lisa Dunlop and punched the appropriate digits on her mobile.

CHAPTER 19

Emma attempted to park her car outside the block of flats as a uniformed garda officer gestured to a small crowd to move back. Taking great care, she nosed the Hyundai Coupé into a tight spot behind a squad car and an ambulance. The address, Leinster Close, Rathmines, had been given to her half an hour earlier when she'd spoken to Lisa Dunlop on the mobile.

Emma got out of the car, eased her way through the crowd, and approached the garda. 'What's happened?' she asked.

'Accident,' he said, giving her that typical all-encompassing glance that policemen have honed to perfection. 'A woman fell down the stairs.'

'You have her name?'

'No, sorry, ma'am, I'm not party to that information.'

'OK if I go inside? I'm supposed to meet someone.'

'You'll have to hang on, ma'am; nobody's allowed in till they get her to the ambulance. Shouldn't be long.'

As though on cue, the door opened and paramedics emerged carrying a stretcher. Emma, like those around her, craned her neck to look at the injured party. Only part of the face was visible but she recognized the woman. It was Lisa Dunlop. Today, the Cleopatra wig was missing. Emma remembered the scene in the Social Alliance Party's reception area when Lisa Dunlop, after losing her cool, spun on her heel and stormed out of the building. The fringe of her wig had slightly parted to reveal part of a tattoo. Today Emma could see it in its entirety. The letters S L U T were branded on her forehead.

She was about to push forward when a familiar figure emerged from the buildings. No mistaking DI Seán Grennan's big gut. Some instinct made her pull back to the rear of the onlookers. Grennan and a younger man, obviously a detective, waited until the ambulance departed before getting into their unmarked car and pulling away. Each onlooker had a different theory as to what happened, most of it fanciful speculation. Emma returned to her car; she needed time to evaluate the situation before venturing inside the building.

Earlier, in her conversation on the mobile, Lisa Dunlop had sounded distraught. 'What kept you so long?' she'd asked, in barely more than a croak, 'It's been a whole day since I called.'

'I've been out of the office,' Emma replied. 'Just got your message this minute. What's the problem?'

A deep sigh came from Lisa 'They're after me.'

'Sorry, *who* is after you? Why are you telling *me*?'

'Last week, you were in Maurice Elliott's office, right?'

'Yes, I was, but I didn't think you knew me.'

'I didn't know you then, hadn't the foggiest. Saw your picture in the papers since, remembered where I'd seen you.'

'What did you want to talk about?'

'The killings! But not on the phone; they're listening.'

'Who's listening? You've lost me.'

'I'm being followed. They want to shut me up.'

'Who exactly are *they*?'

'Can't say over the phone,' Lisa said in a conspiratorial whisper. 'Call to my flat, I'll talk to you before they get me; I'll tell you who's behind the killing. You coming?'

'Give me your address.'

Emma had set out straightaway but the traffic on the way to Rathmines had been badly congested. She'd inched her way along by the canal, cursing the hold-up as she went. Stalled completely at one point, she decided to contact Vinny, get him off her back. She couldn't get through to his mobile so she tried the Antiques and Fine Art Studio in Little Bray. Vinny's father, Ciarán, answered. 'Vinny's gone to an auction,' he informed her, 'won't be back till late this evening.'

Emma was fond of Ciarán and knew her feelings were reciprocated. In the past, when the odd difference of opinion between her and Vinny surfaced, Ciarán usually took her side. Today, he'd avoided all mention of the marriage break-up, sticking to small talk instead. Before hanging up he'd wished Emma happiness and expressed a wish to see her soon. Emma had promised to visit, knowing that such a meeting was highly unlikely.

Moving at a snail's pace, she'd attempted to make contact with her father's office. Arthur Boylan, a solicitor, ran a busy practice in the town of Navan. The receptionist there informed her that he was out and wouldn't return for some hours. Cursing softly to herself, she resolved to try again later. She put the mobile away just as the tailback eased. She was curious to know what lay behind Lisa Dunlop's panic call, wondering if perhaps Lisa could give her that one vital piece of information that would resolve the whole puzzle. Tragically, Lisa had already come to grief by the time she got to the flat.

Five minutes after the ambulance and the detectives departed the scene, Emma decided to take a look inside. The garda officer, like the onlookers, had found something better to do. Two young women, both carrying books under their arms, emerged from the flats as Emma approached. 'Excuse me,' she said, 'can either of you tell me what happened? I was supposed to meet Lisa Dunlop but she's just been taken away in an ambulance.'

One of the women, 19, maybe 20, with a freckled face and sandy hair, dressed in typical student attire, spoke. 'She fell down the stairs.'

Her companion, dark-haired and slightly younger, cut in. 'A nurse on the top floor says she thinks the woman was pushed. It was her that called the cops and ambulance.'

'Do you know Lisa Dunlop?'

They shook their heads in unison. 'We're on the ground floor,' the sandy-haired girl said. 'We've been studying like mad lately, don't have time to mix with anyone.'

'This nurse, do you have her name?'

'That's Rosaleen Doyle. She's on the fifth floor, flat twenty-two. She's on night duty this week.'

Emma thanked them and made her way up the stairs. There was a lift in the hallway but she decided to use the stairs instead, hoping it might be possible to spot the place where Lisa had taken her tumble. The building was well maintained, clean and brightly lit. It fell midway between the lower range of accommodation and the newer, more expensive apartments springing up across the capital. Emma paused on the fourth landing and tried door No. 19, the number Lisa had mentioned over the phone. It was locked. Pity. She would like to have seen inside. She examined the landing and the stairway but nothing out of the ordinary caught her eye, certainly no blood splatters or evidence of a struggle.

A narrow stair led to the fifth floor. A series of skylights in the arched roof gave an abundance of light but the height of the rooms had been slightly truncated. Emma knocked on No. 22. A young woman in a dressing-gown opened the door. 'Hello,' she said, stifling a yawn. 'Can I help you?'

'Sorry to bother you – Rosaleen, isn't it? – I spoke to two students below who said you'd witnessed what happened. I was wondering if you—'

'Excuse me, but who are you?'

'I'm Emma Boylan; I'm an investigative journalist. I was hoping to have a word with you about Lisa Dunlop.'

'I've already spoken to a detective.'

'Right, but I'd really appreciate if you could spare a few minutes. You see, I received a call from Lisa Dunlop before she fell; she said she'd something important to tell me.'

'I'm not sure I can help, but you may as well come in,' Rosaleen said, 'looks as though I'm not going to get any sleep today.'

Rosaleen Doyle's flat consisted of a small, tidy sitting-room divided from a tiny kitchen by a counter. An open door led to a brightly lit bedroom.

'I really don't have a whole lot to tell you,' Rosaleen said.

'One of the girls from the ground floor said you thought Lisa Dunlop might have been pushed.'

'Well, yes, I thought that at first but I'm not so sure now. I was in bed when the noise started, sounded like she was crashing into things, making a bit of a racket.'

'Does she usually make a lot of noise?'

'Yeah, she can be a right pain, especially when she's got friends in; they're the absolute pits.'

'You've seen her friends, yeah?'

'Yes, once or twice.'

'What are they like?'

'Snooty bitches, horsy set, I'd say.'

'Did she have anyone with her today?'

'Not too sure, like I told you, I was trying to sleep. I heard her shout a few times but I'd no idea what she was saying.'

'Just the one voice?'

'Hard to say; there might have been others; couldn't tell with the racket. I thought I heard her out on the landing, sounded like she was staggering about, bumping into things, muttering and shouting. After a while I heard this really loud scream followed by a thumping sound. I leaped out of bed and ran to the landing, saw Lisa lying in a heap at the bottom of the stairs. I dashed down to her, saw the way her head was twisted and thought, oh, my God, her neck's broken. I looked for signs of life, discovered she was still breathing and raced back up here, rang for an ambulance and called the police.'

'There was no one to help you?'

'Not really, most of the people in the flats are at work during the day. Apart from the students on the ground floor, the place is pretty much empty.'

'So, you didn't see anybody near Lisa?'

'You mean, did I see someone push her?'

'Did you?'

Rosaleen paused before answering. 'Well no, not exactly.'

'Not exactly? What does that mean?'

'Oh, I don't know,' Rosaleen said, a confused look on her face. 'It's probably my imagination, but when I first saw Lisa at the bottom of the stairs I thought I saw a shadow in the stairwell, thought it might be someone moving quickly downstairs.'

'Could you tell if the shadow was that of a man or a woman?'

Rosaleen gave a nervous laugh. 'I'm not even sure I saw a shadow. I'm not sure what I saw ... if anything. I told the detective all this. I overheard him tell the other detective that he thought Lisa might have been on a very bad trip. To be honest, I think he's probably right.'

'Which hospital have they taken her to?'

'I called an ambulance from All Saints, that's where I work.'

'Could you do something for me?' Emma asked. 'Could you ring All Saints and ask how Lisa Dunlop's doing? Find out which ward she's in? I want to visit her.'

Rosaleen picked up her mobile from the counter. Within seconds she was talking to someone called Charles. She looked at Emma, said, 'They're putting me through to A and E.' She spoke into the phone again and after a small delay spoke to someone. Rosaleen asked about Lisa and nodded her head several times before putting the phone down.

'What's the story?' Emma asked.

'Lisa's dead. She died in the ambulance.'

CHAPTER 20

Nine months before Iseult Connolly met her death she had been a guest at the charity banquet hosted by her great friend Diana Elliott. It was a July evening on the Costa del Sol, high season for the Marbella set. Daylight had slipped away but an oven-warm breeze continued to waft gently outward from Spain's vast interior. The super-rich, armed with platinum credit cards and matching bank balances, were determined to make their presence felt beneath the balmy Iberian sky. Diana Elliott, dressed in her best summer wear and holding a mobile to her ear, learned that the first limousines were *en route* on the Golden Mile, making their way via the Istan road. The 'beautiful people' were about to descend on her holiday home in the exclusive Olivia Valeres district of Marbella. As she talked animatedly on her mobile, her brunette hair, full and glossy, moved with natural ease in the soft evening breeze.

Diana greeted each guest with air kisses on both cheeks and thanked them for their generous patronage of her nominated charity. She'd lost none of the skills learned as a public relations practitioner back in another life. In a well-oiled operation, photographers were on hand to record the 'names' as they were greeted. These photographs, along with a press release, would later be dispatched to the media. Coverage of the event was important to both hostess and those donating chunks of cash. At €1,750 a plate, plus a contribution to the auction scheduled for later in the evening, the cost represented little more than pin money for most. These were the fat cats, the captains, kings and queens of Irish industry, many of whom had temporarily abandoned their palatial piles in Dublin's Ailesbury Road in favour of Marbella's Golden Mile.

Diana had an especially warm welcome for Iseult Connolly and took the opportunity to whisper how gorgeous her new escort looked. As a frequent visitor to the Elliott's Costa del Sol home,

Iseult habitually turned up with a handsome beau in tow. Diana, a stickler for protocol, had included Iseult's detective husband on the invitation but, as expected, he would not show. In his absence Iseult liked to pick a partner more in tune with the glamour and razzmatazz that went hand in hand with such high-toned bashes. Later in the evening Diana would quiz Iseult for a rundown on her latest paramour's prowess. Descriptions employed by Iseult to measure her lover's performance borrowed heavily from equine speak: Alisdair, she would declare, was worthy of the Blue Riband. Mark was a good three-day event rider. Trevor was hung like a young stallion and quick to his oats. James reacted well to the whip. Charles was good in the saddle and had stamina to take her all the way to the final puissance. And so it would go.

Diana's bash allowed the *soi disant* 'top society' to flaunt their wealth unabashedly while easing their conscience in the vague belief that they were helping unfortunates in some far-flung hell-hole in the third world. Quite a few of the guests had no need to dip into their own pockets at all; they were the cute ones who had arranged corporate sponsorship, or availed of the tax breaks doled out for such charitable events. For the past seven years Diana had presided over the glittering event, raising millions in the process. Rather than tie herself to a specific charity she selected her causes on an annual basis. It helped that each 'cause' she chose to favour with her largesse had prime media focus at the time.

Her husband Maurice would handle the auction later in the evening. As a successful real estate operator he knew a thing or two about buying and selling. Fifteen years earlier he had come to the Costa and seen the potential. He'd purchased a beachfront villa in the Oasis complex for what seemed like an extraordinary sum at the time; he'd sold it recently for ten times that amount. With something of a Midas touch he had bought and sold properties in Edificio Parque, Las Brisas, and Terrazas de Banus, always returning huge profits.

Marbella had been good for the Elliotts but keeping a tight rein on Maurice had caused major headaches for Diana. He liked to visit Milady's Palace, a five-star bordello in the Olivia Valeres, to sample the wares on offer. Diana no longer had, or wanted, a physical relationship with her husband, but she worried about his indiscretions. She had no objections on moral grounds. Indeed, she had carved out her own special route to pleasures of the flesh but, unlike him, she'd been careful in her choice of lover and never less than discreet. That Maurice should be so cavalier about his libidinous behaviour bothered her. She shuddered to think what would happen should some tabloid capture him in a compromising situation. His proposed entry into mainstream politics and her own high profile fundraising activities necessitated that they project a certain degree of decorum and respectability.

Diana had first singled out Maurice for special attention when he had hired her firm to create publicity for a housing project he had on the market at the time. It was obvious to her, even then, that Elliott was destined to become very successful and very rich. From her earliest days, Diana had decided she would marry money. Maurice Elliott fitted the bill; apart from his wealth he had a lot going for him. An accomplished charmer, he was easy on the eye, knew how to pass himself in society, and could provide entrée to the sort of people she desired to know and cultivate. From the start she'd known that he had an eye for women – all women – but she believed, wrongly as it turned out, that she could change his erring ways. With skill and determination she played him like an angler plays a fish. It hadn't taken her too long to land him.

They had come to Spain on their honeymoon, stayed in Marbella's Hotel Le Meridien. Her worst fears were realized as she watched him flirt with barmaids, female room attendants, and pretty girls on the beach. This was a mere precursor to what lay in store for the duration of their marriage. Post honeymoon, back in Ireland, he continued on his merry way, making money and screwing anything that moved. One-night stands were his stock in trade, but occasionally he got caught up in more protracted affairs. When this happened, Diana intervened.

His latest madcap notion to front a political party was causing her some disquiet. Why he should want to go into politics was something she didn't understand. Probably a power thing was her best guess. He'd been greatly impressed by the multimillionaire financier Sir James Goldsmith who had set up his own political party in Britain back in the nineties. Goldsmith had rocked the establishment with a very personalized brand of politics, pitching into the fray with a passion, commitment and motivation that led to his early death. Diana didn't think Maurice had an ideological bone in his body, having never displayed a passionate feeling about politics one way or another. Apart from the accumulation of money and chasing tail

there wasn't a lot he stood for. She'd once read an article about his political aspirations in the *Phoenix* magazine where the reporter had finished with the line – *Other than the national anthem there's not a lot Elliott stands for.* Diana had hoped this new-found interest in politics might divert his mind from sexual pursuits but the same old problems persisted.

Maurice had recently hired a young receptionist named Lisa Dunlop. Within a matter of days she'd been seen on his arm at Lillie's Bordello, one of Dublin's trendiest nightclubs. If she remained in the background, Diana could have let it pass. In her opinion, Lisa Dunlop had airs above her station. Hailing from the north side of the River Liffey – an insurmountable disadvantage in Diana's book – Lisa tried to mix it with the horsy crowd from south side. But the bit that hurt, the bit that crushed her spirit, was the fact that Lisa Dunlop was almost a decade younger than her. That was intolerable.

At the first opportunity, Diana had introduced herself to the receptionist and made it clear, without putting it in so many words, that it would be in her best interest to desist from going out with the boss. So far, Lisa had heeded the warning, but if the situation persisted she would call on her close band of friends to devise a more drastic plan to keep Lisa and Maurice apart.

Diana moved indoors as soon as she'd finished welcoming the guests. She was pleased with the turn out. Edmund Smyth-O'Brien and glamorous partner – his wife, Iseult's mother, had passed away two years earlier – had flown in from Rome where they had been attending a wedding. Norbert Hillary and wife Margot arrived from the South of France, both looking radiant, sporting mahogany tans but barely speaking to each other. Diana's hug and kiss for her friend Margot had been especially welcoming. She complimented Margot's magnificent outfit and asked what was wrong with 'soggy bottom' aka Norbert. 'Tell you later when I've offloaded him,' Margot said, with a conspiratorial wink. 'I've persuaded him to help with the charity auction.'

Elizabeth Telford, another of Diana's close friends, and her husband Jeffery, chairman of the Telford & Spencer corporate bank, had come over from their villa beside the old lighthouse at the marina in Puerto Banus. Elizabeth's dress – a Dolce classic – probably cost more than it would take to feed an entire African village for a year. Since Elizabeth's time in banking, since the day she'd been dumped by Gordon Dankar, she'd harboured a fear of rejection. Her display of opulence on show this evening represented one of the weapons she employed to ensure nobody ignored her. She was in good company; all the women competed for the lime-light, clad in everything from Pucci to Gucci, while their male counterparts, not to be outdone, personified the height of sartorial elegance. None looked more elegant than Ann Buckley and her father Shane. Accompanied by the whiff of his Romeo y Juliet corona cigar, Shane beamed proudly as he introduced his daughter to all and sundry.

In an enormous lounge that spread beyond a series of open patio doors through to the gardens and swimming pool, guests were already busy picking through the lobster and prawn appetizers and quaffing champagne. Later they would dine on the best gourmet foods Spain had to offer while downing cases of Ornellaia Cabernet Sauvignon and New World Chardonnay. Diana was pleased with how the bash was going, but she no longer possessed the energy she once had, the effort to host the event seeming to take a little more out of her each year.

Keeping up appearance had become an obsession. In the beauty stakes, it was important to hold the edge she perceived she had over the seriously good-looking women of forty-something in attendance. She'd seen too many women her age become invisible, boring and irrelevant. It was important that people continue to admire her, and for that to happen she must retain a youthful appearance; looking young and vibrant meant looking sexy, and sexy equated to power. She had zapped the wrinkles before they gained the upper-hand. Thanks to collagen-boosting facials, vitamin shots, yoga exercise and intense pulsed-light treatment, her skin retained its smoothness. Her legs were good, maybe not as outstanding as Elizabeth Telford's shapely pins, but good nevertheless; the few squiggly blue veins that struggled to make it to the surface were held in check by her well-toned and tanned skin. The rest of her five-foot-seven figure was holding its own … just. Her great abiding fear, that of developing cancer – the condition that killed her mother – was ever present. Not a day passed that she didn't search for the tell-tale lump that would signal the lethal malignancy. That aside, she'd had all the other medical tests done – diagnoses of her hormones, bone mass, heart condition and the like; she'd availed of all the anti-ageing treatments, everything from simple detox through to live cell injections. If these treatments failed she would consider the scalpel, but right now she was holding back the tide, successfully masking the worst that nature could inflict.

Four hours later, Diana bid farewell to the guests in a flurry of hugs and air kisses, relieved that everything had gone without a hitch. The band and special surprise celeb singer had met with enthusiastic approval. The main courses, a three-way choice – salmon with tarragon mayonnaise, pepper steak with leek mash, and veal escalope with herbs, had gone down a treat. Maurice, assisted by a reluctant Norbert Hillary, had managed to make a cool million plus on the auction. Proceedings concluded with a grand fireworks display, set to musical snippets from the better-known classics.

This was the moment Diana had been waiting for. Maurice and Norbert Hillary had wandered off into the night – they said they were going to the casino but Diana doubted if that was their destination. A few guests had been invited to stay overnight and she'd managed to get them to their respective rooms. It was 4.15 a.m. by the time she made it to her bedroom. She pressed her hands together as though in prayer, excited by the prospect of what lay ahead; she was about to make love to the person waiting in the room. She need not worry about Maurice because his room was situated on the opposite wing of the house. Besides, he already knew about her lover; it was something he'd learned to live with.

Diana took a deep breath and opened the door to her bedroom. Margot Hillary sat on the side of her bed wearing nothing but a minuscule negligee and an alluring, if somewhat lop sided, smile. Margot was already a little stoned, her flaming hair in disarray, but that didn't matter to Diana. Experience had taught her that the nose candy on offer had the power to remove all inhibition from their love play. She would take a snort before beginning her quest for the ultimate in sexual release.

CHAPTER 21

Emma drove out from the city along the N4, gripping the wheel tighter than was necessary, trickles of sweat rolling down her back and an impending headache sending advance warnings of its arrival. She was unfamiliar with the Cloverhill district, but it wasn't this lack of awareness that sparked her anxiety; it was the very thought of visiting the Cloverhill Remand Prison. She had an unreasonable disdain for prisons and all things associated with institutions of that nature. That Connolly should be locked up in one was, for her, the ultimate nightmare scenario.

The last time she'd visited a place of detention had been five years earlier. On that occasion Vinny had persuaded her to accompany him to Arbour Hill prison. Thankfully, that visit had nothing to do with law-breaking or anything untoward. She'd gone with him to view one of the prison's most interesting structures: the chapel. She'd been impressed that such a place of worship could coexist amid sinners, lawbreakers and the odd, wrongly incarcerated innocent victim. It had been the Harry Clarke stained glass window, situated behind the altar that had enticed Vinny to visit the place. He had been in raptures but, if Emma were to be honest, the window hadn't done a lot for her.

She dispelled all thoughts of the Arbour Hill visit as she pulled into the car-park of The Horse's Leap public house and went inside to seek directions. A handsome young barman seemed overly keen to give her the benefit of his knowledge as he abandoned his place behind the counter and walked her to the car, gesticulating all the while with both hands. 'Proceed along that road you see in front of you; turn right at the first set of traffic lights ... that'll bring you on to Coldcut Road. Take the next left at the lights on to Cloverhill Road. You can't miss it after that.'

Emma thanked him and got back into the car. The barman held on to her door for a moment before she closed it. 'Call in on your way back,' he said, giving her a lecherous wink. 'I'll be off duty by then; might be able to provide you with the TLC you're missing while your man's in the clink.'

In another life perhaps, Sunshine.

Emma suppressed a smile, closed the door, gunned the engine and pulled on to the road. She'd forgotten the incident by the time she checked in at the visitor's reception desk in the prison. She was instructed to wait alongside a small group of people to be processed through the security vetting system. Most of them had the bored expressions of routine visitors while others, like her, appeared ill-at-ease and unfamiliar with proceedings. After what seemed like an interminable wait, but was probably no more than ten minutes, a female prison officer escorted her to the visiting area. Emma was granted twenty minutes with the detainee. Nervously, she took a seat opposite Connolly at a narrow table, experiencing an unaccountable sense of guilt at being there. He was wearing prison regulation grey corduroy trousers and green shirt.

'Could be worse,' Connolly said, trying for a smile, 'they have dividing screens in the visiting area next door.'

'Why so?' Emma asked, glancing at the other inmates and visitors in their section. A bespectacled middle-aged prison officer stood by the door, his eyes appearing enlarged behind thick lenses, keeping watch on all activity.

'Because drug addicts and dealers are physically separated from their visitors ... for obvious reasons.'

'Well, let's be grateful for small mercies,' Emma said, reaching to hold his hand. She tried to blank the surroundings and make the most of the limited time available. They took it in turns to bring each other up to speed on current developments. Connolly confirmed that he'd been charged with double murder and would be held on remand until a date was set for trial. That could take anything up to six months, maybe longer. Bail was not an option.

'Did you know that Iseult was buried this morning?' Emma asked.

'Yes. I saw it on the early news, saw the reporters baying for pictures of me at the graveside. They'd love that – just as well I'm locked up here.'

'They'll still splash your photograph next to shots of Iseult and Nuala.'

'Tell me about it; every time my name's mentioned, it's prefixed with the words – *double-murder suspect*.' Connolly squeezed

Emma's hand. 'I'm not too bothered,' he said. 'I've done nothing wrong, justice will prevail. Have to admit though, I'd like to be out there with you gathering evidence on whoever's trying to frame me.'

Emma asked what seemed like an obvious question. 'Who hates your guts enough to kill in order to frame you?'

'I've got a whole bagful of theories ... I just don't have anything substantial enough to finger a suspect.'

'Come on, Jim, there must be a name on top of that list.'

'Well, yes, but it makes no sense. My prime suspect is dead.'

Emma nodded knowingly. 'You mean Iseult, right?'

'Right. It's crazy but there you have it.'

'Wait a minute, when this began, I suggested Iseult might have staged the whole thing to make it look like murder; you disagreed, remember? What's changed your mind?'

'I told you then that she'd never take her own life – I still believe that, but the crazy bit is, she must have been involved. She phoned me that morning, made sure I'd be there when the action went down, but for some inexplicable reason, she became a victim.'

'And what about Nuala Buckley, was she also in on the conspiracy?'

'I don't know. Maybe she was, maybe she wasn't. I think Iseult and her friends might have planned to accuse me of raping Nuala.'

Emma nodded. 'Well, yes, that'd tie in with her phone call to her father. It might explain why her friends are so quick to give evidence against you.'

'It's definitely a conspiracy,' Connolly said, interlocking his fingers. 'For reasons that escape me, they're hell-bent on destroying me.'

'Is Edmund Smyth-O'Brien one of the plotters? Was *he* telling lies when he said Iseult called him?'

'No, I think he got the call all right. It's what she's supposed to have said that I don't believe: all that stuff about finding me with Nuala Buckley and then chasing her into the garage ... it never happened.'

'And yet the door to the garage had been busted, like she said.'

An expression of dread crossed Connolly's face. 'Are you saying you believe Smyth-O'Brien? You think that I—'

'No Jim, I never said ... shit, now you're being paranoid.'

'Is it any wonder? I'm banged up in here behind bars like some—'

'Listen to me, Jim, I know you didn't rape Nuala, OK? And I

know you didn't kill Iseult, right? It's just that, given what Smyth-O'Brien was told, and given how Iseult's body was found, it looks bad. That aside, the thing that baffles me is *why*, why are Iseult's friends lying? They hardly know you. What reason do they have for concocting such stories?'

'Beats me, Emma; beats the hell out of me.'

'OK, let's try another tack. Who, besides Iseult, hates you enough to set up this elaborate frame?'

'Iseult's father? From the day he discovered I was engaged to Iseult, he took pleasure in humiliating me. I was never good enough for his precious daughter. But I can't see him harming *her* to get to me, can you?'

'No, I can't. So, who else out there has it in for you?'

'Well, I've put a fair number of criminals away in my time, but I can't see any of them being behind this. No one else springs to mind ... unless ...'

'Unless what ... who?'

'Unless you count Seán Grennan.'

'Yeah?'

'We trained together in Templemore. Back then we seemed destined to be pitted against each other. I've never thought about it much since – we were young lads at the time, burning off excess hormones, having a bit of fun, at least that's how I saw it. Since this murder business I'm not so sure, but you never can tell with Grennan. Behind that redneck persona he projects, he's cunning as a fox; not near as green as he's cabbage looking. Right now, he appears to be going all out to stitch me up.'

'That's very interesting,' Emma said. Mention of Grennan brought to mind the scene she'd witnessed outside Lisa Dunlop's flat. The press had allocated the incident to sidebars on their inside pages, recording the death as accidental. Her own paper, despite her protestations, consigned the report to the 'News in Brief' column. *The Times* implied that drugs had been involved. It occurred to Emma that people like Lisa seemed destined to be swept to the margins of society, even in death. She told Connolly about seeing the detective outside the flat in Rathmines and related the strange episode of the tattoo on Lisa's forehead. 'There has to be a connection with your case; Lisa told me she wanted to talk about the killings.'

'She also told you she had an affair with Maurice Elliott?'

'Well, actually I picked that titbit up when I visited Elliott's reception. It was obvious from what Lisa said to Elliott on the phone that a degree of hanky-panky had been going on.'

'And this tattoo business? Who would organize that?'

Emma shrugged her shoulders. 'Elliott's wife?'

'Not Diana! I don't think she'd get involved in that sort of thing.'

Emma raised both eyebrows. 'You know Diana Elliott?'

'Yes, met her a few times with Iseult. Tough woman! Never could understand how she tolerates Maurice Elliott.'

'The man certainly appears to spread his favours. According to Ann Buckley, he was carrying on with her sister Nuala.'

'I'm going to tell you something I've never mentioned before,' he said, looking directly into her eyes. 'In my job I hear rumour, gossip, innuendo, bad-mouthing, downright lies and so forth; most of it I can take or leave, but one piece of tittle-tattle I heard involved Maurice and Iseult, just whispers ... nudges ... winks.'

'But Nuala Buckley and Iseult were friends. Nuala worked for Iseult. Are you saying Maurice was having a relationship with both of them?'

'The way I heard it, Maurice used Nuala as a sort of cover for his time with Iseult. I'm not sure how much of this to believe. I've heard so many stories that in the end I stuck my head in the sand ostrich-style.'

'I find it interesting,' Emma said, suddenly animated, 'that Elliott was involved with three women who are now dead. How weird is that?'

'Yeah, weird maybe, but proves what? Just means Elliott has an over-active sex drive; hardly means he's going around knocking off people.'

'Maybe his wife Diana is cleaning up after him?'

'As a fanciful theory, I like it, Emma, but in the real world, well it's hardly likely, is it? No, we're missing something. Just can't figure what it is.'

'Me neither,' Emma admitted. 'But ponder this: *if* Lisa Dunlop was pushed down the stairs, *if* her tumble was not accidental, it means she was killed. And, *if* she was killed, then her murder must be linked to Iseult and Nuala's murders. And *if* I'm right about that, it exonerates you. You were here under lock and key when Lisa went sailing through the air.'

'Yes,' Connolly said, 'but *was* she pushed? That's the question.'

The expression on Norbert Hillary's face was inscrutable. 'We could be of mutual benefit to each other,' he said, peering over his glasses at Emma.

'I'm in favour of anything that helps.' Emma replied, having no idea what specifically was on offer. The meeting had been his idea. He had contacted Bob Crosby earlier and Crosby had passed the message on to her. They were now seated in the Crystal Lake Lounge at the Belhavel Hotel and Leisure Complex, the venue Hillary had chosen for the rendezvous.

Hillary ordered a brandy for himself and, for Emma, a mineral water. It was early afternoon and, apart from a young barman who seemed preoccupied with the racing pages, the lounge was empty. Sunlight shafted through large picture windows filling the lounge with a hazy, amber quality.

'I asked you here for a particular reason,' he explained, twirling the cognac about in its glass, not as yet imbibing. 'Margot and I, and our son Ronan, are members here.'

'Oh, I didn't know you had a son.'

'No reason you should; he's in boarding-school at present so you wouldn't have seen him when you called to see Margot. Actually, what I want to talk to you about concerns Ronan ... in a way.'

Emma looked perplexed. Hillary caught the expression. 'I can see I'm confusing you. Let me explain. What I have to say may have a bearing on the dreadful business of Iseult and Nuala's deaths. Your concern, I know, is for Detective Inspector Connolly's welfare. The other day when you talked to Margot, I was impressed by your utter conviction of his innocence.'

'That's because he *is* innocent.'

'Have you discovered anything since to help prove it?'

'Nothing concrete so far but I'm following up a few leads.'

He nodded and allowed his fingers to stroke his neatly trimmed moustache. It had only been a matter of days since Emma had last seen Norbert Hillary but it seemed to her he had aged considerably in the interim. On their first encounter his eyes had been all encompassing and penetrative but today they were wells of sadness. His rimless spectacles had slipped halfway down his large nose. 'I know I should go to the police with my suspicions but ...'

'Suspicions? Police? Sorry, what exactly are you saying?'

'I have information that might have a bearing on Iseult and Nuala's deaths ... I know I should go to the authorities—'

'So, why don't you?'

'Why don't I?' he repeated. 'Truth be told, I have misgivings about the detective in charge.'

'You mean Seán Grennan, yeah?'

'Yes, I think he has a hold over Margot ... some of her friends, too.'

'You think—'

'Let me fill in the background,' Hillary interrupted, 'You've heard of the swimmer Brendan Edwards?'

'Yes,' Emma said, puzzled, 'He had his own television show.'

'Indeed he had. The show was pulled when unsavoury rumours began to circulate. After that Edwards was employed here in the Belhavel as manager of the swimming complex.'

'Ah yes, I remember. He drowned; caused a great hullabaloo.'

'Correct, Emma. A verdict of accidental drowning was returned. It was claimed that the closed-circuit cameras did not begin recording until the pool opened to the public each morning. But I believe CCTV tapes *do* exist. Furthermore, I believe they show other people, apart from Edwards, present in the pool.'

'What are you suggesting?'

'His death might not have been all that straightforward. I believe there's a person out there somewhere in possession of a tape. I think it's possible – in fact I'm pretty sure – that someone's blackmailing the people who were in the pool complex at the time of the drowning.'

Emma drew a short breath. 'Are you saying you know the identity of someone on the tape?'

Hillary's face darkened perceptibly. 'It's possible that someone very close to me is on it.'

'You mean your wife?' Emma asked. 'Are you implying that Margot witnessed the drowning?'

'That, I'm sad to relate, could very well be the case,' Hillary replied gravely, his words underscored with judicious nods.

Emma made no reply, wanting to hear more.

Norbert took his first sip of brandy. 'Now we come to the nub of the problem,' he said, putting the glass down. 'You see, Emma, Margot discovered that Edwards was sexually molesting Ronan. She was afraid to go to the authorities, afraid that Ronan would be destroyed by the scandal. She didn't come to me because of some screwed up notion that I would take it out on Ronan, or some such nonsense.'

'So, how did you find out?'

'Margot told a close friend, swore her to secrecy. That close friend told her husband, a man who happens to be a friend of mine.'

'Margot is unaware that you know?'

'Right. You may have noticed when you talked to her that she is somewhat disengaged from reality?' He looked to Emma for a reaction. She returned his gaze, sipped some water, said nothing. After a short pause he continued, 'Look at me, Emma, I'm not a handsome man ... and I'm not a fool. I've come to terms with why a beautiful woman like Margot marries someone like me. It's funny really; I look at wealthy old guys with their young, trophy wives and I think to myself, how can they be so dumb? Do these old farts really believe these women would look at them twice if it weren't for their money? Then, I think, damn it, I'm not that different myself.'

Norbert removed his spectacles, placed them on the table beside his drink and rubbed his eyes. He shook his head slowly from side to side and then, as though lost in thought, began to polish the spectacles with a tissue. 'I didn't always think like this,' he said, replacing the glasses again. 'When I married Margot I thought I could make it work, I really did. I hoped money, material possessions, a place in society, would outweigh the romantic deficit. I hoped that in time Margot might come to love me. God knows I loved her. First time I saw her, with her red, lion-like mane and stunning looks, I was smitten ... I'm still smitten. Trouble is, I lack the skills to demonstrate my feelings, I thought it was enough to be there for her and Ronan but life's not like that. Margot wanted more than I could ever provide. She turned to drugs for solace, sought love ... elsewhere.' He paused momentarily to collect his thoughts, tapping his forefinger against his pursed lips.

Emma waited, her index finger unconsciously tracing the rim of her glass. She could only guess at the struggle taking place inside his head.

'I'm sorry,' he said at length, 'I hadn't intended to burden you with this but, well, I suppose I'm still trying to make sense of it myself.'

'I understand,' was the best Emma could think to say.

Hillary nodded. 'I make it my business to know everything concerning my family. I allow Margot all the money she needs to feed her habit – until recently I had no cause to check expenditure. That changed with the death of Iseult and Nuala. Inadvertently, I overheard Margot and two of her friends – Elizabeth Telford and Diana Elliott – discussing the death of Brendan Edwards. I can assure you that I don't go around eavesdropping on my wife or her friends, but when I heard the word blackmail being used in the conversation, I was naturally intrigued. I didn't hear the full discussion but I heard enough to know they're all shelling out money.

'The last few days have been the most bizarre of my life. I examined Margot's bank statements and discovered a sizeable monthly withdrawal to a particular account. I contacted the husbands of Margot's two friends. What I had to ask was damned awkward, but they know me well enough to trust my discretion. I avoided all mention of Edwards' death. Within twenty-four hours they confirmed that similar payments had been withdrawn from their spouses' accounts. I asked Elizabeth Telford's husband – he's a big noise in the banking world – to chase down this account. Yesterday he came back to me. He discovered that it's an offshore deposit account in Jersey. He has been unable to uncover the name of the account holder, but I think I can guess at who the blackmailer is.'

'You suspect Seán Grennan?'

'I've no proof it's him but who else can it be? He led the investigation and must have discovered that the cameras were, in fact, live that morning. He probably took away the videotapes for inspection, saw what was on them, and decided to get rich.'

'Who, apart from Margot, was caught on the footage?'

'Elizabeth Telford, Diana Elliott and Iseult Connolly.'

Emma opened her mouth, speechless. Her head buzzed with a million different scenarios. For the first time since she'd seen Iseult's dead body, she felt she was getting somewhere. 'How do you know these women were captured on tape?'

'I don't, but they're the names I overheard being discussed.'

'And you believe they're being blackmailed?'

'Yes, I'm sure of it.'

'But why would Grennan kill Iseult? And what about Nuala Buckley? From what you've told me, I gather she wasn't even present at the pool.'

'Yes, it's a flaw in my argument, one I have no answer for.'

A small prudent voice curbed Emma's enthusiasm. 'Why have you come to me?' she asked. 'If you and the other husbands know your wives are being blackmailed, why not go to the police? Why tell me?'

'I don't have proof that any CCTV actually exists. And, if it does exist, what does it contain? I don't want the other husbands to know about the Edwards affair, at least not until I'm sure their wives are involved. Also, I don't want to betray my wife. There could be a perfectly logical explanation for what they did … or didn't do. The women could be victims of some elaborate hoax. What I'd like you to do, Emma, is investigate the whole affair. I'm happy to cover your expenses. I need you to find the blackmailer, discover the full circumstances behind Edwards' death.'

'My priority, Mr Hillary, is to find whoever put Connolly in the frame for murder. What you've told me might go some way to help me, but I have to warn you, should I discover your wife has been involved in illegal activity I'll have no choice but to go to the authorities.'

'I understand that,' he said, holding his glass out to Emma. 'All I ask is that you come to me with your findings first.'

Emma allowed the glasses to clink. 'You've got yourself a deal.'

The man sitting behind the tinted windows of the parked Subaru Forester was enjoying the rich aroma of his smoke-filled cabin, dragging on his cigarette as though life depended on it. Through the fog of smoke he observed Norbert Hillary escort the female journalist to the hotel's car-park. The journalist had not figured in the initial assignment, an assignment that called for the deaths of Iseult Connolly and Nuala Buckley. It was clear to him that the plan had begun to unravel, that the person behind the scheme had seriously miscalculated. Actions had veered dangerously off course – Lisa Dunlop being a case in point. She had not been part of the original strategy. Improvisation had been required. He'd snapped her neck, sent her arse-over-tit down a flight of stairs because she'd threatened to talk to the journalist.

And now the journalist, this woman named Emma Boylan, had the potential to further upset the apple cart by poking in her nose where it didn't belong. He felt confident that, as yet, she didn't know who'd killed the two women or the motive that lay behind the deaths. It didn't bother him unduly that she had just met with Norbert Hillary; what Hillary would have to tell her would, he hoped, help muddy the waters. Nevertheless, the little he knew about Emma Boylan gave him cause for worry. He didn't doubt her resourcefulness; a bright, intelligent woman like her would, given half a chance, figure out what lay behind the killings. His job was to see to it that she didn't get that half-chance. The instructions he'd been given couldn't be more straightforward: *If Emma Boylan gets too close to the truth, see to it that she meets with an accident, a lethal accident.*

He fired up another cigarette, using what was left of the old one as a lighter, before chucking the fag end out the window. He exhaled a perfectly formed circle of smoke from his mouth and through it watched Emma get into her silver Hyundai Coupé and pull away from the parking lot. Easy enough to keep her under observation: no need to break a tail light or any of that nonsense so often employed on film and television cop shows. In the first place, she wouldn't expect a tail, and in the second, he was damn good at his job.

mma sat beneath the picture of the mackerel-striped cat. Diana Elliott sat next to her. It seemed like no time at all since Bob Crosby had first pointed out Diana in this same venue. When Emma phoned Diana to seek a meeting, Diana had been the one to suggest The Cat's Pyjamas. 'We could do coffee ... say, eleven o'clock?' she'd suggested.

Emma readily agreed. Since talking to Norbert Hillary her brain had been on fire with a profusion of theories, her enthusiasm leading her to believe she was tantalizingly close to some sort of resolve.

Diana, elegantly dressed and perfectly coifed, appeared at ease with the surroundings, exchanging friendly banter with the waitress serving their coffee and croissants. Pleasantries with Emma were markedly less cordial. 'Let me begin,' she said, raising her chin in reproach, 'by telling you that Iseult Connolly and Nuala Buckley are – sorry, *were* – friends of mine. I will do all in my power to help bring their killer to justice.' Before Emma could say a word, Diana waved a magazine in her face. 'Have you seen this week's edition of *Dublin Dispatch*?'

'No, I haven't ... not yet.'

'Take a look,' Diana said, handing her the current affairs magazine.

The cover showed Maurice Elliott alongside the headline – BREAKING THE MOULD IN POLITICS?

'Oh, an article on your husband,' Emma said, somewhat surprised.

'No, no, not that!' Diana said irritably. 'Go to page twenty.'

Emma flicked through the magazine. A colour photograph of Shane Buckley and his two grandchildren occupied three-quarters of page twenty. His arms embraced Chris and Katie in a study that had him beaming with pride. Emma speed-read the accompanying text.

In a rare interview, Shane Buckley admitted to feelings of guilt for having allowed the estrangement between himself and his late daughter to continue for too long: —*Her death came at a time when reconciliation was imminent. I will never allow her memory to fade as long as Chris and Katie are with me.* Emma handed the magazine back to Diana. 'It's good that Nuala's children have found a welcoming home.'

'Should never have come to this. Two beautiful kids left without a mother. Hanging's too good for the person who brought about this tragedy.'

'Yes, it's awful when innocent children are left behind to—'

'Don't insult my intelligence,' Diana snapped, her nose up-tilted, as though offended by an unpleasant odour. 'I'm perfectly aware of your involvement in this beastly business. We both know that the prime suspect is Iseult's ex-husband and that he left her to take up with *you*. So, Ms Boylan, you'll forgive me if I treat your interest with a degree of scepticism.'

Emma was taken aback by Diana's quietly articulated invective. Everything about the woman was controlled; the way she walked, the way she talked, her haute-couture clothes, her meticulous attention to make-up and hairstyle. Her movements were graceful and thoroughly feminine, but her ultimate achievement lay in her ability to make the whole package look natural and casual. Emma, who prided herself on her own appearance, felt lacklustre by comparison. Attempting to get things on a more agreeable footing, she pointed to the picture of Maurice Elliott on the cover of the magazine. 'You know I almost got a job as media manager for your husband's political party,' she said, trying to steer the conversation in the direction she'd come to discuss. 'I visited your home quite recently; it's a beautiful place.'

Diana responded with a tight little smile as she dabbed a napkin on the corners of her mouth to remove croissant flakes. 'Look, you'll forgive me, but I think I know where you're going with this.'

'You do?' Emma said, surprised.

'Every half-decent-looking female who comes in contact with Maurice makes a similar complaint and I guess you're no different; you're going to tell me that my husband propositioned you, yes?'

'No, as a matter of fact he didn't,' Emma said, not knowing whether to feel pleased or slighted. 'He decided not to hire me when he discovered I was – what he termed – Connolly's "live-in lover".'

'Hmmm, well now, it's a relief to know we don't have to travel that particular well-worn track. So, if it's not Maurice, what is it?'

Sensing a softening in Diana's attitude, Emma threw caution to the wind, decided to go for broke. 'I need to know who's blackmailing you?'

'What?' Diana asked, losing her composure for a split second but recovering it just as quickly. 'What on earth are you talking about?'

'I'm talking about the swimmer Brendan Edwards. His death was captured on CCTV. The tape shows a number of people poolside at the time.'

'Are you implying I was there when this Edwards chap drowned?'

'Yes, according to a reliable source, you, Iseult, Margot Hillary and Elizabeth Telford, witnessed the drowning.'

Diana's reaction was more pronounced this time. 'I can't imagine who'd spread such lies. Besides, were such a preposterous story true, what exactly would it have to do with what we're talking about?'

Same question I've asked myself a dozen times.

Emma took a mouthful of coffee to allow herself time to marshal her thoughts. A new strategy was required. 'Did you know Lisa Dunlop is dead?' she asked.

'What? No, I didn't know.' Diana said, unable to hide the flicker of shock in her eyes. 'How did it happen?'

'Fell down the stairs; could have been pushed. You *do* know Lisa Dunlop had an affair with your husband?'

Diana sighed. 'Yes, yes, God-damn-it, here we go again. I know about it. I met her once in the reception of the Social Alliance Party. I'm sorry to hear she's dead but that doesn't alter my opinion; Lisa was a social climber, an ambitious little nobody on the make. Maurice is quite insufferable when it comes to such women. Trouble is, they take him seriously. Fools! They fall for his silver-tongued flattery. They mean absolutely nothing; they're a disposable commodity, something for him to *use* and discard at will.'

'Does it not strike you as odd,' Emma asked, 'that two of the women Maurice knew on intimate terms are now dead?'

'Odd? I don't know,' she said, the tight little smile resurfacing again. 'Which two in particular do you have in mind?'

'Nuala Buckley and Lisa Dunlop.'

'You've got that wrong,' she said, smirking. 'I think you'll find that Maurice used Nuala Buckley as a cover for his affair with Iseult, an affair, I hasten to add, that preceded her marriage break-up.'

Emma's mind flashed back to the conversation she'd had with Connolly. His suspicions in regard to Iseult and Elliott had just been confirmed. This information added yet another layer of confusion to the events surrounding the deaths. Before she had time to frame her next question, Diana continued, 'It's like this Ms Boylan: our marriage has been a dysfunctional, adulterous charade from the word go, it's no big thing. And yet, in spite of our marital malaise, we stay together for the most practical of reasons: putting on a front helps our various business interests.'

Emma returned to the subject of blackmail, believing that it held the key to unlocking the log jam clogging her brain. 'I know for a fact that you are making monthly payments to an offshore account.'

The tight little smile again, this time accompanied by eyes ablaze with defiance. 'You're flying kites, Ms Boylan. If what you say were true you'd have it plastered over that rag you work for, right? You're on a fishing expedition, but I can assure you, no one's biting.'

'I'm not flying kites, or fishing for that matter,' Emma said, recycling Diane's mixed metaphors, 'I'm stating facts. You haven't seen it in the *Post* because I no longer work there. My sole interest is in proving that Connolly had nothing to do with anybody's death.'

'Well, I hate to piss on your little parade, Ms Boylan, but I can assure you that Detective Connolly *did* kill Iseult and Nuala. You don't believe me, ask my friends. You've already mentioned their names so talk to them, they'll confirm what I'm telling you – your lover is a cold-blooded monster who kills what he can't have.'

Emma remained silent, struck by the conviction in Diana's voice. She would have to look elsewhere for evidence. There was still one person from the so-called swimming pool incident that she hadn't tackled yet; that person was Elizabeth Telford.

CHAPTER 25

'I don't talk to reporters,' Elizabeth Telford said, in a smoky drawl that sounded offhand over the phone.

Emma was in no mood to take no for an answer. 'I've spoken with Margot Hillary and Diana Elliott: They're anxious, as I'm sure you must be, to discover who's behind the deaths of your friends.'

With some reluctance, Elizabeth condescended to meet her. She named the Lansdowne Palace as the venue, the time, seven o'clock that evening.

Before setting out for the hotel, Emma booted her laptop and logged on to the *Post* data bank. She needed to discover what the files had on Elizabeth Telford. Not a lot as it turned out, just a note to say Elizabeth had worked for Thackaberry's, Anglo Celtic Securities, and Shannon & Dockrell Bank. The rest of the entry concentrated on her husband's achievements. Jeffery Telford held the position of chairman at Telford & Spencer, one of the top corporate banks in the state. Somewhat of a recluse, he had managed to avoid recent controversies involving fraudulent banking practices. Highly respected, he had the ear of the finance minister and the country's top politicians.

Separate photographs of Jeffery and Elizabeth, dated two years earlier, appeared on the screen. Jeffery had that successful aura about him that so often surrounds people who wield power. His wife Elizabeth looked no less successful but whereas he possessed one of those instantly forgettable faces, her looks were striking. Her eyes stared out defiantly from the photograph as though challenging the viewer. Emma was disappointed to find no further background information on Elizabeth; even so, armed with what little she'd found, she felt more confident setting out for her meeting.

Emma manoeuvred the Hyundai Coupé into the hotel's car-park, a high-walled area set back from the hustle and bustle of Lansdowne

Road and controlled by security gates. The digital clock on the dashboard clicked to 18.50 p.m. as she cut the ignition. She hurried through the hotel's lobby, needing to visit the powder-room before engaging with anybody. She evaluated her appearance in the mirror, finger-flicked a hair off her jacket, blinked her eyes and pouted her lips.

You look fine, girl.

Elizabeth Telford was more striking than the photographic image had conveyed. Impeccably dressed, she possessed a figure that any woman half her age would envy, her long shapely legs, crossed at the knees, drawing admiring glances from other hotel guests. She encompassed an aloof sophisticated air of toughness about her and her voice, when she spoke, had a lived-in nicotine and alcohol timbre to it. Emma would not have been in the least bit surprised if Elizabeth drank bourbon on the rocks and smoked Gauloises but, as it turned out, she did neither.

'I've checked with Diana Elliott and Margot Hillary,' Elizabeth informed Emma, after sipping some mineral water, 'so, I know what this is about. Let me be up-front with you Emma – may I call you Emma? – I don't care a whole lot for journalists.'

Emma was tempted to say how she didn't care a whole lot for bankers but resisted. Instead she went for, 'I'm sorry to hear that. Why do you—?'

'Journalists invade people's privacy, accost them when they're off guard, look for glib answers to complicated questions, promise anonymity, guarantee accuracy and then sell them down the Swanee.'

The put-down sounded rehearsed to Emma. 'I'm sorry you feel that way,' she said, keeping her voice in check, 'but it's a bit unfair to tar all of us with the same brush. At the *Post* we believe in coverage that is fair, justified and responsible. Our policy is to—'

'Balderdash! Your paper, like the media in general, thrives on titillation, sensationalism, lurid headlines and downright lies.'

'Well, obviously I disagree with your sweeping generalizations,' Emma said, determined not to get drawn into an argument. 'Besides, in this instance, I'm acting as a private citizen and not as a journalist. I need to get at the truth, establish the innocence of my friend Jim Connolly. You've been up-front – to use your expression – with me, so let me be equally frank with you. My investigation has been unproductive to date; by talking to people like you, people who knew the victims, I'm hoping to discover who the real killer is.'

'You say you want the truth, but when it's comprehensively proved that Connolly killed both women, what then?'

'That's not going to happen! I *know* Connolly. He couldn't have killed either of them.'

'And, I'm told, you think the death of Brendan Edwards is connected to myself and my friends?'

Emma outlined her take on what had happened at the pool and her belief that those present were being blackmailed. 'Do you deny that you were there?' she asked in conclusion.

'I deny any involvement, but let me try to help you. Let's take a hypothetical scenario. Let's suppose we have a woman with a young son, and let's say this boy is groomed and sexually molested by a paedophile. This paedophile we'll assume has already been involved in other similar cases. He has managed to get away with his earlier crimes but has he learned a lesson? Of course not! Paedophiles don't learn. Proven fact! They offend again and again, even castration doesn't work. So, we have this unfortunate woman and her only son and we have this depraved pervert who's hell bent on corrupting the child. What's the woman to do? Let the liberal lobby "rehabilitate" the child molester? Watch helplessly as the monster is allowed back on the streets a few years later, ready to recommence his evil game?'

Emma made no comment. So far, the hypothetical conjecture put forward by Elizabeth appeared remarkably similar to Margot Hillary's experience. She wanted to hear more. Elizabeth duly obliged.

'Imagine the mother's devastation. What options does she have? The police? Will they believe her? It'll be her son's word against the molester's. The child will be shamed, forced to relive the disgusting episode and accused of lying by some smart-arse lawyer. What's the mother to do? Let's take the situation you put forward – the case of Brendan Edwards. We're still speaking hypothetically, but let's assume, for the sake of argument, this mother has some friends who can help. Maybe a few of them happen to be strong swimmers, let's go further, let's say they tackle this pervert, doused him several times, threatening to drown him unless he repents and agrees to steer clear of the boy. How could they know their action would trigger a heart attack ... that the paedophile would die?'

Elizabeth paused again, looked at Emma. 'I'm not saying that anything like that happened, but it's possible, don't you think?'

'Yes, I suppose so,' Emma agreed. 'But surely, even allowing for the fact that your scenario is conjecture, wouldn't the women who assaulted the paedophile be seen by others?'

'It's possible. Anything's possible. Let's assume the action in the pool was picked up on security cameras. Whoever viewed the tape would certainly be in a position to blackmail those featured on the footage. If something like that happened, I'd ask this question: did the pervert in the pool take a bribe from someone who wanted to operate the security cameras ... and did that person confiscate the tape?'

Emma was convinced that Elizabeth Telford's hypothetical account reflected the actuality of what happened. Edwards had been the manager; he knew his clientele and was well aware of their wealth. What if someone bribed Edwards in order to be allowed to video certain female patrons. Edwards could have been sold a cock 'n' bull story about the women's husbands checking up on their wives, or some such excuse. If the money on offer had been substantial enough, Edwards would turn a blind-eye to the covert surveillance. Emma was just guessing but she felt it might not be a million miles away from the truth.

Elizabeth looked at her watch, an indication that the meeting was over. 'I'm sorry I couldn't be of more help,' she said with a dismissive tone. 'I still believe your detective friend is guilty ... and, as for the Edwards drowning, I don't believe it is connected to the deaths of Iseult and Nuala, irrespective of how it happened.'

'And what about the blackmail?' Emma asked.

Elizabeth stood up. 'Now *that*,' she said, walking away from Emma, 'I wouldn't know anything about.'

E mma's second visit to Cloverhill proved far less intimidating. Even the building's granite and red-brick exterior looked more benign, more like a cinema multiplex than a prison. Were prisons rated like hotels, Cloverhill would probably get the full five stars. The purpose built remand centre had a capacity of 456 beds. Its catering and general hygiene standards qualified for the highly coveted Quality Mark, a far cry from the slop-out conditions prevailing in some of the country's older Victorian establishments.

Connolly appeared in good spirits. If he had any complaints about his treatment on the 'inside' he wasn't saying. He was impressed with Emma's account of how she had uncovered new information. He too, in spite of his confinement, had managed to move the investigation along. He'd had a visit from Detective Sergeant Mike Dorsett the previous day. 'Dorsett is part of my unit in Pearse Street,' Connolly explained. 'He's been keeping his eyes and ears open on my behalf. He's worked with me long enough to know the charges against me are a load of bollocks. He's taken it upon himself to do a little snooping and he's been able to get a few tip-offs from a colleague in the Dun Laoghaire division. Looks like Seán Grennan has been busy working on the case against me – nothing new there – but he's been following some rather strange avenues of enquiry. He brought Darren Dempsey in for questioning.'

'Darren Dempsey? He's the father of Nuala Buckley's two children.'

'That's the one! What do you know about him?'

'Only what Ann Buckley told me. He's a piece of work; tried to have it off with Ann while Nuala was in hospital. Nuala parted company with him after he'd been arrested for rape.'

'That's our boy all right. Dorsett looked up the records to see why the case was dumped. The facts are straightforward enough; the victim left a city centre pub with Dempsey late one Saturday night. The rape happened after midnight, which meant technically, the offence took place on Sunday. The date on the warrant was Saturday so the case was thrown out. But here's the stinger: Seán Grennan was the arresting officer.'

'The same Seán Grennan who is now—'

'The very one! Mind you, Grennan hadn't earned his stripes back then. He'd been working out of Tallaght at the time, not Dun Laoghaire.'

'So, Sherlock, what do you deduce from this.'

'Grennan and Dempsey have a history.'

'But does it have a bearing on this case?'

'Grennan could be on to something that'll prove I had nothing to do with the deaths, or – and here's the bit that bothers me – it could mean he's going all out to stitch me up. Can't figure Grennan on this one. I'd like you to do something for me, if you don't mind?'

'Like what?'

'I'd like you to get what you can on Darren Dempsey, maybe ask Ann Buckley about the relationship that existed between Nuala and Dempsey.'

'I'll see what I can do.'

Connolly became silent, suddenly lost in thought.

'Something else on your mind?' Emma asked.

'Yeah!' he sighed. 'Being locked up here, solitary confinement you might say, gives me time to think. When the lights go out at night I lie awake and blank my mind of all extraneous thoughts, try to revisit the events that've put me here. It's a bit like self-hypnotism ... helps me get a fix on what took place with a new degree of clarity. Does this make sense to you?'

Emma failed to hide her scepticism. 'I don't know, Jim, it might help if you told me which events you've returned to.'

'The day I went to see Iseult! I had to swerve to avoid a collision as I entered the driveway.'

'Yes, I remember; you said you didn't get a decent look at the driver.'

'I didn't! But I've reconstructed the scene and I think I might have been wrong about the driver being a woman. I got a subliminal image of the face behind the windscreen. I think it's possible *a man* drove that car.'

'You don't mean Grennan?'

'No, definitely not Grennan ... if it was a man at all. The vague – *very vague* – impression I got was of a younger man.'

'It would help if you could get a better fix on the face. Whoever drove that car could very well have been the killer. So, I suggest you try a little more self-hypnotism when you're alone on your bunk tonight.'

'Yeah, right, Emma. Only problem is, every time I try to clear my mind, you come floating in and occupy the space. And when that happens my body behaves in the only way it knows how.' Connolly gave Emma a sheepish grin. 'I feel like I've returned to the college dormitory, and you can imagine what the main preoccupation of every adolescent young male was there, once the lights went out at night.'

Too much information.

'I'd better go,' Emma said, taking his hand in hers. 'Anything else I can do for you, big boy?'

'Now that really is a dumb question,' he said, seeing the laughter in her eyes. 'Unfortunately, that kind of thing is not permitted in Cloverhill.'

'Well then, I'll just have to work a little harder to get you out of here. A girl can get lonely too, you know.'

'Yeah, don't I just know it.'

The first Friday in March had been the date set aside for conclave. The five women involved could not have imagined the dire consequences their deliberations would wreak on their lives. Two of them, Iseult Connolly and Nuala Buckley, would be dead one month later. Like the first Friday of each month, they came together to devise a project to challenge and enliven their lives for the following four weeks. These projects sometimes overran to a second or third month; other times, several schemes proceeded in tandem. They took it in turns to come up with fresh ideas. No rules, no limitations governed what they proposed. However, unless the person doing the proposing got wholehearted support from the four co-conspirators, it failed to get the go-ahead. They tried (unsuccessfully) to avoid subjects like fashion, television programmes, and whatever current trivia happened to be doing the rounds in favour of more profound or cultured subject matters. On this occasion, Iseult Connolly had been the one putting forward a proposal.

Diana Elliott's luxurious conservatory was, as always, the designated venue. For weekly updates they would convene over breakfast in The Cat's Pyjamas restaurant. Diana had been the one to suggest they hold their meetings on the first Friday of each month. She'd ceased to concern herself with religion, but a memory from childhood – that of her mother's devotion to the Sacred Heart – prompted the dateline. Her mother, a devout Catholic, observed a church ritual that guaranteed a happy death and a place in Heaven; all she had to do was attend Mass and receive Holy Communion on the first Friday of each month for nine consecutive months. Except that the contract she'd engaged in proved a hollow covenant. In a cruel mockery of her mother's faith, her death had been prolonged and horrific. Skin cancer had eaten away at her body until there was nothing left of the disfigured woman to recognize. Towards the end, even the drugs failed to kill the unremitting pain. Diana and her family watched, grief-stricken, as, after months of unimaginable agony, a silent scream brought the suffering to an end. It was then that Diana had fallen out with God and resolved never to allow herself depart this world in such an undignified fashion. Her mother's death and blind devotion to the First-Friday ritual had left an indelible impression on Diana's mind.

The women met at 8.00 p.m. and usually carried on till midnight, sometimes later. Each paid an agreed contribution towards an operational fund and for liberal quantities of booze and recreational drugs.

The concept Iseult had prepared for the March meeting was, she believed, every bit as devious as any of the previous escapades they'd hatched. Even so, she felt a little giddy, almost light-headed. Her fellow conspirators were, it seemed to her, in a receptive mood, all of them comfortable in the warmth and luxury of their surroundings. Margot Hillary was a little stoned but her movements, as ever, remained graceful, thoroughly feminine. With her trademark crimson and mahogany mop, she sat next to Diana Elliott. It was an open secret among them that Margot and Diana had a thing going for each other but it was never openly commented on.

Elizabeth Telford sat back in an oversized easy chair with her knees pulled up and her legs and shoeless feet tucked decorously to one side. Of the five women, she was the quietest, usually restricting her comments to more serious aspects of debate, her soul-piercing stare, an affectation she'd developed from her time as a banker, observing all. She understood, better than the others, that the cordiality they displayed to each other concealed a barely hidden sense of rivalry.

Next to her, Nuala Buckley lounged in a wicker chair, an oriental basket affair with a great circular backrest. Back in the 1980s Maurice Elliott had brought it back from Samoa or somewhere in the South Seas on the understanding that Somerset Maughan had once sat in it. It was unlikely that Nuala, were she familiar with the chair's history, would be remotely impressed. She'd just assembled Rizla papers and was busy rolling a joint of cannabis resin. Unlike the others, she had dressed down for the occasion. She wore designer jeans and a fleece and didn't seem in the least bit bothered by her nonconformity to the unspoken dress code.

'What I'm going to propose,' Iseult said, getting down to the business of the evening, 'is the very essence of bitchiness.'

This brought cat meows from all except Elizabeth; the faint smile on her lips implied forbearance with their childish behaviour.

'I want to humiliate my ex,' Iseult said, 'and I want you lot to help me.'

'Ah, come on, Iseult,' Nuala said, 'haven't you humiliated him enough over the past decade? Get over it.'

'I hear what you're saying,' Iseult said, with a dismissive flick of the wrist, 'but this is different; this is more profound; I want to fuck with his mind, really screw up his life.'

'What brought this on?' Diana asked.

'Saw him the other day with the press hack he's hanging with, wanted to knee him in the balls and pluck her eyes out.'

Diana laughed from deep inside her throat and poured herself a half measure of Remy Martin with a double helping of Baileys. 'You are utterly depraved,' she said as her house cat, a tortoiseshell named Sasha, arose from the cashmere sweater he'd been snoozing on, arched his back, yawned and slunk on to her lap. 'What do you have in mind?'

'To destroy him; have him fired from his job in disgrace, turn the Boylan bitch against him.'

'But why?' Elizabeth queried. 'He's out of your life. Why bother with him and this ... this Boylan bitch, as you call her? What's the point?'

Iseult turned to Elizabeth. 'Remember when you worked in the bank, when you got us to help destroy your stockbroker boyfriend, *Dankar-the-wanker*, after he'd dumped you and took up with Avril Coyle?'

Elizabeth's face flushed. 'That was different,' she said, annoyed by Iseult's comment, 'that was—'

'No, it's the same. I despise Jim Connolly every bit as much—'

'Sorry, Iseult,' Margot cut in. 'I can see where Elizabeth is coming from on this. I can't think why you still—'

Iseult swallowed her irritation. 'Remember how you felt when the swimmer molested your son?'

Nuala Buckley exhaled a bloom of hash-laden smoke. 'Hey, guys,' she implored, 'let's not get our knickers in a twist; let's keep it nice and mellow, see what Iseult has to say. If we like it, we'll discuss it; if we don't, we'll pass. So for frig's sake let's get on with it, OK?'

Assenting nods all around.

'Thank you,' Iseult said. 'I don't blame you for wanting to know why I despise Connolly and I wish I could give you a straightforward answer. The burning hatred I feel is hard to put in words. I mean, how do any of us explain why we love or hate? We're talking about irrational emotions; not something based on logic, not something you can measure by conventional yardsticks.'

'Did he ever hit you?' Nuala asked.

'Or cheat on you?' Diane added.

'No he didn't. It'd be easier to explain my deep loathing had he done so, but that's not his way. And that's the problem. He is Mister Perfect. Living with him, trying to measure up to his perfection was like living in a convent. As a husband he made the perfect overzealous jailer.'

'How come you married him?' Margot asked.

'Every day I ask myself the same damn question. I could put it down to a prolonged bout of temporary insanity, but even that wouldn't come close to explaining it. Before we married, I admired his handsome, suave looks, his impeccable manners, his elegant dress sense, and – huh! you won't believe this – I was attracted to the idea of being married to a detective. How sad is that? I was a true romantic, saw him as one of those dashing detectives you see on television. You know, a Dirty Harry kind of guy who lives hard 'n' dangerous, beats up the baddies, drinks to beat the band, makes unending love, and takes crap from nobody. Except, of course, he turned out to be nothing like Dirty Harry. My father, to be fair to him, warned me, insisted I was making a mistake. We argued hot 'n' heavy over it. I was determined to prove him wrong, but it soon became evident that he was right. Only in one area did Connolly score: he's a good stud, has amazing staying power and is hung like Delaney's donkey.'

This comment brought a chorus of yelps and groans from the others.

'Yeah, right,' Iseult said, dismissing their lusty outpouring. 'Rumpy-pumpy's fine but there's twenty-four hours in every day and I wanted a whole lot more. I wanted a full-blooded life; I wanted my friends; I wanted wild weekends; I wanted to remain one of the party circuit, to live it up, enjoy the money Daddy gave me.'

'And Connolly stopped you?' Diana said.

'He didn't have to; the disapproval in his eyes was enough. He refused to be part of my set, really screwed my social diary.'

'You should have brought him to a few functions,' Diane suggested.

'I did. Big mistake! He refused to join in, wouldn't let his hair down. He was no swinger; the most innocuous of things shocked him. He refused to participate in key-swap parties and walked out rather than smoke dope. In the end he just stayed at home and sulked.'

'There's girls I know,' Nuala said with a smile, 'would be glad to have their hubbies stay at home.'

'Yeah, and it would've been fine except every time I returned home from a late party or brought friends to the house he had a face on him like boiled shite. I mean, fuck it all, the house was mine to start with; Daddy paid for it. Connolly should have been grateful, but instead he held it against me. Can you believe it? He thought I'd forsake my lifestyle to become a copper's mousy little wife and live on the pittance he earned. Christ, you'd think it'd be enough that I sacrificed the Smyth-O'Brien name for his? Did he appreciate it? Did he fuck? He believed *he* was better than me. I saw it in his eyes; he looked down on me, looked down on my friends.

'I'll give you a laugh; he once told me he felt sorry for me. *He* felt sorry for *me*. The worst part was he meant it, the prick actually felt sorry for me. That was when I knew I hated him. That hatred became an obsession.

'And then, a few months before we split, I saw him in Grafton Street walking with the Boylan bitch. I damn-well near lost it; the man who'd made my life a misery was smiling at the little nobody, chatting happily like he hadn't a care in the world. I saw red; I tell you my blood boiled. That was when I decided enough was enough; I had to take him down a peg or two. All I ask is that you lot help me.'

Sasha, who'd been snoozing on Diana's lap, raised his head and glanced at the women before rolling beneath the hand of his mistress. This cat, could he talk, would tell wondrous tales. For five years, he'd been privy to the deliberations. He'd reacted with indifference to the various intrigues, allowed Diana to stroke his belly as plans to settle scores were ventilated. When Sasha was little more than a kitten, he'd first attracted the group's attention with his antics in the garden. They watched him crouch low on all fours as he played with his prey, a small field mouse. He would release the mouse every so often then pounce down on the terrified victim with his paws again before finally delivering the deathblow with his teeth. They were impressed. The cat's action was spiteful and somewhat cruel but ultimately efficient. Sasha became the First-Friday mascot from then onwards.

Diana Elliott, unofficial chairperson for the group, was first to react to Iseult's words. 'Connolly's only crime, it seems to me, is that he failed to play your game, failed to follow your rules and ultimately failed to appreciate your needs. On the scale of causes we've taken up over the years it's no big thing.'

'It is to me,' Iseult said defiantly.

'Well, it's OK by me,' Diana said, with measured reluctance. 'Provided you come up with a punishment that fits the crime.'

'Yeah, let's bring Connolly down a peg or two,' Nuala Buckley said. 'It sounds to me like he's a bit too big for his jocks.'

'It's fine by me,' Margot said, her fingers decorously stroking her throat. 'I just wonder if the man is worth the bother.'

'Believe me,' Iseult assured her, 'what I'm asking for is well worth the bother. What do you think, Elizabeth?'

'I agree with Diana, provided the punishment fits the crime.'

'Good,' Iseult said, 'here's what I have in mind.' She outlined her plan in minute detail, aware of her audience hanging on her every word, conscious of the renewed current of excitement evident in the room.

Yes, yes, yes, I have them.

One by one, Diana Elliott, Margot Hillary, Elizabeth Telford and Nuala Buckley gave their nods of approval. The expression on Iseult's face was triumphant. 'We can meet a few mornings a week to go over the finer details. I see this action going down in a month from today; that'll be 1 April. That'll give us time to get our act together.'

'Yes, why not?' Diana agreed. 'April Fool's Day, how very appropriate.'

Sasha leaped down from Diana's lap, stretched and made his way out of the room. Could it be possible that Sasha was the only one in the room to sense that Iseult's scheme would change all their lives irrevocably?

CHAPTER 28

'Look, I'm worried about you,' Vinny repeated.

'Well, there's no need; I'd be a darn sight happier if you stopped creating such a God-almighty fuss.' Emma sat across from her ex-husband in the lounge of her apartment, finding it hard to keep her tongue in check. Vinny's unannounced, but expected, visit had lasted twenty minutes already and her patience had reached breaking point. He'd gone over all the old ground, everything from losing their baby to the ending of their marriage. But when he began to probe the current difficulties, she saw red.

'I'm here for you, Emma,' he insisted. 'I still *care* about you and it pains me to see what's happening ... all this ugly stuff about you being an accessory to Connolly's criminality ... it's upsetting your parents and your friends. It's time you got away from all this—'

'No Vinny, hold it right there,' Emma demanded, her voice rising. 'What I do is my business ... *mine alone*; it no longer concerns you. Why can't you get that into your head? I can look after myself and—'

'—and you're making a right dog's dinner of it,' Vinny said, rising to his feet, his hands gesticulating like some mad, fire-and-brimstone preacher. 'Connolly's got you running around like a slapper on heat. I saw the pictures in the papers; you both looked totally out of it, pissed as coots, and his wife's body barely cold, lying in the morgue. What's anyone to think? My friends look at me; they want to know if this is the woman I married; they want—'

'OUT!' Emma roared, pushing Vinny away from her. 'Get out before I do something I'm bound to regret.' In a blind fury, she forced him out of the apartment. The last thing she saw before slamming the door was the look of dazed incomprehension in his eyes. She'd seen that look once before: the time she'd lost the baby. Back then it had been her fault, no one else's. Vinny had seen the danger all along, had warned her, begged her to be careful. The whole world, it seemed, had screamed its warning but she'd remained deaf to it all, believing she was wiser, invulnerable to the frailties of others. Christ, what a grand conceit! And when the inevitable happened, when she'd lost the baby, Vinny's eyes reflected the recrimination and guilt tearing her apart.

That look was back in his eyes today.

She pressed her back against the panels of the door and slithered slowly to the floor. She sat with her backside to the door's base, her thighs angled towards her chest, elbows propped on the knees and her head canted forward, cradled in her hands. Tears rolled down her cheeks. Echoes from her time with Vinny flashed through her head like a kaleidoscopic lightning storm.

There had been good times, certainly, but towards the end, the relationship had become awkward and self-conscious. It was only after Connolly had become her lover that she appreciated what had been missing from the marriage. Making love with Connolly was a roller-coaster ride; it exposed every nerve end in her body to the most exquisite torture and delight. With him, she'd discovered the earth-shattering experience of multiple orgasms, an explosive convulsion that brought animal-like utterances of unbearable pleasure from deep down in her soul. Bound together, their hearts thumped as one in sublime ecstasy. They touched, teased, kissed, devoured and explored each other, clinging to the earth's crust as it rotated beneath them, gasping for breath, their naked, sweating bodies rising and falling in perfect rhythm.

And what of Vinny, the man she'd lived with for ten years? Thinking about that period made her feel guilty. She knew that Vinny loved her. If he had been a cad, a bad husband, a drunk or a gambler, she'd have had some justification for how she'd ended it. But he was none of those things; Vinny was a nice person, and *nice* was a description that, for Emma, equated to *forgiving*. He wanted to forgive her, but absolution was never going to be an option for as long as he remained part of the equation. If Connolly hadn't been there for her it's possible she might have settled for the ongoing suffocating marital state she found herself in, but even before his arrival she'd known her marriage had become defective, a living lie. Was it wrong to crave escape from the guilt trip she laboured under for so long? Was it wrong to seek happiness, sexual fulfilment and a greater degree of contentment? If it was, then so be it, she pleaded guilty.

Towards the end, making love had become a passionless predictable ritual. She no longer felt the need to fake orgasms, a factor Vinny seemed not to have noticed. What went through his mind during those times? God knows! He was probably contemplating procreation as he huffed and puffed his way to ejaculation. Emma had no intention of going down that road again; the very thought of conceiving was akin to a nightmare of epic proportions.

The telephone brought her out of her stupor. She took her hands away from her head and wiped the tears. In no hurry, she wandered listlessly to the kitchen and picked up before the answering service kicked in.

Her father was on the line. 'Emma, ah, good, you're there; I was just about to hang up. How are you doing?'

'Hello, Dad,' she said wearily, fearing another earful. Coming fast on the heels of Vinny's call, she wasn't sure how much abuse she could take in one day. Arthur Boylan always seemed the most conservative of men to her, both in manner and dress. Once, in a rash moment, back in her early teens, Emma had asked her mother why she'd married him. Her parents' contrasting looks had prompted the question. Hazel, her mother, was beautiful – even to this day she retained a remarkable appearance – whereas Arthur Boylan, in marked contrast, could never be considered handsome. 'I married your dad,' her mother had replied, 'because he's beautiful from the inside.'

Over the years Emma had come to understand the remark. She learned to appreciate his wise counsel and his unswerving adherence to a very personal code that had 'honest dealing' as its central plank. A little old-fashioned, he could be vivacious and charming at times; on other occasions he could be downright crusty, but in one aspect he remained constant: he never made a judgement without hearing the other side of the story. Emma hoped that today she'd caught him in one of his better moods.

'I've been meaning to talk to you, Dad. Sorry to take so long about—'

'That's OK, I know; I heard in the office that you'd been on. So, tell me, how are you coping with this ... this unfortunate business?'

'Well, Dad, to tell you the truth, until about half an hour ago I thought I was doing pretty damn good. Then Vinny called; after that my world seemed to implode. I've disappointed him; I've let you and Mum down and—'

'Hey, hey, stop that, Emma. You haven't let anyone down. Your mother and I are as proud of you as we've always been. We worry of course; we read the newspapers and we fret. I'm ringing to let you know I'm here for you – both your mum and I – we're here to help if you think there's anything we can do.'

'Thanks, Dad. I'll take you up on that offer if things get out of hand.'

'Good, I hope you do. Can you tell me what stage it's at now?'

'Well, I can tell you that Connolly is being accused of something he didn't do. Of that, I'm one hundred per cent certain.'

'I believe you, Emma, your instincts have always been sound. Do you have any idea who the guilty party is?'

'That's the real problem. I've got a whole bunch of soft suspects; could be any of them. I don't want to mention names on the phone, but they range from people on the inside track of the law to some well-heeled friends of the victims. Motive and opportunity is proving a real problem. To be honest, Dad, I feel like a blind person in a maze.'

'I know the feeling. I just wish I could do something to help.'

'You already have, Dad. I was so afraid you and Mum would be mad at me, ashamed of—'

'Don't be daft, girl, that'll never happen, just go on doing what you know to be right; we'll be behind you every step of the way.'

'Thanks, Dad, you're a tonic. Before you rang I was starting to feel sorry for myself, but now, well, I don't know how you did it but I'm ready to get stuck in again.'

'That's my girl. Go get the bad guys.'

Emma hung up. She smiled and nodded with satisfaction. She had a job to do, an innocent man – her lover – to set free. A resurgence of energy coursed through her body, propelling her into action.

CHAPTER 29

etective Sergeant Mike Dorsett, a lanky Donegal man of few words, had agreed to meet Emma in O'Neill's. The venue, his choice, was a large traditional-style public house on the corner of Suffolk Street, directly opposite the tourist office that operated out of the deconsecrated Church of St Andrew. Sectionalized by a warren of nooks, crannies and alcoves, the pub had filled to capacity for the lunch hour. Dorsett's accent, a rich hybrid of Scottish/Donegal dialects, meant Emma had to listen extra carefully to catch what he was saying. Noise volume presented a further hindrance in deciphering the detective's limited utterances.

Emma had met Dorsett on a few previous occasions in the company of Connolly. His lack of dress sense had made a lasting impression, an aspect of his personality made all the more striking when viewed alongside Connolly, the epitome of the sharp-dressed man. Single, and in his early forties, Dorsett had a long chiselled face with as many peaks, hollows, plains and hard lines as his native Donegal landscape. Today, he was sporting a week's stubble and wore one of those woollen hats that looked like an old-fashioned tea cosy. His long legs were clad in jeans that had seen better days; his jacket and shirt could have been retrieved from the Oxfam rejects basket.

'Undercover, I see,' Emma remarked, giving him the once-over.

'No, not really,' Dorsett replied, pouring water into his Paddy whiskey.

'Connolly says you looked up the file on Darren Dempsey's rape case.'

'I did,' Dorsett agreed, taking a sip of whiskey.

'Seán Grennan was the arresting officer, right?'

'He was, aye.'

'And he messed up on the warrant?'

'He did, aye.'

'D'you think Grennan got it wrong on purpose?'

'That, I wouldn't know.'

Emma was beginning to feel a little pissed with Dorsett's minimalist responses. 'Look, Mike,' she said, allowing an edge to show, 'Connolly led me to believe you would help, said you'd fill me in on what happened to Darren Dempsey. Can you tell me, for instance, if you think Dempsey got away with rape, or whether Seán Grennan might have helped set him free?'

A smile broke on Dorsett's craggy face. 'Easy on, girl, hold yer horses. Can I make a suggestion?'

Emma nodded gratefully. Dorsett had strung more than three words together. 'All suggestions welcome,' she replied.

'Talk to Dempsey.'

'You think that's a good idea?'

'Aye, I do.'

'You don't think he might be in league with Seán Grennan?'

'Could be.'

'What if the two of them are working against Connolly?'

Dorsett drank more whiskey. 'One way to find out,' he offered.

'And that is—?' Emma asked, falling in with his speech pattern.

'Talk to him.'

'How do I get in touch with him?'

Dorsett extracted a piece of paper from the pocket of his jacket and handed it to Emma. Before she could examine it, he downed the remainder of his drink, tipped his forehead in salute, and exited the pub.

Great talking to you.

Emma looked at the paper, saw that it contained, written in neat script, Darren Dempsey's business address.

The man studied the reflections of Emma Boylan and the detective in the antique mirror behind the bar. A timber and frosted-glass counter partition blocked their view of him. It was important to the man that the observed did not spot the observer. He badly needed to light up a cigarette but the state had denied him that pleasure, at least in public places.

He averted his eyes momentarily from the reflections in the mirror to see how his Guinness was coming along. As a connoisseur of the good pint he was every bit as fussy as the most fastidious wine expert. It was important to him that the glass should be angled correctly while it filled to four-fifths its height. For best results, he knew the stout should then be allowed settle for 119.5 seconds to give the nitrogen and carbon dioxide time to create a creamy head. Once the perfect collared head has fully formed, the glass could then be topped to the brim.

He swished the first sip around his mouth before swallowing. Perfect! With this ceremony out of the way, he could now drink the contents at his leisure. The fact that the Reverend Ian Paisley, Ulster's firebrand preacher and maverick politician, once labelled the black liquid 'Devil's buttermilk', added to its allure.

The man at the counter could only think of two activities that gave him more pleasure than drinking pints: sex and killing people.

CHAPTER 30

KIDNAPPED. The word sent shivers down her spine. That Emma should hear the word on what was turning out to be a God-awful morning propelled her heartbeat to overdrive.

Inklings of difficulties to come had been evident from early morning.

Armed with the slip of paper Dorsett had given her, she'd gone to Darren Dempsey's place of work, a small business called Blue Pencil on Leixlip's main street. Owned by Dempsey, the enterprise employed a staff of five and provided editorial services for local businesses and the computer giants on its doorstep. It specialized in producing, designing and scripting newsletters, mail shots, stationery, workers' manuals and marketing leaflets.

Sinéad, a young attractive receptionist, told Emma that Dempsey hadn't arrived for work that morning. 'Most unusual,' she'd insisted, concern in her voice. 'He has a whole heap of appointments lined up. He normally contacts me if there's a problem.'

Prompted by Emma, Sinéad tried contacting him on both mobile and landline. There were no replies. When Emma offered to call to Dempsey's house, Sinéad was happy to supply the address.

There was no response at his home, a detached two-storey of recent vintage. The house, with its small, manicured front garden, was part of a development created for the mushrooming IT industry in Leixlip, a onetime sleepy village on the outskirts of Dublin City. Heavyweight global players like Intel and Hewlett Packard had increased the population tenfold, and in doing so had caused havoc with the environment and infrastructure.

Cursing softly at the wasted journey, she decided to head back for the city. With luck, she'd make it before midday. But she hadn't counted on the unusually heavy traffic. A bus had ploughed into the railings of Leixlip Bridge, known locally as the Salmon Leap Bridge, causing major disruptions to those entering or leaving the village. This same bridge had been the scene of a tragic accident back in 1932 when a distillery lorry, returning from the Eucharistic Congress in the Phoenix Park with thirty pilgrims on board, had crashed through the railings and ended up in the river below. More than seventy years later, the bridge layout remained much as it had been back then. Today's accident saw no loss of life, but it caused the traffic to back up all the way to the Lucan bypass.

It was here, stuck in traffic, her fingers drumming impatiently on the steering wheel, that the news of the kidnapping came from the car radio. She increased the volume, barely believing what she was hearing. Shane Buckley had received a ransom note for the release of his two grandchildren. The kidnappers were demanding a ransom of five million euro.

Honking horns behind her signalled a movement in traffic. She waved an apology and drove forward, her head buzzing with the breaking news. Further along the road she swung left on to a filling station forecourt. She needed to contact the *Post*, find out what the newsroom knew about this latest development. She had just brought the car to a halt when her mobile rang. It was Bob Crosby. 'That you, Emma?' he asked.

'Yeah, Bob, I was about to call you; just heard the news.'

'How soon can you get here?' he asked without preamble.

'About fifteen, no, make that twenty minutes; traffic's crazy.'

'Get here quick as you can. Come to my office. There's something I'd like you to see.'

'What Bob? What is it?'

'You'll see when you get here. Hurry … be careful.'

'Right, Bob. See you.'

In the newsroom for the first time since her enforced absence, Emma could see reports of the kidnapping on every monitor. Phones rang incessantly; some tucked between ear and shoulder, allowing journalists to scribble furiously on notepads. Mugs of coffee remained unconsumed; donuts and croissants lay untouched in their wrappings. Nobody, it seemed, had time to drink or eat but it was imperative that the crutch remain at arm's length.

The *Post* newsroom resembled a pressure cooker, the news hounds on the scent of a sensational headline. In the background the ever present rumble of the huge printing presses vibrated up from the basement. Passing her workstation, Emma was pleased to note that her desk remained unmanned.

Good, they haven't replaced me yet.

Bob Crosby and two sub editors, John Kavanagh and Rebecca Gibney, sat at the central table in Crosby's office. Crosby asked Emma to take a seat, indicating a space next to the subs. Rebecca Gibney a black woman in her thirties was dressed in a colourful, floral design, ankle-length dress with a wide, multi-beaded waistband. Her elaborate hairstyle and chunky jewellery gave the allure of exotica and cosmopolitan chic, an illusion that crumbled as soon as she opened her mouth. Born and bred in the heart of Dublin's Liberties, her utterances could best be described as 'inner-city vernacular'. 'How ar'ya Emma?' she enquired kindly.

'I'm fine, thank you, Rebecca,' Emma replied, nodding to her and the others. 'I take it, this is about the kidnapping, right?'

'Right,' Crosby affirmed. 'We're trying to figure how best to react. I thought you should be here on account of your prior involvement.' He closed the timber slat blinds that screened his office from the newsroom, crossed to his desk and swivelled his monitor towards the central table. 'The kidnappers have posted a video on the Internet. Take a look.'

The screen filled with silver static before a shaky picture appeared. A single naked light bulb illuminated a row of rafters, crossbeams and a sloped ceiling. The camera lens panned in jerky movements to a chimney breast with raw cement blocks and rough grouting, an area identifiable as an attic.

What appeared next brought a gasp from Emma; the faces of two children stared out at her. Emma recognized Chris and Katie. They appeared bewildered, frightened and lost. Holding hands and huddled together, both sets of tiny shoulders hunched inward as though warding off the cold. A rope secured their waists to a timber beam. No sound accompanied the picture. The focus shifted away from the faces and on to the naked bulb. Slowly, the bulb began to dim until there was no light at all. The screen remained black for several seconds before returning to static-filled grey.

Crosby and the two subs looked to Emma for reaction. They'd watched the images prior to her arrival but it was evident that the impact had not lessened with repetition.

'Sweet ... sweet Jesus,' Emma stuttered. 'Who ... who would—?'

'You may well ask,' Crosby said, 'but you'll get a better measure of the perpetrator when you see the message that accompanies the footage.'

Words began to appear on the screen.

CHRIS AND KATIE WILL REMAIN HUNGRY AND
COLD UNTIL OUR DEMANDS ARE MET.
MR BUCKLEY MUST APPEAR ON THE RTE NEWS
THIS EVENING AND SIGNAL HIS WILLINGNESS TO
PAY FIVE MILLION EUROS. WE WILL THEN CONTACT
HIM WITH AN OVERSEAS BANK ACCOUNT NUMBER.

Emma felt her throat constrict. 'Those poor little souls,' she said. 'Who would use children to—?'

'They're the bleedin' pits,' Rebecca Gibney said. 'But what connection is there between the kidnapping and the killings?'

'I don't know ... I don't know. This is crazy stuff,' Emma said, her thoughts fixated on the images she'd seen on the screen. 'You've had time to absorb the situation; what's your take?'

'Well, it's obvious there *is* a connection,' John Kavanagh said, 'but *how* it's connected is the big question.' Kavanagh, a young man with watery grey eyes, pale skin and a bookish appearance was on the first steps of the corporate ladder. He hadn't spoken to Emma more than a dozen times in the two-year period they'd worked on the same floor.

'Someone could have read about Shane Buckley taking the children under his wing,' Emma suggested. 'Buckley's rich; they see his involvement with his grandchildren as an opportunity to put the squeeze on him?'

'You think it's opportunistic?' Crosby asked.

'Could be, Bob; could be somebody jumping on the bandwagon, but I'd say it's more likely part of an overall strategy.'

Rebecca Gibney looked sceptical. 'Are we saying the kidnappers killed Nuala Buckley knowing that her father would take in the children?'

'Unlikely,' Emma admitted. 'According to Ann Buckley, her father had little or no time for the children and refused to see them *or* their mother. As it turns out, he's had a change of heart, but it's hard to see how the kidnappers – if they are the same people who did the killing – could have foreseen that.'

'My point exactly,' Rebecca said.

'So, where does that leave us?' Crosby asked.

'I think I know who's behind the kidnapping,' Emma said, 'It's only a hunch – nothing I can back up with facts.'

'Well, come on,' Crosby urged, 'who do you have in mind?'

'Can't say just yet. I need to run something by Connolly.' She turned to face Crosby. 'I need copies of last week's editions; the ones with pictures of Nuala Buckley's funeral.'

Crosby went to a cabinet and flicked through the recent editions. 'You think the people responsible are among the mourners?' he asked, handing the papers to her.

'Yes, well, at least I'm almost positive that the main instigator is among that group. Connolly told me he saw someone drive out from Iseult's house on the day of the murders. I think he might recognize that person when I show him the photographs.'

'Keep us informed,' Crosby said. 'I'm still not sure how we should handle this story.'

'Does that mean I'm back working for the *Post*?'

Crosby smiled. 'Didn't think you'd ever quit.'

CHAPTER 31

mma decided on a change of clothes, something with a dash of feminine flair, something to cheer up Connolly. She whittled the options on offer down to two outfits before eventually singling out her final preference: a demure grey dress that came to a fraction above the knee, with short puff sleeves, a low V neck and a white vest underneath. Choosing from her eclectic mix of accessories, she plumped for a wide, tan leather belt and high-heeled boots that came a little below the knee, enough to show off her artificially tanned legs. She felt confident that her choice looked expensive, restrained and, hopefully, just a little raunchy. Happy with her selection, she phoned Cloverhill.

Rules and regulations restricted visitors to a single period of twenty minutes duration per day. Up to three people could avail of the same time slot. When informed that Connolly's allotted time had been used up, she employed her most seductive voice to coax the authorities into bending the rules. The man at the end of the line was having none of it. 'D'you think we're running a hotel or what? Be here tomorrow and we'll let you in' – the man sniggered – 'wanna see if you look as sexy as you sound.'

Sexy, my arse.

Emma hung up, regretting the cheap tactics she'd used, annoyed at having to wait another twenty-four hours to put her new theory to the test. She was still fuming when Mike Dorsett called her, wanting to know if she'd spoken to Darren Dempsey. She told him she'd called to his office and home and had missed him in both places. 'Has something happened?' she asked.

'Not sure. There's been an altercation between two men in the car-park off Leixlip's main street. We found an empty car with the driver's door open and the keys on the ground. Ran the car's registration through the system, discovered Darren Dempsey is the owner.'

149

'Interesting!' Emma said, 'I know that car-park; it's opposite his office. He was probably on his way into work.'

'Both men were gone when we got there. If you catch up with Dempsey, contact me.'

'Will do,' Emma said.

As soon as Dorsett hung up, a call from Diana Elliott awaited her, 'You've heard about the kidnapping?' she said.

'Yes, I have.' Emma said, surprised that Diana should call her.

'Can we talk? There's a few things I'd like to ... to clarify.'

'I see, sure, why not? You want me to call to the house?'

'No. How about The Cat's Pyjamas? Half an hour?'

'I'll be there.'

Emma wore the clothes she'd chosen for the prison to the restaurant, still feeling peeved at being denied her visit to Connolly. The waiter's effusive greeting was in marked contrast to what she'd been used to. Whether this was because of what she was wearing, or because she had become something of a regular, she couldn't tell. Diana Elliott, Elizabeth Telford and Margot Hillary were in earnest conversation, ensconced at their usual table. Each in turn shook her hand, their greetings, like that of the waiter, less reticent than had been the case previously. Attempts to inject warmth into their smiles, however, failed.

'Glad you could make it,' Diana Elliott said. 'Would you like a menu?'

'No thanks,' Emma said, noting that they were not eating, 'coffee will do grand, thanks.'

'Fine! We'll have the same. Elizabeth and I are dining later this evening ... with the Lord Mayor – a charity do.'

'I'll have wine,' Margot Hillary said, her voice slightly slurred. She made no attempt to remove her shades even though the light in the restaurant was subdued. As soon as they'd been served, Diana dispensed with small talk. 'We'd like to talk to you off the record, if that's all right with you?'

'Why off the record?' Emma asked, in no mood for affability.

'What we have to say is not for publication; we are not talking to you as a journalist, but as an interested party who—'

'OK, fine, whatever,' Emma said wearily, 'if I can deal with the subject on an off-the-record basis then that's what I'll do, OK?'

Elizabeth and Margot murmured consent. 'Good!' Diana said,

'We'll proceed on the basis that what we say is strictly between the four of us.'

'OK,' Emma snapped. 'What's this about?'

Diana gave Emma the benefit of her, by now familiar, tight little smile. 'This kidnapping business has forced us to re-evaluate recent events.'

'In what way exactly?'

Diana paused before answering. 'You've talked to all of us in recent days and we've told you that Connolly was guilty. We believed it at the time.'

'And what ... now you don't, is that it?'

Elizabeth Telford nodded. 'We're not so sure any more, we—'

'Look, Emma,' Diana cut in, 'this is difficult for us but we need to get a few peripherals sorted out first.'

Emma guessed what was coming, asked nevertheless, 'Like what?'

'Blackmail! The subject is not relevant. Suffice to say that as a group we sometimes band together to achieve objectives that are pertinent to no one but ourselves.'

'And framing Connolly for murder and rape was one such project?' Emma said, failing to stifle the onset of anger.

'You're wrong, Emma,' Elizabeth said. 'There was never any intention of framing him for murder.'

'What? Oh, I see; you just wanted to frame him for rape?'

Elizabeth looked shamefaced. 'Yes, I regret to say that was the plan.'

'And *whose* idea was it?'

Diana glanced at Elizabeth and Margot before speaking. 'I hate to speak ill of the dead but, well, the truth is, it was Iseult's idea. She wanted to humiliate her ex. The *why* is more difficult to rationalize.'

'It was daft,' Elizabeth said, uneasily. 'How she ever persuaded us to go along with it is beyond me. We must've been mad.'

'Yes, in hindsight it does seem inexplicable,' Diana conceded, 'but, for reasons that were important to Iseult, she convinced us to get involved.'

'What exactly did she get you to do?' Emma demanded.

Diana glanced at her two friends. Their consenting nods prompted her to proceed. 'Iseult's plan was to have Connolly arrive at her house on the stroke of noon. Nuala Buckley would pretend to be alone while Iseult remained hidden. Nuala would invite Connolly in, tell him to wait for Iseult's arrival. And then, when Iseult appeared,

Nuala would pretend she'd been raped by Connolly. Iseult would have called her father by that stage. My job was to ring the police and report the rape. Iseult and Nuala would accuse Connolly when the cops arrived.'

'To back up their story,' Elizabeth said, 'I would give evidence to suggest that the detective had been pestering Nuala and that I had seen him alone in the house with Nuala.'

The conversation halted to allow a waiter place a fresh bottle of wine in front of Margot, who, with trembling hands, filled her glass, took a sip, and looked at Emma from behind her shades. 'Iseult wanted to mess with Connolly's head, have him fired from his job and in the process, split you and him apart. None of the other stuff was supposed to happen.'

Emma could no longer contain her fury. 'But why in God's name did you stick to your stories when it became obvious that Iseult and Nuala were murdered? Surely then, you knew that the time for daft games and intrigue was over. Why did you persist with your ... your lies?'

'We genuinely believed Connolly *had* killed both women,' Diana said.

'That's the truth,' Elizabeth assured Emma. 'We assumed he sussed Iseult's plan and went berserk ... struck out at them ... I don't know....'

Margot lowered her shades down her nose and stared at Emma. 'There was no other rationale that made sense.'

'So, when did you first realize you might be wrong?' Emma asked, finding it difficult to remain civil.

Diana seemed about to place the palm of her hand on the back of Emma's hand but held back. 'As soon as you told me Lisa Dunlop was dead I knew we'd got it wrong. Connolly was locked up at the time, so he couldn't have done it. There had to be someone else. I wondered if Maurice could have been involved. Three women were dead, all of them having had relationships with him. But then I thought, if Maurice wanted to kill all the women he slept with we'd have a bloody massacre on our hands. The only weapon he carries dangles between his legs ... shoots semen, not bullets.' A pained smile creased her face, then disappeared. Her eyes fixed on Emma, as though seeking to be understood. 'Maurice is a lot of things, most of them thoroughly unpleasant, but he's no murderer.'

Emma, in no mood for conciliation, felt her breathing become

shallow. 'If you now accept that neither Connolly or your husband
are guilty, whom do you suspect?'

'We've thought about nothing else these past few days,' Diana
said. 'The kidnapping has shaken us. Initially, when our plan went
off the rails, we still believed Connolly was guilty. We convinced
ourselves we were doing the right thing. There's only three of our
group left – the three you see in front of you – and I can assure you
that none of us talked to outsiders. Yet, there's no doubt that
someone familiar with our intentions hijacked our plan and used it
for an altogether different purpose.'

How can intelligent women be so bloody stupid?

'Just what the hell did you think you were playing at?' Emma said,
giving full vent to her anger.

'There'll be plenty of time for recriminations later on,' Margot
said, looking over the rims of her shades. 'Our concern should be
that there is someone out there killing people and kidnapping children.'

'Yes, and meanwhile Connolly remains locked up, accused of—'

'He's still alive,' Elizabeth snapped, 'which is more than can be
said for our friends. In time, he'll be vindicated, probably get promo-
tion.'

'Can we concentrate on the more serious problem, please?' Diana
asked. 'I feel guilty enough as it is; I don't want the deaths of Nuala's
kids on my conscience as well.'

Breathing through flared nostrils, Emma wanted to lash out at the
women, punish them, but she acknowledged that Diana was right:
the children were what mattered now. 'Have you any idea who
rumbled your plan? Did someone put the squeeze on one of you,
force you to—?'

Diana stopped her. 'You're on about blackmail again?'

'Yes, I happen to think it's relevant. I *know* you're being blackmailed yet you persist in denying it. Why, in God's name, are you still
lying?'

'You're barking up the wrong tree,' Elizabeth said.

'It really isn't relevant,' Margot added.

'I've already told you,' Diana insisted, 'that the blackmailing business is unconnected to what's happened. I must insist that you desist
from—'

'Look,' Emma said, gripping the edge of the table, 'this is not
about you. I don't give a shit what the three of you got up to in the

past to amuse yourselves. Far as I'm concerned you're just a bunch of rich biddies who, for devious pleasure, play nasty little games with other people's lives.' Emma paused, her knuckles white from the pressure exerted on the table. The compulsion to up-end the table and storm out of the restaurant was overwhelming, but a more prudent thought forced her to remain. She took a deep breath, stared at the three women in turn before continuing, 'Three people are *dead*; the lives of two children are in grave danger, so cut the bullshit, tell me what you know. Are you being used, willingly or unwillingly, to participate in what's happening?'

Diana Elliott, unaccustomed to being spoken to in such a manner, stared open-eyed at Emma. Emma returned the gaze, wondering what exactly it was that emanated from Diana's mercurial inspection: fury, curiosity, surprise, or contempt? Hard to tell at first, but the expression appeared eventually to settle for a barely decipherable measure of admiration. It was as though Emma had passed some kind of secret initiation rite into Diana's unholy sisterhood.

'All right,' Diane said, nodding her head gravely, 'I think we might just have reached an understanding.' She paused, looked to the other women, got their nods of approval, then continued. 'We think Detective Grennan could be involved. We have no evidence, just gut feelings.'

'What about Darren Dempsey?' Emma asked.

Diana looked puzzled. 'What? You think Dempsey's the kidnapper?'

'Well yes, I've considered that possibility.'

'You don't know Darren Dempsey then,' Diana said. 'He'd never harm Chris or Katie; those kids mean the world to him.'

Emma didn't like what she was hearing. 'I understood there was quite a history of hostility between him and the kids and their mother.'

'Well yes ... after the rape business,' Diana said. 'But Nuala never stopped loving Dempsey. He was the love of her life. She was devastated when he was accused of rape. It split them up, but more recently there's been a thawing of hostilities. Darren Dempsey would never harm Nuala ... or Chris and Katie ... not in a million years.'

Diana Elliott had just blown a great big hole in the one theory Emma had banked on. 'Did you know that Darren Dempsey has gone to ground?' she asked Diana. 'Odd that he should go missing at the same time that his two children are being held captive, don't you think?'

'It may be odd,' Diana conceded, 'but I can assure you he would never dream of harming a hair on the head of either of those children.'

'And you've no idea who's behind the kidnapping ... or the murders?'

'No ... but I'll bet Grennan's involved. Whether he's working on his own or with someone else I really don't know.'

Elizabeth and Margot nodded in agreement.

onnolly put aside the book he'd been reading to look at the television, a modern flat screen, bracketed high on the wall of the recreational room. It was 6.01 p.m. and the RTE evening news beamed its signal into Cloverhill. Top item, the kidnapping, was spliced with a package that portrayed him as chief villain. Luckily, there was none of the hardened criminals in the room at the time; they liked nothing better than to give him a hard time every time his mug appeared. Already, he'd been locked up for four days, well aware that prison – even a remand centre – represented a hostile environment for a cop. A number of refugees and asylum seekers were, however, present in the room; they'd been detained under section 9 of the Refugee Act. One of them, a burly Russian, pointed at Connolly, then to the image on the screen, and said, 'Is you, ya?'

Connolly sighed. 'Yes, my friend, yours truly, none other.'

A live transmission of a press conference flashed on to the screen. Chief Superintendent Rochford appeared harassed as he handled proceedings. Grennan, looking pleased with himself, sat to Rochford's right; Shane Buckley and his daughter Ann to his left. Behind a clutch of logo-labelled microphones, Rochford talked about the ransom, outlining his objection to giving in to the demands, before handing over to Shane Buckley.

Buckley, bereft of the velvet-collared overcoat and felt hat so beloved of the racing fraternity, looking pale and red-eyed, appealed directly to those holding his grandchildren. 'Please,' he implored, 'give them food and water and allow them light. I've just buried my daughter ... I don't want to lose her babies. Please do the right thing; contact me; my family have suffered enough.' He gave his e-mail address, his mobile, fax and landline numbers before pleading once again that no harm should come to the children.

Off camera, a commotion interrupted proceedings. 'I want to

speak!' a voice from the back of the room bellowed. Cameras panned across the assembled press and zoomed on to a big man. 'My name's Edmund Smyth-O'Brien,' the man said. 'I'm here to support the Buckley family. I, too, have lost a daughter, so I know what they're going through. I'll pay the ransom.'

Shane and Ann Buckley appeared shocked by the intervention. Chief Superintendent Rochford stood up, his face contorted with fury. 'Please, Mr Smyth-O'Brien, this is highly irregular. Could you come with me so that—?'

'No, to hell with all that, there's been too much death already, it's got to stop. Let the kidnappers contact the Buckley family; let them make arrangements to pick up the money; let them hand over the children.' Edmund Smyth-O'Brien sat down to a stunned silence. The camera picked out a teary-eyed Ann Buckley as she reached out to hold her father's hand. The man sitting next to Ann clasped her shoulder in a gesture of support.

Seeing so much emotion exposed on television made Connolly feel like an intruder; he'd never felt comfortable watching grieving parents or siblings exposed to the camera in such a cruel fashion. Rochford was set to speak again when the segment ended. An item about Iraq took over.

Connolly returned to the book he'd been reading, *The Guards*, a crime fiction novel by Ken Bruen. The prison officers who'd given it to him had said, 'This one's right up your street; it's about a disgraced, alcoholic garda who's been drummed out of the force.' If the intention had been to heap further ignominy on his plight, then the gesture failed. The book, Connolly discovered, was a mesmerizing, hilarious, eccentric take on how the Garda Síochána dealt with a renegade member. But right now Connolly's concentration remained fixated on the televised images he'd just seen. He was thinking about Chris and Katie's ordeal when suddenly he closed the book. Something on the news footage had taken hold of his subconscious, a subliminal message endeavouring to break through, yet stubbornly refusing to reveal its mystery.

Think, think, man.
What did I see that's ringing bells?

CHAPTER 33

Could this be the afterlife? Had he been buried alive in a coffin? Was he hallucinating, lost in some intangible nightmare? Slowly, too slowly, with the dawning of consciousness came a measure of reality. He was sitting on a cold hard surface, his legs stretched horizontally in front of him. Engulfed in darkness, Darren Dempsey's senses kicked in. He was learning an interesting fact: no matter how remorseless the dark appears initially, it gradually permits the eye to penetrate. He could smell wood, a whiff he associated with hardware stores, the kind that stocked timber beams and flooring. He could hear something. Movement. Scratching. Was he in the company of mice or rats? He hated rodents. Moving shapes materialized, his imagination now playing tricks on him. He needed to take hold of his senses. The sound of breathing came from the area where he'd first heard the scratching. 'Who's there?' he asked, a quiver in his voice. The sound of breathing became more pronounced. 'Please, who is there?' he asked again.

He heard a child whimper. His eyes narrowed in an effort to pinpoint the source. He sensed faint movement. Two barely visible spherical shapes hovered into vision. Spirits? No! He realized he was seeing the heads of two small children. 'Who are you?' he asked, his confusion overwhelming. There was no answer apart from the continual whimpering coming from their direction. Dempsey tried to move but discovered he was secured to a timber beam, his arms pulled behind his back, his wrists tied with plastic cord. He tried to prise his wrists apart but only succeeded in forcing the cord to tighten and dig into his flesh. Every time he moved or stretched, the mobile phone in his inside breast pocket dug into his ribs. If he could get to it he'd be able to summon help but, with his hands out of commission, he had no way of reaching or activating it.

He tried to move his bottom and legs but in doing so discovered that his ankles were bound. 'Talk to me,' he said. 'How did we get here? Why are *you* here? Can you move?' There was no answer but the whimpering stopped. The darkness appeared to ease fractionally. Gradually he got a sense of his surroundings. He could now see a sliver of faint diffused light. It appeared to be created by a series of roof rafters and horizontal beams meeting the exterior walls of an attic.

What am I doing in an attic?

He'd been unconscious, that much was clear. But how long had he been out for? Measuring time without the aid of a watch was diffi- cult if not impossible. His watch was still on his wrist but he had no way of looking at it. He tried to remember his last recollections before unconsciousness. It was like trying to recapture fragments from a dream but eventually details began to solidify. It had been morning time. He'd found a tight space to park his car and had been cautiously edging into it. What then? His door would only open halfway because of its closeness to the next car. To exit the car, he'd been forced to back his body through the narrow space. It had been then that everything went blank. No, wait, there had been something else; he'd sensed a movement behind him. Then pain. A blinding flash of pain ... then nothingness. What happened in the interim, he'd no idea.

'Are you going to hurt us?' a child asked.

Hearing the child speak gave him a start. The voice asking the question belonged to a young boy, a very frightened young boy.

'No, of course I'm not going to hurt you. Tell me, what's your name?'

'I'm Chris. This is my sister Katie.'

The names hit him like a strike of lightning. He wanted to scream, demand to know what kind of madness had descended.

Oh, sweet Jesus, please tell me I'm hallucinating.

The realization that he was sitting across from his own two chil- dren was simply too much to comprehend. He took long breaths to stop from hyperventilating. He had seen the children with Nuala as recently as three weeks earlier. She had wanted to ease him into a relationship with them, allow him to get to know them, and vice versa. Her intention had been to tell Chris and Katie that they might be seeing a lot more of him, and eventually, depending how things worked out, to let them know he was their father. Tentative moves had been set in motion. It was a delicate situation but the attraction that had drawn Nuala and him together in the first place had found new beginnings. In spite of the awful things that had happened, in spite of those who sought to poison the affection they had for each other, he'd never stopped loving Nuala. He had been encouraged to believe she felt the same way about him.

Nuala's murder had crushed him. Just when it seemed like he'd been given a second shot at happiness, his world had been torn asunder. He had begun to plan all the wonderful things the four of them would do together. The prospect of getting to know Chris and Katie had seemed tantalizingly close but with Nuala's death, that promise had been cruelly snatched away. Yet, here he was, confronted by the children in circumstances that seemed scarcely credible. He knew they could not see him in the darkness and wondered what would happen if they could; would they remember him from his recent meetings with their mother?

'Hello Chris and Katie,' he said, aware that the hairs on his arms were bristling. 'How did you get here ... how long have you been here?'

'A man with a funny face brought us here,' Chris said. 'He told Granddad he'd kill me and Katie if he didn't get a whole lot of money.'

'Your grandfather? He was here? He was with the man?'

'No. The man with the funny face spoke into a microphone.'

'When did this happen?'

'Don't know ... a long time ago; yesterday I think. He gave us nothing to eat and Katie has wee-weed her pants.'

'Have not,' Katie said with as much indignity as a 4 year old could muster.

Dempsey remembered Nuala telling him that Katie was a feisty young lady. Even in these trying circumstances, she was determined that her brother should not dent her dignity.

'Has anybody come to see you since you came here?' he asked.

'Yes,' Chris said. 'The man comes up and puts on the light and then turns it off. One time he took pictures of me and Katie. You came after that. We thought you were dead ... or sleeping. Two men tied you up.'

'There were two of them?'

'Yes.'

'This second person, did he have a funny face too?'

'No, his face was covered with a scarf.'

'And you didn't recognize his voice?'

'I don't know. I think he said nothing.'

'Please,' Katie said, 'I want to go home.'

'Yes I know. I'm your ...' He stopped, aware he'd almost blurted out something he shouldn't say. 'My name is Darren,' he said, quickly recovering, 'I'm a good friend of your mum's. I met both of you a few weeks back ... but I don't expect you'll remember me.' He waited for an indication of recognition but none came. 'I'll try my best to get us all out of—'

'Mum's dead,' Katie cut in.

'Yes, yes, Katie, I know about—'

'My aunty Ann says that Mum smiles down from Heaven each night when she sees me and Chris going to bed. Can she see us here ... in the dark?'

'Yes, I'm sure she can,' Darren said with a lump in his throat, 'she can see how brave you and Chris are right now.' Darren stopped talking. He could hear sounds coming from below them.

'Someone's coming,' Chris said.

'Good,' Darren said, 'Maybe now we'll get some answers.'

CHAPTER 34

Emma would never claim to be the most spiritual person on the planet, yet she embraced a profound notion concerning the redemptive benefits to be gained from soaking in a hot bath. It was, she firmly believed, the perfect place to soothe the soul and meditate without distraction. No longer a practising Catholic, she bestowed her hot bath with the same degree of sanctity she once conferred on the absolution and sanctifying grace imparted in the Sacrament of Penance. How profound was that? And yet, she'd allowed her fast-paced lifestyle to trick her into the habit of making do with the shower, cheating her of the spiritual goodness conferred by near total submersion. Since Connolly's arrest she'd been spinning in circles, getting nowhere, her brain overwhelmed with half-baked leads, all of them terminating in cul-de-sacs. Meltdown beckoned. She needed to purify body and soul, cleanse herself of extraneous baggage.

Stepping out of the tub, she felt loose-limbed, invigorated, her mind once more receptive to uncluttered thoughts. Wrapped in a big, fluffy white bathrobe, her toes brushing against the tufted carpet, she moved to the front lounge as though walking on air. She switched off the light and approached the front window, the sweet smell of bath essence embracing her in a full-body aureole. How many times had she watched Connolly stand on this very spot as he gazed on the river, cogitating conundrums he'd brought home from work?

Tonight, it was her turn. Standing in the darkness, she felt wholesome, soaking up the city's nightscape, her face up close to the glass, her body liberated beneath the bathrobe, her arms free of the sleeves. She could sense the pulse and flow of the city in the ink-black waters of the river, its shimmering surface alive with reflections of a thousand twinkling lights. Traffic had eased since the chaotic daytime grind but the side streets, footpaths and alleyways had taken on a

162

darker, nocturnal life of their own. The triple-glazed window screened the sounds but her mind could hear and see all: the vacant laughter, the false gaiety, the artificial masks. The underbelly of Dublin's fair city lay exposed; drug pushers, villains and pimps, like evil puppeteers, like vultures and leeches, mercilessly plying their trades, manipulating the lives of their victims. Desire and despair were, it seemed to her, inseparable bedfellows.

She thought about Vinny and the baby – *his* baby, *her* baby – the baby she'd lost. Like some great stormcloud, the loss hovered above her, refusing to dissipate, its presence a continual reminder of her negligence in the affair. Vinny had wanted to pick up the pieces, put Humpty Dumpty back together again but she didn't possess that kind of fortitude; for her, the loss had sapped the colour and vitality from their relationship. Something had burned out inside her, an intangible fear inserted in its place, a fear that prevented her from revisiting the path of procreation.

Earlier, before disrobing for her bath, Vinny had telephoned. Seeing his number, she'd let the call transfer to the answerphone and listened with a mixture of sorrow and annoyance. Poor Vinny, would he ever give up his self-imposed mission to save her from the demons he perceived to have taken possession of her soul? She fervently hoped that he would not become one of the lost souls abandoned to the mercies of the darkened metropolis.

Her bathrobe slipped from her shoulders and crumpled to the floor. She hardly noticed, couldn't be bothered to retrieve it. She just stood there, naked, exposed to the inky silhouettes of the buildings and the dark brooding quayside walls, a witness to Dublin's nocturnal populace as they participated in clandestine rendezvous, safe from the harsh scrutiny of daylight, sucking sustenance from the ether of the night. Thoughts of Vinny continued to invade her inner peace. When all this murder and kidnapping was done with, she would take time out with him, convince him to get a life of his own … set her free – set himself free – once and for all.

Thoughts of her lost baby took hold of her consciousness. Had she condemned its soul to the nothingness of limbo, waiting there for her, accusing her, saying *How could you do this to me?* Emma's thoughts merged into images of little Chris and Katie. They, too, were lost, out there somewhere in the vastness of the night. She dreaded to contemplate the terror going through their heads. What manner of monster had stolen them? Earlier in the day, she'd thought she had the answer, felt sure that Darren Dempsey – with the possible connivance of DS Seán Grennan – represented the guilty party. But, after her talk with Diana Elliott and friends, she no longer felt so sure. The possibility that the three women were lying had to be considered. They'd been less than forthcoming when it came to discussing the episode in the pool and the subsequent blackmail threats. But why would they lie about Dempsey? Why indeed? Tomorrow, she would show Connolly the picture of Darren Dempsey taken by the graveside. If the face in the picture resembled the person he had seen drive away from Iseult's house, then all bets were off.

Thoughts of Connolly brought a shudder to her body. She remembered the bathrobe at her feet and retrieved it. She slipped it on, this time putting her arms through the sleeves before wrapping them around her body. She hugged herself, evoking memories of his embrace. For one glorious moment he was there with her, real enough to hold, his breath on her lips, his fingertips soft as a whisper, touching her body ... but quickly, all too quickly, the illusion shimmered and melted away like a wisp of morning mist. Now, all she saw was the dark arches of O'Connell's bridge and the HEINEKEN sign on the O'Connell's Bridge House, its green, vertically arranged illuminated characters reflected as NEKENIEH on the Liffey's surface. She stood like that for an age, pressed against the window, unaware that tears were running down her face.

orning traffic on the N4 had been chock-a-block but Emma managed to pull into the prison car-park by ten o'clock. Three minutes later – and a full day later than intended – she sat in front of Connolly. The outfit she'd chosen on the previous day had been dropped; wearing it to The Cat's Pyjamas to meet Diana and her friends had put a damper on the feel-good effect she'd initially experienced. Instead, she'd selected a chic white, pleat-fronted dress and a flattering coat. Connolly's appraisal of her, as she faced him in the visitor's area, made the change seem well worth the bother.

'Got something,' she said, after fast tracking initial pleasantries.

'Oh, good, because I think I've got something too,' he replied.

'You start,' Emma offered.

'No, beauty before age, you first.'

'OK, then,' Emma said, pleased to see Connolly's recently departed *bonhomie* restored. She took a folded piece of newsprint from her pocket and showed it to him. 'See this,' she said, indicating the graveside photograph. 'Recognize anyone?'

Connolly angled his head to study the picture. 'Is there someone in particular you want me to look at?' he asked.

Emma pointed to Darren Dempsey. 'Could this be the driver you saw at Iseult's house?'

'That's Darren Dempsey,' he said. 'Mike Dorsett showed me his mugshot when he filled me in on the rape case. Like you, he thought it might ring a bell … but it didn't. Dempsey wasn't the driver.'

'Damn! I was so sure … I'd hoped that—'

'Don't look so glum, Emma. I now *know* who drove the car.'

'You're serious! You know? That's great. How did you—?'

'God, it does my heart good to see your eyes light up, Emma. That's what I miss most of all in this Godforsaken place – your smile.'

'Smile my backside. Just tell me who drove the bloody car.'

'First, let me tell you how it came to me. Did you see the news on television yesterday evening, the piece where my ex-father-in-law interrupted proceedings and offered to meet the kidnapper's demands?'

'Yes. Never saw Rochford so fired up. What of it?'

'Did you notice the man caressing Ann Buckley's shoulder?'

'Yeah, that's Sam Cline. I met him at Nuala's apartment.'

'Well, he is my mysterious driver.'

'You're serious? Damn, I never gave him a second thought. He helped Ann clear out Nuala's house. You're sure it was him?'

'Positive! Which means he knew Nuala Buckley ... probably got to know the sister Ann through her. I'll bet you a pound to a penny he's central to all that's happening.'

'You think Ann Buckley might be involved?'

'I doubt that; it's more likely she's in danger.'

'What makes you say that?'

'Can't see her having anything to do with the kidnapping. We both heard her that day in the courthouse. She loves those kids. And last night on the telly, you saw those tears running down her face....'

'I agree. The sisters were very close.'

'Exactly! If we accept that Sam Cline is involved, it's more than likely he's *using* Ann Buckley. She could be in real danger.'

'But what's in it for Cline?'

'Blackmail! Big money! First he goes after a bunch of rich biddies. Now, he's upped the stakes. By kidnapping the children he hopes to get millions from Shane Buckley. God knows how long he's been planning this.'

Emma nodded. 'I only saw Cline briefly ... Ann told me he was a musician – he certainly didn't come across as the criminal kind.'

'Well, you know what they say – never judge a book ... But you could be right; he might just be the hired help.'

'I don't know. I think I'll have another word with Ann.'

Connolly held out his hand. 'Show me that press clipping again.'

'Sure,' Emma said, handing it back. She watched intently as he pored over the photograph. 'What exactly are you looking for?'

'Ah ha! Found it,' he said, holding the cutting so that both could see it. 'What do I spy with my little eye?' he said, indicating a half-hidden face to the rear of the chief mourners.

'Yes I see, that's him, that's Sam Cline.'

'Right, but look who's standing next to him.'

'Oh yes, I see, that's Diana Elliott. I don't see any significance in that, do you? I mean, you can hardly choose who stands next to you at a funeral.'

'I suppose not. It's my cop training; seeing conspiracies everywhere.'

'Speaking of Diana Elliott,' Emma said, retrieving the press cutting, 'I saw her give dagger looks to Maurice as he drove from the cemetery with Ann Buckley. I don't understand Diana. I mean, she claims tolerance towards her husband's womanizing, but I don't think there's a woman born who would put up with that sort of behaviour without feeling resentment.'

'Yes, I agree, but Diana Elliott would never stoop to murder.'

'Maybe not, but you have to admit she's got motive. What if Diana couldn't take it any more, decided she'd had enough?'

Connolly shook his head, smiled. 'No, Emma, I *know* Diana. That's not her style. If she went after Maurice's women, Mount Jerome cemetery wouldn't be able to cope with the bodies.'

'Yeah, you've got a point there.'

'There *is* something I'd like you to do for me. I managed to get a message out to Mike Dorsett; told him what I'd seen on the television. Dorsett is working this unofficially – can't let Grennan know what he's up to as yet – so I've arranged for you to meet him at one o'clock today in O'Neill's if that's OK with you?'

'Yeah, sure, but why?'

'I'd like you to dig up all there is on Cline before you go charging out to see Ann. Dorsett has agreed, albeit reluctantly, to let you act as a sort of go-between ... if you're comfortable with that?'

'Yeah, that's fine. I just want to get you the hell out of here ... and see if I can find those children before—'

'Be careful, Emma, we don't know what we're up against here.'

Emma watched, bemused, as DS Mike Dorsett drank his Paddy and water, sitting in the same alcove they'd used on their first meeting. He still looked like a throwback to the hippie era. If his intention was to blend with O'Neill's regulars then he'd seriously misread the scene. His designer stubble had progressed to tramp bristle and the tea-cosy affair on his head appeared to have taken root. Describing his jacket and jeans as stressed would be to confer on them a respectability they didn't deserve.

'Did Connolly tell you what this is about?' he asked Emma.

'Yeah,' she said, 'you're checking on Sam Cline. Have you come up with anything?'

'I have, aye,' Dorsett said, with some reluctance.

'You going to tell me or not?'

Dorsett fiddled with his cigarette pack, thumbing it from end to end like a pack of cards, occasionally tapping it on the tabletop. An elderly man at the next table, nursing a pint of shandy, watched the detective intently. Emma figured him for one of the no-smoking vigilantes who had taken it upon themselves to enforce the smoking ban. To judge from his expression, he hoped to see Dorsett light up, an action that would allow him point to the no-smoking signs and demand compliance. If Dorsett was aware of this mini drama, he ignored it. He ceased playing with the cigarettes and looked Emma straight in the eye. 'I'm not happy 'bout this.'

'You mean the smoking ban?' Emma asked, facetiously.

'No! Dealing with you, I mean.'

'And why would that be?'

'Isn't it obvious? You're a journalist....'

'Well, in that case, let's stop wasting each other's time.' Emma got up and was about to walk when Dorsett caught the sleeve of her jacket. 'Whoa!' he said. '*Not happy* don't mean *I won't*. Connolly says you're OK, I'll live with that. Drink?'

'Thanks, I'll have a coffee.'

Dorsett ordered a coffee and remained tight-lipped while it was being served. Emma sat in silence, giving as good as she got.

'This Sam Cline fellow,' Dorsett said after Emma had taken a sip from her coffee, 'has been to the funny farm.'

'A mental institution, you mean?'

'Aye, I do. He was a child prodigy. Musically gifted but disruptive. Won all sorts of competitions. Played the fiddle – or should that be *violin* – won scholarships and bursaries to the world's top schools of music. Had a brush with the law while studying in London. Got pulled over by a bobby for eating an ice-cream cone while driving. When the cop gave him a tongue lashing for driving without due care, Cline leaped out of the car, shoved what remained of the ice-cream into the cop's face and began punching him. It took a crowd of onlookers to pull Cline off the cop. He got charged with GBH and was lucky to escape jail.'

'You ask me, the cop got what he deserved. I mean, come on, eating an ice cream!'

'Perhaps, but the incident set the tone for what was to follow.'

'How come?'

'A year later, Cline was rehearsing with the chamber orchestra here in Ireland when he took exception to something the conductor said. He snatched the baton from the conductor and smashed it over the poor man's head.'

'Sounds like Cline has serious anger management problems. So, what happened?'

'Once again, he escaped a custodial sentence, but this time he was sent for psychiatric evaluation. Went to St Mary's Psychiatric Clinic, met another patient there, someone relevant to current events.'

'And that patient's name is...?'

'*Was!* The patient with Cline *was* Nuala Buckley.'

'You're serious? I wonder why Ann Buckley never told me Nuala had psychiatric problems.'

'It's not the sort of thing people talk about.'

'Do you think Ann knows Cline was a fellow patient with her sister?'

'She might, aye ... then again, she might not.'

'I'm going to meet Ann again, see what she has to say for herself.'

169

'What if Cline is with her?'

'So much the better! I'd like to get all the facts this time.'

Dorsett stroked his stubble. 'There's something else,' he said. 'I found another file on the Dempsey rape case.'

'You say *found*? Was it lost?'

'It was buried ... not meant to be found.'

'Interesting! Does it shed any light on current events?'

'Depends on how Lisa Dunlop died. Did she fall? Was she pushed?'

'You saying Lisa Dunlop figures in Darren Dempsey's *lost* file?'

'At Dempsey's trial, the rape-victim's identity was withheld. Turns out that the person who'd accused Dempsey was Lisa Dunlop.'

'Wow!' Emma said. 'Seán Grennan handled that case. His negligence meant the case got thrown out ... and Darren Dempsey got away with it. And now, just when Lisa Dunlop was about to talk to me, she fell – *or* was pushed – down a flight of stairs, who should turn up to investigate her death? None other than our friend, Detective Inspector Seán Grennan.'

'And ... there's something else.'

'What?' Emma asked impatiently. 'Extracting information from you is like getting sperm from a eunuch.'

Dorsett smiled; a first from him. 'Well,' he said, pausing to restore his grim countenance, 'Lisa Dunlop's movements were secretly observed for a period around the time of the trial. It appears she was having an affair with a married man. His name was—'

'—Maurice Elliott,' Emma said.

'Hey! Now who's the tight arse?'

CHAPTER 37

Emma had done her research on Carrigmore Stud. Home to racing tycoon Shane Buckley, the place was a virtual fortress. Surrounded by high walls, the 3,000-acre estate was patrolled by security guards using state-of-the-art technology. As part of their brief, the guards were charged with the protection of legendary stallion, Tulferris, a champion sire responsible for winning more than €2 million in prize money during his racing career. Clients who enlisted the services of the stallion had made Buckley a rich man. Staggering sums of money were exchanged in the hope of breeding a champion racehorse. The Stud farm had another eighteen stallions, each capable of servicing thirty-five to forty-five mares per annum, but, in this regard, there was one piece of information that brought a smile to Emma's face. Tulferris was a slave to the reproductive requirements asked of him; he could service almost twice that of his fellow stallions in any one season.

Driving through Donnybrook, *en route* to Carrigmore, Emma first noticed the black Ford Mondeo. When she changed lanes, the Mondeo changed lanes; it slowed when she slowed; picked up speed when she did, an action that continued as she drove through Galloping Green and Foxrock. At one point, on the roundabout next to Loughlinstown Hospital, she got a glimpse of the driver in the mirror. There was no mistaking that face: it was Seán Grennan. As Emma took the Bray bypass and entered Wicklow's picturesque countryside, Grennan's Mondeo remained steadfastly behind her. It wasn't till she came to the village of Kilpedder and saw the approach signpost for Carrigmore Stud that he overtook her. She watched as the security guard waved him through without delay. For her, gaining admission was not quite so simple.

Security had been stepped up since the kidnapping. The guard refused to let her through without the say-so from someone within the Carrigmore complex. Emma gave Ann Buckley's name, hoping Ann would remember her. After making several phone calls, the guard instructed Emma to wait for an escort. Five minutes later Ann arrived in a Land Rover and invited her to hop aboard. 'Welcome to Carrigmore Stud,' she said. 'We'll go to my house if that's all right with you. My father is in the main residence ... with the police ... oh, yeah, and Edmund Smyth-O'Brien. They've set up a nerve centre to deal with the kidnapping ... tracer lines and all that paraphernalia.'

'How do you feel about Smyth-O'Brien's offer to pay the ransom?'

'If it helps get the children back, then, great. 'Course we all know his offer is really an attempt at *one-upmanship*. Even with something as serious as this, he feels compelled to compete with father. Pathetic, really.'

'Have the kidnappers made contact since?'

'No, not a word. Everyone's on tenterhooks.'

While Ann talked of the ordeal they were experiencing, Emma could not help but be impressed by the scale and grandeur of the place. What Ann called the main residence was a stunning nineteenth-century Victorian mansion. Grennan's Mondeo, along with a Mercedes and two squad cars, was parked in a gravelled courtyard to the front of the house. She recognized Shane Buckley standing on the porch and the bulky back view of Edmund Smyth-O'Brien. Both men were smoking – Smyth-O'Brien had a cigar, Buckley, a slim cheroot. Some distance from the mansion several smaller houses stood, each with their own driveways and outhouses. A series of creosote-finished fences separated this area from the stables and yards. In the distance Emma could see the paddocks, horse tracks and the roofs of two huge hangar-like buildings.

'This is like a whole world in itself,' Emma said, pointing to the buildings.

'Yes,' Ann said with a shrug, 'and it keeps growing, expanding ... the price we pay for success. On the positive side, though, we're pretty much self-contained; over three hundred people are employed here and some of the stewards reside within the complex. We have a full veterinary service, shops, a gym, and visitors' accommodation suites for overseas buyers.'

'I'd no idea the bloodstock business was so sophisticated,' Emma said, genuinely impressed.

'Sophisticated, huh? I don't know about that. What you see all around you,' she said, pointing to a newly constructed house, still clad in scaffolding, 'is part and parcel of what my father likes to imagine is progress; he thinks it's necessary to provide more and more accommodation for clients.'

'You don't agree?' Emma asked, sensing resentment.

'Can't stand in the way of progress ... isn't that the mantra we're all supposed to buy into? Trouble is, I like my own space and privacy.

'This is my house,' Ann said, pulling in next to the new building and parking in front of a modest two-storey, ivy-clad, cut-stone building. 'I mostly stay in the big house with Father but I like to crash here when I have friends over. With all that's happening right now I thought it best to bring you here.'

'That's fine, thanks,' Emma said, stepping down from the Land Rover. Inside the house, a warm log fire awaited them in a comfortable sitting-room.

'What a lovely place,' Emma remarked, 'you live here on your own?'

'Yes, I do. I'm quite a private person; I like to live the way I want to, eat food that suits me. I'm a vegetarian so I prefer to do my own cooking; can't stand to see Father and his friends foul the air with their stinking cigars while they gorge on red meat. Ugh! Would you like a coffee?'

'Yeah, please.'

Ann handed Emma a cup of steaming coffee. 'It's instant I'm afraid,' she said by way of apology, 'hope you don't mind.'

'It'll do fine,' Emma said, surprised that Ann, who made a virtue of caring about her food, should lack similar discretion when it came to coffee.

'So, tell me, what's this about?' Ann asked, cocking an eyebrow.

'I was hoping we might talk about Sam Cline?'

'Sam? What about Sam?'

'Well, you could tell me about his relationship with Nuala.'

'Relationship? Didn't think he had one; they were just good friends.'

'Nuala and Cline were patients in St Mary's psychiatric clinic at one time. I just wondered why you never mentioned it.'

Ann's eyes opened a little wider. She took a mouthful of coffee, put her mug down and nodded. 'Yes, Sam and Nuala were in St Mary's together ... what of it?'

'Well, it's just that when we spoke before, you told me Nuala was into sex, drugs and rock 'n' roll and that she was a free spirit; you made no mention of psychiatric problems—'

Ann appeared to blush. 'I'm sorry. I wasn't trying to fob you off, it's just that, well, it's hardly the kind of thing I'm likely to broadcast, is it? It was some years ago and I saw no good reason to dredge it up. There's no big secret. Nuala suffered from bipolar disorder; what we used to call manic depression. She was creative, exuberant, impulsive, passionate, and – I'm sorry to say – sexually permissive; she had the ability to dazzle with her brilliance. For the most part she could be witty, articulate and loving, but her behaviour was unpredictable. Sometimes it got ugly.'

Ann hesitated, a look of unease on her face, but Emma wanted to hear more. 'In what way did it get ugly?' she asked.

Ann scrunched her shoulders. 'It started in school. Nuala was subject to serious temper tantrums and had great difficulty studying. The school labelled her a "problem child". A specialist psychiatrist who examined her at the time prescribed a drug called Ritalin for what he defined as Attention Deficit Disorder. I remember this because Nuala got me to try it. We crushed and inhaled the tablets through a piece of rolled cardboard instead of swallowing them with water as instructed.'

'What effect did that have?'

'Not good, not good at all. At first I experienced an intense feeling of euphoria but later the exuberance was replaced by extreme fatigue. I kept well away from drugs after that but Nuala was not so easily put off.'

'She was hooked, yeah?'

'Right! The death of our mother triggered Nuala's first breakdown. She'd moved on to cannabis by then and was experimenting with acid – LSD – I think, and amphetamines. God knows what else. It was then that she was diagnosed as bipolar. Father had her taken away in the middle of the night to a psychiatric hospital on the outskirts of Cork. They subjected her to a combination of therapy and medication in an effort to stabilize her. She was given a month-long course of ECTs and the usual cocktail of anti-psychotic neuroleptics – Risperdal, Melloril, Zyprexa, as well as uppers like lithium and downers like Largactil. Trouble was, she often dispensed with the medication, went for several days at a time taking nothing.'

'How did that affect her?'

'It was a mixed blessing. I firmly believe they over-prescribed anti-depressants for Nuala; the doctors seemed to rely way too readily on handing out pills to those they considered mentally ill. For a while she acted like a zombie, as though she'd been chemically lobotomized; it was just too awful to watch. Nuala's condition did improve though, albeit very slowly. She had hyperactive days with overwhelming highs followed by crippling lows. The truth is, bipolar destroyed Nuala. She found it impossible to work or retain a stable relationship. Sometimes, she treated Dad and me as though *we* were the enemy, rejecting all our efforts to help her. That broke my heart. She might have coped better if she'd had a better relationship but her choice of male companions left a lot to be desired.'

'You're talking about Darren Dempsey?'

'I'm talking about *all* her men, but yes, Dempsey was the worst. After the rape business Nuala spent a second period in St Mary's. During that time she met Sam Cline. They were there for each other when life got too much to bear. It was a platonic relationship, nothing more. Sam's been a great help since Nuala's death.'

'Did you know he visited Nuala at Iseult's home on the day that … that she was—'

'No, but it doesn't surprise me; Sam called on her frequently.'

'You don't think he's involved in what happened?'

'Not a chance! Sam looked out for Nuala. They were kindred spirits.'

'How does he get on with Chris and Katie?'

'He dotes on them. They call him Uncle Sam. He's distraught over their disappearance. We all are!'

'When did you last see Sam?'

'The day we moved Nuala's stuff here. He calls me every other day, wants to know how I'm doing. Sam's part of the family.'

'Do you know about the group of women that Nuala hung with?'

Ann's brow furrowed. 'You mean Diana Elliott's ladies?'

'Yes – Elizabeth Telford and Margot Hillary … and, before their deaths, Iseult and Nuala. They had formed, what? – some sort of secret society.'

Ann laughed. 'Hardly that. They're a bunch of old hags in search of eternal youth – not Nuala, of course – with too much time on their hands, too many disposable assets, and husbands who pay too little attention to them.'

'Did Nuala ever talk about the activities they got up to?'

'No, and I never asked.'

'Is it possible that Nuala talked to Sam Cline about the group?'

'Could have, I suppose. I wouldn't know. Like I told you, they were close – been through Hell together. Yeah, it's possible. Why ask?'

'Did you know that Iseult asked Connolly to her house on the day that the murders took place?'

'No, I didn't.'

'I only ask because it's possible that Nuala may have told someone about the women's plan to inveigle him there.'

'Have you spoken to Darren Dempsey yet?'

'No. As you know he's gone missing.'

'How very convenient.'

'You think Dempsey's behind the kidnapping?'

'Yes, I do. He'd made strenuous efforts to get back with Nuala. He's quite the charmer; could twist her round his little finger. He would go to any lengths, invent any excuse, to get the children back.'

'I see!' Emma said. 'But why kill Nuala, or Iseult for that matter?'

'You've got me there, but I know Dempsey; he's one devious shit.'

'Can we talk about Darren Dempsey's rape case?'

'I've already told you what I know.'

'Yes, but you didn't mention the name of the rape victim.'

'The identity was never made public.'

'Yes, but I assume you know the victim's name.'

'I do, as a matter of fact. Why do you ask?'

'Because that person is now dead. Lisa Dunlop fell down a flight of stairs last week and died. Did you know that?'

Ann Buckley's hand shot to her mouth in shock. 'Oh my God. No, I didn't know. Jesus, God, how did it happen?'

'The police are saying it was an accident. Her autopsy revealed that she'd been stoned at the time.'

'You said the police *are saying* it's an accident. Is there a doubt?'

'I'm keeping an open mind. How well did you know Lisa Dunlop?'

'Scarcely at all. Nuala and I used to see her in the pony club, but we weren't close. She was a bit of an outsider, always trying to ingratiate herself with the more affluent members.'

'By the *more affluent members* you mean Nuala, Iseult and yourself?'

'Well yes, I suppose I do,' Ann said, casting her eyes downward. 'Not a whole lot I can do about my family's wealth.'

'Of course not. Did you know that Lisa Dunlop had an affair with your friend Maurice Elliott?'

'*Affair*? I wouldn't put it quite like that. Maurice is a twat when it comes to women, has a twitch in his loins for every one he claps an eye on. He saw Lisa as little more than an easy lay, paid her for services rendered in the form of expensive gifts … gave her money, God knows what else. He tired of her very quickly but had difficulty offloading her. By way of settlement, he gave her a job in his organization. He thought she'd leave him alone once he paid her a good wage. Didn't work out though. She continued to make a nuisance of herself. I only know this because Nuala told me. Maurice's wife got wind of the affair. You've met Diana so I don't need to tell you she's not someone you mess with. She set about teaching Lisa a lesson. That's the last I heard of Lisa Dunlop … until now.'

Emma finished her coffee and thanked Ann for her time. Ann drove her back to where she'd parked the car. Leaving Carrigmore Stud, Emma felt no nearer to resolving what lay behind the murders and kidnappings. Ann Buckley had given Sam Cline a clean bill of health. Yet he was the one Connolly had seen leaving the scene of the crime. Could he have fooled both the Buckley sisters as to his true nature? Was he the killer? Was he a blackmailer? Could he have kidnapped the children? According to Ann, he had open access to Carrigmore Stud.

And what of Darren Dempsey? Ann Buckley's opinion of him was tainted by her earlier experience at his hands, so her views had to be treated with a degree of scepticism. Yet, Emma could not dismiss Dempsey as a suspect. It was possible he'd pushed Lisa Dunlop down the stairs as an act of revenge for having accused him of rape. Equally, revenge could be the motive for killing Nuala. She'd left him and denied him access to Chris and Katie. It followed that he could easily be the kidnapper. But why kill Iseult Connolly? That was the stumbling block. And why leave the door of his car open and the keys on the ground? That didn't sound like the action of someone planning to kidnap two children.

What role did Seán Grennan play in the aborted rape case, and more recently, in Lisa's mysterious death? The detective's name kept cropping up. Even so, one of Emma's usually reliable gut instincts warned her that Grennan was not the prime mover. What reason would he have to kill Iseult or Nuala, or Lisa Dunlop for that matter? His apparent dislike of Connolly could never be construed as a motive for killing Connolly's wife. He could very well be the blackmailer – it was not unknown for coppers to be bent – but did she seriously believe he would kidnap two little children?

Who else was in the frame? Well, there was, what Connolly liked to term, the rich bitch club: first up, Diana Elliott, the socialite and fundraiser and wife of Maurice. It looked like she'd been responsible for the tattoo on Lisa Dunlop's forehead, but did it follow that she had something to do with Lisa's death? What of Margot Hillary? Dependent on drugs, her son had been sexually molested by Brendan Edwards. It was probable that Margot had been involved in the swimmer's death ... but what else had she done? And then there was Elizabeth Telford, ex-banker and dark horse among the women. As part of Diana's group, there's no doubt Elizabeth had been involved in some dubious escapades, but her role in recent events was unclear. All three women had been friends of Iseult and Nuala; did that rule them out as suspects for their murders?

What of Maurice Elliott? He had been on intimate terms with Iseult and Nuala. He'd also had a relationship with the unfortunate Lisa Dunlop. It could be argued that he had cause to get rid of Lisa but what reason would he have for killing the other two? She ran through the list again. Lurking there, was the name of someone who was capable of orchestrating all that had happened.

All I have to do is identify that person.

CHAPTER 38

The hatch door opened. Dim light seeped in. Dempsey could now make out the features on the children's faces. He wanted to study them, assure them that everything would be fine but his attention focused on the silhouetted figure emerging through the trap door. With half the body visible, it was possible to make out the shape of a smiling Tony Blair mask. Dempsey saw the grinning British Prime Minister reach with gloved hand to a timber beam and switch on a light. The glare blinded him initially but Dempsey forced his eyes open. The light was aimed at him and the children but, like an interrogation lamp, deflected away from the controller.

'Why are we here?' Dempsey demanded to know.'

No answer.

'I'm hungry,' Chris said. 'I want a drink.'

'Say something, goddamn you,' Dempsey challenged. 'Why are we tied up? You can't torture children like this.'

No answer from the grinning visage, just the sound of breathing from behind the mask. Dempsey screwed his eyes up in an attempt to penetrate the glare. The overall shape appeared to take on a more discernible outline – dungarees and donkey jacket – but then, in an instant, darkness descended. The faint glow from the hatch dissolved. The comic Prime Minister was gone.

Chris started to cry. 'I want to go home,' he sobbed, 'Please, let me out of here, I'm afraid ...'

'Don't cry,' Katie said. 'Grandad will come ... I know he will.'

Dempsey wanted to reach out, comfort them, but he couldn't move. 'You're right, Katie,' he said, 'People *are* looking for you. Your grandfather will find you.' Dempsey wasn't sure if he believed his own words; he had no idea if Shane Buckley was even aware of his grandchildren's predicament. Pondering this dilemma, he thought about the children's late mother and his own relationship with her.

Nuala had told him about a meeting she'd had with her father some weeks before her death. She expressed her wish to return Carrigmore. Her father had assured her she'd be welcome. A week before she'd been murdered, Nuala and the children visited Carrigmore Stud. Chris and Katie had the time of their lives. Seeing baby foals had really excited them. A special dinner had been laid on to mark the occasion. All had gone well until Shane proposed a toast at the conclusion of the feast. Replying to the toast, Nuala dropped the bombshell – 'I'm getting back with the children's dad, Darren Dempsey.'

The celebration ended in bitter acrimony. However, three days before the dreadful events in Iseult Connolly's house, a contrite Shane Buckley contacted Nuala. They agreed to meet the following week to sort things out. By the following week, Nuala was dead.

While this scene replayed in Darren Dempsey's head, he thought about the person who'd appeared at the hatch door. The mask had distorted the shape, but there had been something familiar about the body outline, the way it moved, the tilt of the head, the dip of the shoulders, the way the gloved hand reached for the light switch. He felt sure he'd seen those moves before. He was still trying to figure out what it was that struck a chord when a bleep sound startled him.

'What's that?' Chris asked.

'That's my mobile phone, it's telling me it's about to run out of juice.'

'Juice?' Chris said. 'You put juice in your phone?'

Darren smiled. 'No, Chris, the battery needs to be charged.'

'Is it dead?' Chris asked dejectedly.

'Afraid so,' Darren said, 'but it's only a matter of time before help comes. We're getting out of here, I promise you.'

CHAPTER 39

The man kept Emma Boylan in his sights as she drove through the Glen of the Downs. Two hours earlier, he'd tailed her on this same stretch of motorway, going in the opposite direction. Her visit to Carrigmore Stud had sealed her fate. The investigative journalist was now a serious threat. Thus far, she hadn't put it together ... but it was only a matter of time before she twigged. Such a development would jeopardize the final phase of the operation. His job was to stop her. A tingle of excitement ran through his body.

I Still Haven't Found What I'm Looking For boomed from the radio's speakers, filling the car's interior with an irony that Emma acknowledged with a wry smile. She certainly hadn't found what she was looking for. Talking to Ann Buckley had only served to further confuse an already muddled situation.

She was busy constructing multiple scenarios and demolishing them just as quickly when something caught her eye. A familiar car appeared in her rear-view mirror.

Damn! I don't believe this.

Four cars separated her from Grennan's Mondeo. She wanted to believe it was just a coincidence; after all, he was the detective in charge of the case. It would be natural enough for him to meet Shane Buckley in Carrigmore Stud. No reason why Grennan would not use the same route as Emma to get there and back. Coincidence? Could be, but she doubted it.

To put her mind to rest, she pulled into the Dunnes Store car-park in Cornelscourt. She didn't need anything from the supermarket but the diversion would give her time to think, and to ditch the tail, if tail it was. Basket in hand, she strolled the aisles, selected a few household needs: milk, wholemeal bread, tomatoes and satsumas. Since Connolly's absence she'd been living on a low-calorie diet of salad, vegetables and coffee. There didn't seem much point in cooking food without having someone to enjoy it with. It was different when Connolly was around; he liked to eat well but, unlike her, he never appeared to gain an extra pound. Over the years, but more especially of late, she'd been having difficulty in retaining her slim figure. On a few occasions, after over-indulging in Connolly's favourite restaurant, she'd felt the need to purge the food. Well aware of the dangers of getting sucked into the realm of eating disorders, behaviour that smacked of anorexia and bulimia nervosa, she was determined never to allow herself get drawn down that particular path.

Emma paid for her meagre purchases at the checkout and got back on the road again, ready to complete her journey. She watched to see if the black Mondeo reappeared but could see no sign of the detective. An audible sigh escaped as her body relaxed.

In the apartment, she put away her purchases and activated the percolator. She would brew some proper coffee, using her favourite Sugar Loaf blend, and pop a slice of bread in the toaster. Sustenance was required before driving to Cloverhill. She was anxious to see what Connolly would make of her visit to Carrigmore Stud.

As she poured her coffee, she sensed movement behind her. Before she could turn around, an arm wrapped around her waist. She screamed. A hand clamped over her mouth. Her waist was held in a crushing grip. Her feet shot from beneath her, her upper body jerked backwards. The hand on her mouth stifled her screams. She couldn't breathe. Worse, she couldn't see her assailant.

In the second that it took to realize what was happening, her survival instincts kicked in. The moves she'd learned in self-defence class came into their own. She rammed her elbow into the intruder's rib cage with the force of a sledgehammer. The attacker groaned, a sound that let her know it was a man. Emma bit into the flesh on the side of his palm, drawing blood. The hand covering her mouth loosened. She struggled to free herself but the attacker's other hand, the one that had secured her waist grabbed a milk jug and brought it crashing down on her head. Her strength began to fade. The blood in her ears roared like a tempest, the discordant peal of a bell reverberating inside her head, her body sagged and went limp. The world she knew spun out of control, the ceiling above her melted like a Dali painting. In the last moments of consciousness she saw, or imagined she saw, her door burst open and a second man materialize. It was Seán Grennan.

Oh, my God, there's two of them.

This was the last conscious thought she had before darkness descended.

er eyes flicked open. A blurred apparition hovered above her. It took a second to realize it was Grennan's face. 'Come on, girl,' he was saying. 'You're grand now ... ne'er a bother on you. The fooker's gone! Can you hear me?'

She was half sitting, half lying on her couch, her head leaning awkwardly on the armrest. Feeling Grennan's breath on her face, she pressed her head back into the armrest. The realization that he was holding her hand added further confusion. She struggled to string her words together. 'What are you ... why are you ... what...?'

'You're safe now,' Grennan said, his face red as beetroot. 'He's skedaddled; gone with his tail between his legs. I got here just in time. I was—'

In a flash, Emma remembered. 'You broke in here, you attacked me. I saw you.'

'Don't talk rubbish, girl, I didn't touch you. I saved your bacon, saw you were in trouble and I—'

'But how?' Emma asked, aware that Grennan still held her hand, aware of the blood on his fingers. 'You've got blood on your hands,' she said, jerking her hand free. It was then she saw the blood on her own hand. 'Look what you've done,' she said. 'Can you explain—?'

''Twasn't me done that,' Grennan cut in, 'you musta hurt your attacker in the tussle; 'tis probably *his* blood.'

Emma stared at Grennan, struggling to assess the situation. Something in his eyes made her want to believe him. He stared back, saying nothing.

'Yes, I bit him,' she said, a measure of clarity returning. 'I bit his hand. Shit, what if he's got AIDS?'

'You'd want to see a doctor, get a tetanus shot.'

'Yeah, right, that'll be a fat lot of good if he's got ...' She didn't finish the sentence. Instead, she ran her fingers through the hair on the back of her head. A swelling had started but she could find no break in the flesh. 'How did you know I had an intruder?' she asked. 'I don't believe—'

'Let me tell you what happened, OK? I was on my way to Carrigmore Stud when I copped your car ahead of me.'

'You were tailing me; I saw you.'

'Yeah, but not the way you think. Just happens we picked the same route. I saw another car – not yours – acting suspiciously. A four-wheel drive – a Subaru Forester – made some erratic moves, the sort of moves I associate with surveillance. It wasn't until I got to within spitting distance of Carrigmore Stud that it dawned on me the Subaru was tailing you. I made a note of the registration with the intention of checking it out when I got back to the station. I had business with Shane Buckley ... the kidnapping and the ransom money. When I was leaving, the guard at the gate told me you were with Ann Buckley. So, I hung around until I saw Ann drive you to the gate before hitting the road myself.'

'Sounds to me like you *were* following me.'

'Keeping an eye on you, more like. You'd only gone half a mile when I spotted your man in the four-wheel sniffing your tail again.'

Emma was defiant. 'I never noticed any ... what, Subaru Forester,' she said, still massaging the back of her head.

'I'm not surprised; you were hell-bent on keeping my car in your mirror, blind to all other road users. When you branched off at the supermarket I followed the four-wheel to this apartment, watched it being parked in Lower Liffey Street. Had a job finding a space myself. By the time I walked back to the Subaru, the driver was gone. I figured he'd made it on foot to your apartment so I did a little reconnoitring ... couldn't catch sight of the bugger. I hung around until you arrived, thinking he'd show his face. I moved to the lobby, had a gut feeling something could happen. Me, I can smell trouble. I remembered about the fire-escape that's attached to these blocks so I thought I'd better warn you in case you had an unwelcome visitor. I was about to press your doorbell when I heard a scream. I stuck my ear to the door and heard the commotion inside. I rang the bell but nothing—'

'Wait a sec,' Emma cut in, 'I did hear a bell. But, I thought it came from inside my head.'

'Ah, now we're sucking diesel. You believe me, huh?'

'I don't know, tell me more.'

'Well, for once, my considerable bulk came in handy. I smashed the door in, saw your man doin' a number on you. Soon as he saw me he bolted for the fire escape like a scalded cat.'

'You mean to say you let him go?'

'Jaysus, there's gratitude. D'you have to be such a pain in the hole? Look, I wanted to see if you were seriously hurt. Wouldn't have bothered me bollocks if I'd known the thanks I'd get. Anyway, soon as I saw you were still breathing, I gave chase, but by then he'd cleared the fire escape. I already had the number of his vehicle so I came back to check up on you. By then you had started to come around.'

'Did you get a look at him?'

'Yes, I did, but I haven't the foggiest who he is.'

'It wasn't Darren Dempsey by any chance?'

'Why would it be Darren Dempsey? What gave you that idea?'

'Doesn't matter! Can you describe the attacker? I didn't see his face.'

'Youngish, tall, needed a haircut.'

'Sounds like Sam Cline.'

'Who the fook is Sam Cline?'

Emma decided not to answer, at least not straight away. She needed time to get her brain up to speed; time to decide how much she should trust Grennan. Still feeling a little dizzy, she stood up. 'I was about to have some coffee before all hell broke loose,' she said, moving to the kitchen. 'Why don't we both have a cup? Then you can tell me about Darren Dempsey and Lisa Dunlop ... and the rape case you managed to screw up.'

If Grennan was surprised by the direction she'd taken, it didn't show. 'Now, why would I want to discuss details of that nature with you?' he asked.

'Because, if what I hear makes sense, I might tell you what I know about Sam Cline. Who knows, between us we just might discover who murdered Nuala Buckley and Iseult Connolly. We might also find out who's holding the children.'

'Look, Ms Boylan, if you have information pertaining to the offence you've mentioned; if you are in any way obstructing the law—'

'Cut the cop jargon,' Emma said with feigned annoyance, 'I think I prefer it when you pretend to be a country yokel.'

Grennan thought about that for a second, then smiled. 'Oh, right you are then,' he said, offering to shake her hand.

CHAPTER 41

S am Cline ordered a pint of Guinness and moved away from the counter. Today, he couldn't be arsed to watch the barman go through the ritual. Instead, he found a quiet alcove and waited for the drink to be brought to him. He fidgeted with a beer mat, turning it about with his fingers, occasionally breaking off fragments around the edges. In the background, piped music, like an echo from his past life beckoned to him; not the usual insipid orchestral syrup one usually endures in pubs and restaurants but full-blooded classical fare. Haydn and Guinness: a potent cocktail of rare delight. How appropriate, he thought, knowing that Haydn once claimed he'd composed his music for *'the weary and the worn, so that they might enjoy a few moments of solace and refreshment.'*

Right now, though, the heady combination failed to lift his spirits. The adrenaline he'd experienced while attacking Emma Boylan had evaporated. His heartbeat had reverted to its normal rhythm. He'd cleaned the blood from the bite mark on his hand. He would make the bitch pay for that and for the bruising she'd caused when her elbow shot, piston-like, into his ribs.

Things had been going so well for him until today's setback. Although he was a mere bottom-feeder, he had ambitions to make it to the very top, share that position with the person pulling the strings. Now, he'd messed up big time. He'd failed to take out the investigative journalist. Worse, he'd been caught in the act. Grennan had intervened before he'd completed the job. And to cap it all, the detective had seen his face.

Taking a sip of stout, he replayed the scene over again, thinking how he should have reacted. *Should've stood my ground, taken my chances with the big detective.* Involuntarily, he took a second beer mat and demolished it. He'd blown his cover, a factor that meant he now needed a damage limitation exercise. His contributions to the master plan from here on in would have to be conducted underground. The Subaru Forester would have to be jettisoned, new wheels found, and revised rules of engagement employed.

Drinking coffee and conversing with Seán Grennan was not something Emma had envisaged. She still wasn't one hundred per cent sure whether or not he was on the level, but listening to him speak in his flat Midland's accent inclined her towards believing him. When he talked about his colleague Connolly, Emma realized there was more to the big cop than met the eyes.

'I was wrong about Connolly,' he was saying, 'he had nothing to do with the murders, plain as the nose on my face now.'

'So why is he still locked up?'

''Tis a bit like turning the Queen Mary in mid-Atlantic; once the law is set in motion, it takes the devil 'n' all to change it. As soon as the guilty party is apprehended, the DPP will turn Connolly loose.'

'Well, I hope you feel properly ashamed of yourself for—'

'Oh, I do, I do, I know I've made a right dog's bollocks of things. Funny thing is, I've always admired Connolly. Back when we were recruits, he was the one I looked up to.'

'What? I don't believe you. You're saying you—'

'Yeah, I always liked him. He was a hero on the sports field and the one to challenge on the debating team. I tried to compete with him but he wiped the floor with me … brains to burn, he had, way too bright for the rest of us. If I'm honest, he became a sort of role model for me.'

'And yet,' Emma said, finding it hard to believe what she was hearing, 'you had no difficulty thinking he was responsible for the deaths of his ex-wife and Nuala Buckley? How come?'

'Ah yeah, but that's different; that's what I was supposed to believe. The people behind these crimes are crafty buggers. They set up the killings in such a way that Connolly automatically became the prime suspect … the *only* suspect. Every clue pointed in his direction. I didn't want to believe it at first, but when the evidence stacked up I got mad. I couldn't believe that the man I'd thought so highly of for all those years could turn out to have feet of clay.'

'I still don't understand how you could believe a friend – *someone you looked up to, a role model* – could be guilty of—'

'Yeah, I know, I know, 'tis hard to explain but I'll put it to you like this: remember when Michelle Smith won the three Olympic gold medals? Remember how proud we felt? A small country like Ireland and a slip of a girl bringing home the gold? I went on the tear for a whole week. It lifted the whole country; we all basked in the reflected glory. I got mad as hell when the Yanks suggested she'd taken drugs. But then, a few years later the arse fell out of the dream when Michelle was found to have tampered with her urine sample. I was gutted; just couldn't believe it. Well, that's how I felt about Connolly. He'd let me down in similar fashion; I could barely look him in the face.'

'So, when did it dawn on you that you'd got it wrong?'

'I asked myself questions when Lisa Dunlop took her fall. And then, when Darren Dempsey and the kids went missing, I knew which way the wind was blowing.'

Emma wanted to yell at him, punch him in the gut, tell him what a gobshite he'd been, but she held back, determined instead to elicit further useful information. 'Tell me about Darren Dempsey.'

'Darren Dempsey could be in danger. I think the same people who set up Connolly are now framing Dempsey.'

'The way I hear it, Dempsey walked because of your incompetence.'

Grennan smiled. ''Tis true in a way. I knew he was being set up, but I'd no evidence to prove it, so I took the law into my own hands, got Dempsey off on a technicality. I made an error on the charge sheet.'

'Who set him up?'

Before Grennan could answer, his mobile bleeped. The minimalist conversation that followed had Grennan mostly listening, occasionally nodding or saying *yeah*. A minute later he closed the mobile and stood up. 'Got to dash,' he said, making his way to the door. 'I think we've got a break on where the children are located.'

'Are they alive.'

'I'm about to find out. I'll let you know as soon as I hear something definite.'

Emma wanted to ask more. She had a nagging thought that something he'd said contained crucial importance to the case, something that hadn't quite come together in her brain as yet.

CHAPTER 42

It felt like a lifetime since she'd visited the Social Alliance Party office. On that first occasion, Maurice Elliott had not been present but the visit had, nevertheless, been notable in that she'd encounter Lisa Dunlop. There was no hanging about today. Emma had been whisked into Elliott's office as soon as she entered. And, what an office! In marked contrast to the minimalist décor in the reception, Elliott's private suite was sumptuous. Original paintings adorned the walls, plush carpets on the floor and a magnificent display of dwarf trees and shrubs sat atop a green hued marble plinth.

'You like my bonsai display?' Elliott asked, sitting behind a large mahogany desk in a high-backed, leather-studded chair.

'I didn't come here to see stunted growth,' Emma replied.

'I feared you wouldn't come at all.'

'Almost didn't. You said you had important information ... to do with Connolly ... and me. Most urgent, you said. So, here I am.'

'I was less than straight with you when you came to my house.'

'Looked straightforward enough to me,' Emma said, in no mood for condescension. 'You discovered I was living with Connolly – a man suspected of murder – and promptly dumped me. That sums it up, wouldn't you say?'

'Might have looked that way but there was a lot more to it.'

'Really? Like what, for example?'

Elliott got up from his chair and moved to a small bar to one corner of the room. 'Mind if I have a shot?' he asked. 'I have a strange and twisted tale to tell. Not sure where to begin. Get you something to drink?'

'Wouldn't say no to a coffee.'

Elliott moved back to his chair, placed his drink on the desk and rang reception to arrange coffee. 'That day in my house, halfway through our conversation, I got a telephone call.'

'Yes, I remember. And after the call, you told me to—'

'Let me tell you what happened,' Elliott interrupted, 'that call had been from someone wishing to relieve me of an awful lot of dosh. I was being blackmailed. The choices were stark: I could give one million euro to the caller or, I could see my reputation destroyed. As an adjunct to the conditions, I was ordered not to give you the job.'

'Are you saying that my relationship with Connolly was not the reason for refusing me employment?'

'I'm saying that far more profound intrigues were in play. If you'll hear me out, I'll try to explain ...' Elliott ceased talking while the receptionist brought coffee. As soon as she'd left the room, Elliott locked the door and walked to a window and remained motionless for several seconds. With his back to Emma, he appeared to be looking down on the grounds of Trinity College. Emma sipped her coffee, said nothing. One hour earlier, Elliott's call had come out of the blue. She'd barely recovered from Sam Cline's attack and the subsequent rescue performed by Grennan when the call had come.

Elliott returned to his desk. 'Before I talk about the blackmail demand – and your involvement – I need to tell you about the events that have brought us to this point. It might be useful to talk about my wife Diana to begin with. Before marrying me she had a successful career in public relations; she could create illusions, erect veneers around the most superficial products, give them an aura of respectability. Her approach to our marriage wasn't all that different. We were the dream team, a "product" she could fashion into an integral part of what goes for high society in this country. She would ignore my little peccadilloes as long as I remained discreet; for my part I would ignore the fact that her proclivities lay with her own gender. Not your typical dyke I hasten to add; Diana likes women who are thoroughly feminine, hates the butch brigade. Up to a point, this arrangement worked but in recent years cracks appeared.

'Diana began to take a greater interest in my dalliances. She formed a close circle of female friends. Some of the antics they got up to bordered on the insane. Take my affair with Lisa Dunlop for example. I first got to know Lisa when she and Ann Buckley competed as team mates on the equestrian circuit. My company sponsored some of those events, so it was natural enough that I should bump into them from time to time. I had what I thought was a one-off fling with Lisa and assumed she knew the score. Unfortunately, she became a nuisance, refused to bow out gracefully and threatened me with all sorts of unpleasantness. To shut her up, I employed her as a receptionist. Worst mistake I ever made. She refused to back off and Diana got wind of the situation. With the help of her group of ladies, she secured the services of a tattoo artist to do a job on Lisa.

'Diana's not afraid to play rough; neither are her friends. When a certain boyfriend jilted Elizabeth Telford, the women set up a sting to expose him as an inside trader; the guy ended up serving time. Their most recent caper concerned your friend Connolly. On Iseult's behest they set about sullying his name. We now know the plan went disastrously wrong.'

'What exactly happened on the day I went to your house?'

'I received a DVD after you'd left. It contained visual evidence of one of the women's schemes. I watched it in disbelief, saw how my wife and Iseult attacked the swimmer, Edwards, in the pool.'

'But, wasn't he a world-class athlete? How could two women—?'

'You're right, but it so happens, these women were strong swimmers – Iseult had been a school champion; Diana had narrowly missed being picked as a member of Ireland's juvenile Swim Team back in her teens.'

'I see,' Emma said, amazed by what she was hearing. 'Tell me more.'

'Nuala Buckley was not involved in the pool incident, but Elizabeth Telford and Margot Hillary were. They heard Iseult and Diana demand of Edwards that he never again interfere with Margot's son. The poor bastard was scared out of his wits but the women continued to tackle him. At one point, after holding him below the water, he failed to resurface. He'd suffered a heart attack, but, of course, the women weren't to know that at the time. He was dead and they knew they were responsible. The blackmailer threatened to send the footage to the TV networks if I didn't cough up the cash.'

'Are you suggesting that the women never set out to kill Edwards?' Emma asked.

'Of course not. What happened was, at worst, manslaughter. You might think they should have gone to the police, taken their chances, but you'd be wrong. You might think that Diana's fund-raising activities would work in their favour but you'd be wrong again.'

'I think it would—'

'Wrong, I tell you! None of that counts for shit. Diana's had some pretty nasty publicity lately. One article accused her of being morally repulsive, another claimed she focused solely on the glamour end of the aid business. A current-affairs programme pointed out that she'd never bothered to visit any of the disaster areas she collected for. Even the fact that Edwards was a paedophile, the fact that he'd molested Margot's son, wouldn't make the slightest difference. The courts would never condone their action.'

'Nor should they,' Emma said uneasily, unsure of where Elliott was going with his argument.

'You're right,' he said, his concentration appearing to slip. 'And to be fair to Diana, she accepts that her actions, and those of her friends, went way beyond redemption. "I'd rather die", she said to me, "than countenance a public trial". I know she meant it. However, she's had to accept some unpleasant truths in the past few days. Since the kidnapping, she's put a plan of action in train. Today is the first Friday of May. Diana and her friends meet this evening to come up with some sort of strategy. I talked to her earlier today, but she refused to let me in on her thinking ... even so, I sensed something most odd in her behaviour. I got this eerie feeling of doom, something I've never sensed in her before.'

'Sorry, I'm not sure why you're telling me this now?' Emma said, wondering what exactly Elliott was leading to.

'I need your help, Emma. I need a favour from you.'

'You need a favour ... from *me*?'

'I do! You see, I will not be present at their little soirée – it being an all-female affair – but I've been told to offer you an invitation. Diana wants you there at eight o'clock.'

'They want me?'

'Strangely enough, they do. I don't know what the hell they're up to this time. That's why I wanted to see you so urgently. Your presence there could be of vital importance.'

'In what way do you see my presence—?'

'I want you to halt their actions if you think they're doing something totally reckless, something that might prove irreversible.'

'And how am I supposed to do that?'

'You're a smart cookie, you'll find a way.'

CHAPTER 43

The phone rang as Emma entered the apartment. Bob Crosby was on the line. 'Ah, good, caught you,' he said, sounding less grumpy than usual. 'Dempsey's whereabouts has been discovered. Let's hope he has the children with him.'

'You think he's the kidnapper?'

'Well, yes. I thought you did too?'

'I did at first,' Emma admitted, 'but not now.'

'Damn! You'd better tell me what you know. I don't want the *Post* going off half-cocked on this one.'

Emma outlined most of what had transpired in the past forty-eight hours and finished by telling Bob of the invitation she'd received to meet Diana Elliott. She held back on just one detail. Emma now knew who was behind the killings, the kidnappings and the blackmail scam. Talking to Seán Grennan and Maurice Elliott had provided her with the key to the puzzle. Between them they had furnished information that, when linked together, pointed to the culprit. She now had the name but not the motive that prompted the crime. She felt guilty about withholding this information but she needed absolute confirmation before committing herself. She fully expected to receive that confirmation when she got to the Elliott home. 'Diana Elliott is expecting me within the next hour,' she told Crosby. 'I'll give you the full story once I talk to Diana and her lady friends.'

'In that case, you'd better get a lead-in report to the *Post* asap. I want the pumps primed when this breaks.'

'What makes the police think they've pinpointed Dempsey's location?'

'Mobile phone technology. The manufacturers used the triangulation method.'

'The *what* method?'

'Triangulation! It's a technique for measuring the strength of signals coming from handsets to aerial masts. It allows the operators to hone in on the position of a mobile to within a few yards.'

'So, why haven't they found him yet?'

'Apparently, this procedure works best in urban districts where there are lots of masts. Dempsey's location, it seems, is a rural setting with fewer masts. Also, there's a chance he's switched off his mobile or the battery's gone dead. They're working on it as we speak.'

'I see. Let hope they're successful. Let me know when you've got an update. I hope to God that Chris and Katie are with him ... and that they're alive and well.'

'Amen to that.'

'We've never allowed anybody from outside our group join the First-Friday meeting before,' Diana said.

'I am indeed honoured to be—' Emma started to say.

'You're quite the little spitfire,' Diana continued, as though Emma hadn't spoken. 'After the tongue-lashing you gave us in the restaurant we were forced to take what you had to say on board.'

'Look, I know I came on a bit strong, but it's—'

'Your censure, though unpalatable at the time, did act as a wake-up call. So, we thought it appropriate that you should be present for what will be our last First-Friday meeting. With Iseult and Nuala gone, and only Margot, Elizabeth and myself left standing, we've decided to call it quits. The deaths have shocked us to the core, made us think about the shenanigans we've got up to in the past. What started out as a fun way to stimulate our lives has lost its appeal. It never bothered us that we flouted social conventions or stepped outside the law; that's what made it so exciting. We've damaged a few people along the way – most of them, I hasten to add, fully deserving of what they got, but now, with just the three of us left, it's time for a reality check.'

Emma was seeing a new side to Diana Elliott. It was as though she had somehow ditched her affectations, transformed herself to an amiable down-to-earth woman. Not exactly vulnerable, but certainly more humane. They were sitting in the big conservatory that Emma had peered into when she'd visited Maurice Elliott. On the outside, she could see the garden and, in the distance, the silhouette of Bullock Harbour, its shape oppressive in the dwindling light. This evening, Diana, dressed in sober but elegant casual, sat in the same chair she'd used on that first visit. Diana introduced Sasha to Emma; the cat ignored her, content to purr softly on Diana's lap.

'You forced us to look at ourselves, re-evaluate our lifestyles,' Diana was saying, 'and yes, it's true, we were spiteful, selfish and foolhardy in many of the things we've done. The way we treated you and Connolly ... for that I'm truly ashamed, it's why we invited you here this evening ... to make amends.' Diana looked at her watch. 'Ah good,' she said, 'the others have decided to join us.'

With a flourish, Elizabeth Telford and Margot Hillary made their entrance. Larger than life hugs and kisses were exchanged. Margot's hair, shorter than it had been when Emma last saw her, was now styled in mock punk fashion. Tempestuous red spikes integrated with darker shades were set off dramatically by her choice of wardrobe. A black top, black slacks and black boots made her look like a glamorous, if overripe, rock chick. Elizabeth wore an elegant ankle-length grey dress with a mid-thigh split that displayed her shapely legs to full advantage.

Diana organized drinks. They said *cheers*, clinked glasses, but a degree of tension remained evident. Emma had little doubt that her presence was the contributing factor.

'The three of us,' Diana was saying, 'that is, Margot, Elizabeth and I – have pooled our intelligence in a positive way for once and after some soul-searching and straight thinking we have established what really happened. We've gone over recent and past events in painstaking detail, revisiting all aspects of our conduct, especially in regard to how we've behaved with contacts outside our circle, and we've come to a conclusion about what actually happened. We know it will come as a shock to you to know that *we* now know the identity of the person—'

'It won't be a shock,' Emma said, 'I too, know who the murderer is.'

The women stared at her as though she'd dropped in from another planet. 'You know?' Diana said, a sceptical expression in her eyes.

'Yes. I don't have proof or motive as yet. I've only put it together in the last few hours. I believe Ann Buckley is responsible for the murder of her sister Nuala and Iseult Connolly. I also believe she had Lisa Dunlop killed and that she is behind the kidnapping of Chris and Katie.'

'Oh, my God,' Margot said, spilling some of her drink, 'we were right. Ann Buckley really *is* guilty.'

'Yes she is,' Emma said. 'But before I go to the police, I need you ladies to fill in some of the blanks.'

'I think we can do that for you,' Diana said in a solemn tone. 'It's the real reason why we brought you here this evening.'

P ins and needles, cramps and numbness, took turns to inflict misery on Darren Dempsey's constrained body. Chris and Katie were quieter than they'd been since he first joined them. Katie had stopped whimpering fifteen minutes earlier and appeared to be sleeping. Chris moved his head slowly backwards and forward as though in some sort of trance. As Dempsey tried to ease his aches and pains, his mind struggled to identity the person behind the Tony Blair mask. He'd run a mental list of all the people he knew and had drawn a blank. But when he switched to female acquaintances, the truth dawned: the person holding him and the two children captive had to be Ann Buckley.

It seemed too incredible to believe at first but when he allowed the notion to percolate through to his consciousness he saw the twisted logic behind her actions. Ann Buckley resented the fact that her sister Nuala had always been the apple of her father's eye irrespective of what mischief she got up to. Ann spent most of her life seeking an equal share of that paternal approval but always came off second best. She took her work seriously, was good with horses, an asset to Carrigmore Stud and yet Nuala was the one who got the lion's share of fatherly affection.

Darren remembered the time Nuala had introduced him to Ann. Straight away, he'd sensed there was something false and calculating about the younger sibling. It was apparent that Ann did not like the idea of him and Nuala forming a stable relationship. He had tried to warn Nuala, but she'd vehemently rejected any such aspersions. Only later did he realize that Ann had been systematically sowing seeds of doubt in Nuala's head, steadily drip-dripping poisonous innuendo about his character.

But it was not until Ann accused him of sexual molestation that he realized the full extent of her evil intent. How it came about had been partly his own fault. He'd been to the hospital to visit Nuala after the birth of Katie and had taken a few too many drinks before returning home. The birth had left him feeling in high spirits, a factor that caused him to let his defences slip. Ann had been babysitting Chris at the time. On a celebratory impulse, he spun her around in his arms and pecked her on the cheek, inviting her to drink a toast to the new-born baby. She pretended to misinterpret his actions, claiming he was trying to seduce her.

The following day on his visit to the maternity hospital he'd told Nuala about the incident, making light of Ann's mistaken assumption. As he spoke to her, he could see a flicker of doubt in her eye. A day later, on Nuala's return to the house with baby Katie, Ann put on an act fully deserving of an Oscar. When Nuala broached the subject of the misunderstood peck on the cheek Ann hung her head and said nothing, an action calculated to increase Nuala's anxiety. A week later, Nuala made another attempt to get Ann's account of the incident but this time Ann burst into tears and ran from the room. This convinced Nuala that the incident might not have been all that innocent.

One month later Ann delivered her *coup de grace*. He'd been drinking with a few pals after an Ireland/France rugby match played at Lansdowne Road when a group of high-spirited young women joined them. After downing several pints, his friends decided to go to a restaurant. Two of them asked girls along and a young woman who'd been chatting him up invited herself along. After the meal – washed down with several bottles of plonk – the party headed for the Metro Nite Club. Around midnight, the woman who'd attached herself to him asked if he would drop her home. He was not blind to the fact that she was making a play for him but, even allowing for the level of alcohol in his system, he had no intention of allowing her to snare him; he had someone waiting for him at home, the woman he loved, Nuala Buckley.

She told him she lived in Enniskerry, an outlying district in the Dublin Mountains. Following her instructions, he branched off to a narrow side road and had begun to entertain doubts about the final destination when she asked him to pull to the side and stop. He did as instructed, thinking that perhaps she wanted to get sick but fearful that she had something entirely different in mind. His fears were well founded. Without preamble, her hand slipped on to his upper thigh. He made an attempt to rebuff her advances but his body's response melted what little resolve the alcohol hadn't already whittled away. Within minutes the fumbling began. She unhooked the belt of his pants, unzipped the fly and expertly uncovered that part of his body that begged for attention. Feeling reckless, but rather less efficiently than his seducer, he opened her blouse, unhooked her bra and was in the process of removing her panties when the screaming began.

Even now, in a darkened attic, that scream echoed in his mind, the same scream that had blown his life asunder. The subsequent arrest and trial put paid to the future he'd planned with Nuala and the children. Discovery of the bra in his car left little doubt for equivocation. Yet there was one person who had believed his version of events; that person had been Seán Grennan. But it was one thing to avoid going to prison, another thing altogether to expect forgiveness from Nuala or release from his own culpability, shame and guilt.

Only in recent months had the healing process began. He had painstakingly built up a trust between them. The love that had brought them together in the first place had begun to blossom afresh. For Ann, the reunion would put her plans to inherit the Buckley fortune in jeopardy and that was something she could not allow to happen.

He had no idea how Ann had gone from the point of rejecting her sister's 'homecoming' to the position he now found himself in, but he never doubted her resourcefulness. He hadn't suspected Ann when Nuala's dead body had been discovered. Like most people, he'd read the newspaper reports, seen the television coverage, all of it highlighting the arrest and detention of a detective. It was obvious to him now that the wrong man had been apprehended. Recognizing who hid behind the Tony Blair mask clarified everything. Ann Buckley had murdered her sister. He'd never been so sure of anything in his life. Nuala had always been thought of as the flaky one in the family, the one who'd messed with drugs, the one who'd been in psychiatric care. But the sister with the real mental imbalance was Ann. Unlike Nuala, she'd been able to cloak her illness; apart from her phobia about food – she could not remain at a table where red meat was being consumed – no outward signs of abnormality were manifest.

Chris and Katie, whom Ann professed to love, represented, in Ann's mind, a threat to her inheritance. If she could arrange to have her own sister killed, how much more difficult would it be to have the children taken out of the equation? How did she expect to get away with it? Thinking about this, he could envisage the role she'd organized for him. He would be the fall guy. People would naturally assume he had killed the children and then, in a fit of remorse, taken his own life. For Ann, it represented the perfect strategy; it would resolve all her problems and see him out of her life once and for all.

CHAPTER 46

Emma refused to allow darkness to impede her speed. Her determination to confront Ann Buckley meant ignoring speed limits with impunity. Conscious of Chris and Katie's plight, time was of the essence. Forty-eight hours had elapsed since the children had been taken. Their ordeal, she hoped, would soon be over.

Emma's meeting with Diana Elliott, Margot Hillary and Elizabeth Telford had been most informative. What they had to say helped support the case against Ann Buckley. They'd been sure that no one outside their circle knew about their plans but, after some soul-searching and exhaustive brain-storming, they were left with just the one possibility: Nuala must have confided in her sister Ann. A tempestuous relationship existed between Ann and the women's group. Ann had wanted to be part of their set from the beginning but apart from Nuala's support, her inclusion had been blocked by the others. Ann had incurred their displeasure on a number of occasions. Most notably, when she and her friend Lisa Dunlop had, by dubious means, obtained membership to an exclusive pony club that they belonged to. Ann was envious of the company Nuala kept and jealous of the men who befriended her. But it was the proposed reunion between Nuala and their father that spurred her on to the extreme course of action she'd embarked on.

Before leaving Diana Elliott's house, Emma had tried, and failed, to make contact with Grennan. She'd left a message on his answering service advising him to get to Carrigmore Stud asap. Contacting Mike Dorsett had been easier. He'd picked up the note of urgency in her voice and had agreed to meet her at the entrance to the stud farm. He was waiting for her when she got there. The guard on duty remembered Emma from her previous visit but it was Dorsett's status as a *garda* detective that gained them entrance. Emma gave Dorsett a brief outline of what she'd discovered. If he was impressed, he kept it to himself. 'What's my role?' he asked.

'Need someone riding shotgun when I confront Ann Buckley.'

'Fine, but understand this: I'll be acting in an unofficial capacity.'

'That's OK ... as long at Ann doesn't know.'

Dorsett strode to his car and gestured impatiently for her to get on with it. This was Emma's first time to see Dorsett's car. Like his clothes, the twelve-year-old Masda 626 looked as though it had seen better days.

CHAPTER 47

With Dorsett in her wake, Emma hurried towards Ann Buckley's house. Last time she'd made the journey it had been daytime and she'd been a passenger in a Land Rover. Everything looked different by night with only streetlights and the car's main beams to illuminate the way. Oak and sycamore trunks reflected a myriad of ghostly shapes, their overhanging branches taking on frightening proportions. Buildings that had impressed Emma on her first visit now took the form of great hulking monsters, their vastness dwarfing the nightscape vision. Scaffolding attached to the house next to Buckley's looked sinister, its outlines highlighted in the car's headlight beams. The skeletal beams and platforms put Emma in mind of an old-fashioned hanging gibbet. She shuddered and looked away. Ann's Land Rover was parked in the driveway, its silhouette picked out in the diffused light coming through the house's window blinds.

Emma stood at the door, Dorsett by her side, a nervous twitch acting up in her stomach. She was about to press the bell but paused suddenly. 'Shssh,' she said, 'Listen, I thought I heard raised voices inside.' They stood still for a moment, listening intently, but heard nothing. 'I think my imagination's getting the better of me.'

'Probably the television,' Dorsett said with a shrug.

An outside light came on above the door. From inside, the sound of a bolt being pulled preceded Ann Buckley's appearance. She stood in the half-open doorway, surprise and annoyance on her face. 'Emma Boylan,' she said, sounding flustered. 'What brings you here ... and who's this with you?'

'This is Detective Sergeant Dorsett,' Emma said. 'We're here because of Chris and Katie. May we come in?'

'What do you mean ... Chris and Katie? Have you found—?'

'Look, may we come in.'

206

'Yes, of course,' Ann said, guiding them to the lounge and inviting them to sit. Emma and Dorsett continued to stand.

'Is Sam Cline here?' Emma asked.

'Sam? What's he got to do with anything?'

'Is he here?'

'No, he isn't. What's this about?'

'Sam followed me here on my previous visit and tracked me back to the city after I'd left.'

'What are you saying?' Ann asked. 'Why would Sam—?'

'That's what we aim to find out! He broke into my apartment, would have killed me if Detective Inspector Grennan hadn't stopped him.'

Ann seemed genuinely shocked. 'Sorry, I find this very hard to believe but ... what exactly has this got to do with me?'

Dorsett spoke to Ann for the first time. 'We know Cline has the children. You can help us find him before any harm comes—'

'This is crazy! Sam Cline would never touch those children.'

'Yes, it's crazy,' Emma said. 'Cline has access to this place at all times ... *treated as part of the family*, that's what you said. I believe he's being aided and abetted by someone here in Carrigmore.'

'What? You're accusing me?' Ann said, shaking her head in disbelief. 'Have you gone completely nuts? I have absolutely nothing whatsoever to do with Sam Cline. He was Nuala's friend, *not* mine. He helped me move her stuff here; that's all. I don't believe for a second he has anything to do with the kidnapping but even if he had, why on earth would I be involved?'

'I'll tell you why,' Emma said. 'I've just come from a meeting with Diana Elliott, Margot Hillary and Elizabeth Telford. They've told me all about you. Like for example how, after Nuala had made it clear to Cline that their relationship was purely platonic, you moved in on him, pretending friendship.'

'That's not true! I never—'

'In fact, you tried to move in on every friend Nuala had ... with one exception: Darren Dempsey. Him, you decided to destroy.'

'This is madness. Where the hell are you getting this from—?'

'You used Lisa Dunlop to set him up. The first time I spoke to you, you told me you didn't know the person who accused Dempsey of rape. That was a lie. And then, the other day when I asked again about Lisa Dunlop, you claimed to hardly know her. Another lie. You and Lisa competed together on the show-jumping circuits. You put her up to accusing Dempsey.'

'This is outrageous! I told you that the identity of Dempsey's accuser was withheld from the public; I never said I didn't know her. And as for Diana Elliott's junky crones, if you believe anything they say, you're as daft as they are. What other lies did they tell you?'

'They told me how you and Sam Cline blackmailed them.'

'Blackmail? It gets better; what in hell's name are you on about now?'

'Nuala told you about the women's plan to confront the swimmer Brendan Edwards.'

'My sister never—'

'Oh, yes she did. She told you because she had qualms about the plan. You got Cline to video Edward's death, then blackmail the women. Nuala also told you about their conspiracy to destroy Connolly. You decided to reshape their plan. Again, you used Cline to do your dirty work. He killed Nuala and Iseult. Later, when your friend Lisa Dunlop decided to spill the beans, you had Cline shut her up ... *permanently*. And now, even as we speak, you and Cline are holding Chris and Katie captive.'

Ann Buckley laughed, a harsh snort, 'This is ridiculous. I've had absolutely nothing to do with any blackmail, killings or kidnapping.'

'Are you going to deny that you and Cline—'

'I can't speak for Sam Cline,' Ann snapped, her face contorted in fury, 'but we both know he suffers from a mental disorder. I can assure you that I would never in a million years have any truck with him, the very notion is preposterous. What you're suggesting is most offensive to me and now ... if you don't mind, I would like you to leave my house and—'

Ann was still speaking when the lounge door burst inwards. Sam Cline, his mouth open in a scream, charged into the room. He held a carving knife in his hand and lunged straight at Ann Buckley. 'You dirty, double-crossing, lying bitch,' he yelled as he plunged the knife into her stomach. Dorsett was first to react. In a flying tackle, he knocked Cline sideways before the knife struck a second time. The weapon slid beneath the couch as Dorsett wrestled Cline to the ground. Emma went to help Ann who had collapsed. It looked bad. Ann's hands covered the wound to her stomach. 'Oh, Jesus no, you dumb fucking retard,' Ann cried, seeing blood ooze from between her fingers.

'Let me help you,' Emma offered, hunkering down beside her.

'Get the fuck away,' Ann hissed through gritted teeth, driving her knee into the side of Emma's face, sending her sprawling on to her back.

'Hey, you all right, Emma?' Dorsett yelled, still struggling to cuff Cline. The distraction allowed Cline the leverage he needed to wriggle free from beneath Dorsett. He lashed out with his right foot and caught Dorsett's crotch with a sickening thud. The impact brought an agonizing howl of pain from the detective, his hands going instinctively to the source of injury, Cline succeeded in breaking free.

'Stupid fucks, all of you,' he bellowed, heading for the front door. He could hear Dorsett struggle to follow him as he pulled the door open. But the route to freedom was blocked. Seán Grennan's large frame stood in the doorway. 'Got you this time, you hairy fooker,' Grennan said, as he up-ended Cline with a powerful right fist to the lower gut.

CHAPTER 48

Ann Buckley was unconscious by the time they got her into the ambulance.

'She'll not die,' Dorsett insisted.

'You sure?' Emma asked. 'Looks bad to me.'

'Nah, the knife missed the main arteries. She'll stand trial.'

Dorsett struck a match and fired up a cigarette as he stood next to Emma, both of them outside the front door of Ann Buckley's house. The night had grown cold, the sky black as death. In the driveway, behind Ann Buckley's Land Rover, garda officers waited in two squad cars. Emma shivered, unable to say if it was the night air or the recent developments that brought it on. She was still reeling from the dreadful events that had taken place; the sight of Cline bolting through the door, knife in hand, imprinted on her mind like some indelible after-image. 'He was in there all along,' she said. 'The raised voices we heard on our arrived came from the two of them, not the television.'

'Aye, they were arguing.'

'And as soon as we entered, Cline hid.'

'Yeah, but he could still hear everything.'

'Exactly. He'd have heard Ann deny knowing him.'

'And he'd have heard what she said about his mental state o mind.'

'You'd think Ann would've known better; she was aware c Cline's volatility ... his uncontrollable temper.'

'That's women for you,' Dorsett said, suppressing a smile, 'neve can hold their tongues.'

Seán Grennan poked his head outside the door and ordere Dorsett to accompany him while he questioned Cline. Emma made move to join them but Grennan waved his index finger at her, sai 'No way Jose.'

That's men for you.

Emma made her way to the front lounge. She needed to contact the *Post*, bring them up to speed with developments.

In the kitchen, Dorsett smoked a cigarette and watched contemptuously as Grennan straddled a chair, back-to-front style, and interrogated Cline. Grennan's half-arsed technique brought little reward. After failing to elicit any meaningful response, he stormed out of the kitchen and into the front lounge, turning the air blue with his very personalized brand of profanities. He ignored Emma who was busy talking to Bob Crosby on her mobile. Seeing Grennan, she cut the connection, hoping instead to extract information from the detective. Before she had a chance to confront Grennan, Shane Buckley strode into the room. 'Will someone tell me what the hell's going on here?' he demanded, each word harsh and critical. The bloodstock magnate had lost his upright bearing, his eyes were slightly bloodshot and his skin had taken on a waxy pallor. 'My security people tell me my daughter's been rushed away in an ambulance. Why wasn't I informed?'

'We tried to contact you,' Grennan said defensively, 'but we were informed that you weren't available; we *did* leave a message.'

Shane Buckley looked confused. 'Yes, yes I'm sorry, I was on a long-distance call to the Emirates but someone should have … doesn't matter, just tell me what's happened?'

'There's been a development,' Grennan said, stating the obvious. He placed a hand on Buckley's back in an effort to get him out of the room, a none-too-subtle ploy to exclude Emma. Buckley stood firm, his face distorted in anger. 'I demand to know what's happened. *Now!*'

'Fine, Mr Buckley, I'll tell you,' Grennan said, indicating that they should both sit down. Grennan outlined all that had happened, downplaying the seriousness of Ann Buckley's injuries. When he'd finished, Shane Buckley remained silent for several seconds. 'How is this possible?' he said at length, doing his best to remain composed. 'My two lovely girls, dear God, one's dead … the other …' He paused for a moment and blew his nose into a great white handkerchief. 'All I ever wanted was to have them here with me in Carrigmore. I couldn't have done more for them but … seems it wasn't enough. I gave them everything but they've broken my bloody heart … I never meant to drive Nuala away. Thought I knew best. Tried to mend fences … too late. Built the house next door to this one for her, tried to persuade her to come home. Thought I'd sorted it out, but I can see now how Ann might have felt aggrieved ... and yes, it's true, Nuala was my favourite. My fault; my fault entirely.' Buckley rubbed his eyes and looked at Grennan. 'You say Ann's involved in the kidnapping? I can't believe ... Did she say where Chris and Katie are?'

'No, ne'er a word. As for Cline, he won't budge. All we know is that they're hidden in or around Carrigmore Stud.'

'You're sure of that?' Buckley asked.

'Yeah! The mobile people traced the signal to this general area.'

'But every inch of Carrigmore has been searched,' Buckley said.

'True, but somehow we missed them. I've called for reinforcements to search the place again.'

Something that Buckley said struck a chord with Emma. She thought back to the time of her first visit to the house and recalled the disparaging remarks Ann had made about the empty house with the scaffolding, Hearing now that the house had been built for Nuala, it was understandable. Emma had seen something akin to anxiety in Ann's expression at the time. She turned to Grennan. 'Was the house next door searched?' she asked.

'Of course,' Grennan snapped, annoyed by her interruption. 'Every building within the confines of Carrigmore has been searched. Why ask?'

'Just a feeling I have, call it woman's intuition but I think that's where the children are being held.'

'And I told you already, it's been—'

'Yeah, I know, but you also admitted the search missed something.'

'Women's intuitions, huh, just what I need,' Grennan said, then paused, appearing to reflect on Emma's contribution. 'OK, all right,' he said, with a shrug, 'we'll check it out soon as I get Cline away from here.' He made his way out of the room and left Emma with Buckley.

'I'm sorry about what's happened, Mr Buckley,' Emma offered knowing how lame her words must sound to him.

'Thank you,' he replied, without looking at her. 'OK if I have a word with Sam before you take him away?'

Emma saw little point in correcting Buckley's assumption that she was a detective. 'Looks like Mr Cline is in no mood to talk to anyone,' she offered.

'I don't understand it,' Buckley said, dejectedly, 'Sam was like one of the family. He had problems, sure ... mental problems but he was kind to Nuala at a time when she needed friends. And then, when Nuala got better and moved outside Cline's circle, Ann befriended him. She felt sorry for him; at least that's what I thought at the time. I had no idea she was just ...' He stopped talking and stared at Emma. 'No, this is all wrong ... has to be wrong. Ann wouldn't hurt ... kill anyone ... I mean that literally. She's so sensitive ... loves the horses ... all animals, always did, even as a kid. I can remember an incident from her childhood ... something I thought had little significance at the time but now ... now with all that's happened, I think maybe it had a bearing on things.'

'Can you tell me about it?'

'Won't make a whole lot of sense to you.'

'I'd still like to hear it.'

He nodded gravely, his opaque eyes lost to the real world. 'It goes back to a time when Ann was a child. I gave her a lamb to mind one winter. Heavy snow fell that February as I recall ... the lamb's mother died giving birth. Ann loved that lamb; totally devoted to it. She called it Ba-Barbara, fed it from a bottle that I'd fitted with a special teat.

'Easter Sunday fell in mid-April that year and happened to coincide with Ann's eighth birthday. We arranged a special dinner to mark the occasion. Iseult Smyth-O'Brien was invited because she was Nuala's best friend. Ann looked up to the older girls and was thrilled to be in such *grown-up* company. It was the first time she'd been allowed to dine with the adults at the main table. Everything was going fine and we'd just finished the main course when Nuala, always up to mischief, began teasing Ann. She told Ann that we had just eaten Ba-Barbara. Ann started to scream. She wanted me to tell her it wasn't true.'

'And was it true?' Emma asked.

'Yes, unfortunately it was. Should have lied to her I suppose, but I told her that as an eight-year-old she was a big girl and would have to get used to life's more unpleasant aspects. I realize now how insensitive I'd been. It didn't help that Nuala and Iseult were nudging each other and giggling at Ann's distress. The poor child dashed out of the room and threw up. After that she ran to the yard and climbed to the loft in the hay barn. I followed her, tried to cajole her back to the table. I can still see the expression of loathing in her eyes to this day;

it was as though I had become some kind of alien, a monster who'd deceived her, betrayed and humiliated her.'

His story was interrupted by the sound of Grennan and Dorsett escorting Cline through the hallway towards the front door. With surprising agility, Buckley hurried after them and confronted Cline. 'Just tell me one thing,' he demanded, 'what have you done with the children?'

The handcuffed Cline looked at Buckley with a blank expression, making no effort to speak.

'Look, please, I have to know,' Buckley implored. 'Chris and Katie are all I've got left.' He paused to indicate Emma. 'Could what this woman says be true: are they being held in the house next door?'

A look of surprise flitted across Cline's face. He glanced at Emma for a moment, then returned his gaze to Shane Buckley. In barely more than a whisper he said, 'Yes, your precious, psychopathic bitch of a daughter had them put in the attic.' He then moved on, anxious to get out of the house.

CHAPTER 49

I n her younger days, Diana listened to middle-of-the-road music, Bryan Adams, Elton John and George Michael being among her favourites, but this evening she felt the prevailing atmosphere called for more contemplative fare. After a search through her CD collection she selected Mendelssohn. She liked the feeling of warmth she experienced when listening to *A Midsummer Night's Dream* and the tranquillity that flowed from *Calm Sea and Prosperous Voyage*. Her choice, she hoped, would create an appropriate mood for what would be the last of the First-Friday meetings. To complement the general milieu, she lit half a dozen Chinese joss sticks she'd saved from her student days and placed them around the conservatory.

In the half-hour that had elapsed since Emma Boylan left they had spoken but few words. They'd hugged and kissed, alternating between bouts of manic laughter and uncontrolled tears, steadily consumed alcohol and snorted lines. They had dimmed the lights and closed the blinds to the outside world. Diana and Margot, both high, made love to each other, unconcerned that Elizabeth should witness what was a beautiful, tender and sensual display of devotion. In the aftermath, all three grouped together and embraced.

'And so, my dear friends,' Diana said, struggling for words, 'we must do … what we must do. I expect that Emma Boylan and the police have sorted things by now. What lies ahead, should we do nothing, is … distasteful … ugly … degrading. Mustn't let that happen. What we told the journalist earlier was not off the record. That means—'

'—our goose is cooked,' Margot said, every word slurred.

'Yes, we've run out of rope,' Elizabeth agreed with a giggle.

Diana swayed a little, sloshing her drink as she did so, her eyes lazed. The music had stopped but they seemed not to have noticed. 'Part of me wants to see Maurice suffer,' she said, 'but another part of me says no. Truth is, we've both sinned, but this time I've sinned exceedingly … in thought, word, and deed, through my own fault, through my own grievous fault … gone to the Devil entirely … gone too far altogether. And another thing, the old fraud has given me the life I craved … and in his own way – the only way Maurice knows – he has done his best for me. Can't say the same for myself. Salvation is out the window, an act of contrition won't do this time; for me, girls, the course is clear.'

'I hear what you're saying,' Margot butted in, 'my feelings for dear old soggy bottom are not too dissimilar. God knows, Norbert didn't have a clue how to love a woman, couldn't find the man in the boat even if I drew a diagram for him, but he *was* always good to me … even when I behaved abominably. I spent most of my time putting him down, something he hardly deserved. He's a good man really and I think it's time I stopped destroying him. As for my boy Ronan, well, he'll have enough difficulties getting through life as it is; he'll have too much money, too much responsibility and too many male parasites hanging on to him. The least I can do is spare both of them from … further hurt and humiliation. I'm with you all the way, Diana.'

Elizabeth laughed out loud. 'Hey, you crazy pair of bitches, don't you dare get all soppy and sentimental now; this is our last First-Friday, our ultimate experience, so let's be merry. This whole world's a crock of shit when all's said and done, but hey, we've given it our best shot … at least up to now, so let's make ourselves presentable, put on our party faces, and do the only sensible thing that needs doing.'

'You're right, Elizabeth,' Diana said, 'for three old broads we're never going to look better than we do right now. I always think of my namesake, Princess Di, she never got to grow old; she'll always be beautiful.'

'And Marilyn Monroe,' Margot said, 'she'll always be remembered for her beauty.'

Elizabeth hiccupped, said, 'Not like Debbie Harry or Cher .. *Jesus!*'

'So, my special friends,' Diana slurred, 'are we ready for this .. this our last great walk on the wild side … *together?*'

'Ready as we'll ever be,' Margot said.

'Best idea we've ever had,' Elizabeth said defiantly. 'Let's do it.'

'Will they … do you think they'll understand?' Diana asked. 'Will they even be bothered?'

Margot shook her head. 'They never understood before, sure as hell won't bother them now.'

'I can't be bothered ... to bother about who's bothered,' Elizabeth said, through giggles and tears.

CHAPTER 50

Blue lights flashed and sirens blared as the ambulance sped away, its occupants, Chris and Katie, dazed and bewildered, lost in the general confusion. Shane Buckley, his tears streaming freely, accompanied them, his arms gently cradling their exhausted bodies. Darren Dempsey, who seemed to have suffered more than the children, wanted to accompany them but was prevented from doing so by Grennan who insisted that he travel back to the city with him for a debriefing session.

A quick search of the house by the uniformed officers turned up the Tony Blair mask, lighting equipment, a camera and various items of clothing. Questions would be asked as to why these items had been missed on the initial search. But that hardly mattered now, the children and their father had been rescued.

Emma and Dorsett stayed behind. A cordon had been placed around the house and a squad car remained on duty. Dorsett was in no hurry to leave; he hung around, examining the scene, hungrily dragging on his cigarette while Emma fetched her laptop from the car. She set it up in the kitchen and sent a report to the *Post*, hoping to catch the later editions of the Saturday morning paper. She was about to leave when Dorsett approached her. 'Emma,' he said, smoke drifting out of his mouth with each word, 'I'd like to apologize.'

'What for?'

'For my boorish behaviour when we first met. You see the—'

'Forget it,' Emma cut in. 'What's important is that everything worked out in the end.'

'Aye, that's true enough but it doesn't alter the fact that I was wrong about you ... Connolly's right, you're OK. To make amends, I'd like to buy you a drink. We could stop at the Silver Tassie on the way back to the city, what do you say?'

Emma hadn't expected this. There were a lot of things she needed to do right now but shooting the breeze with Dorsett was not one of them. Given a choice, she'd prefer it if he kept to his minimalist uttering. 'I'll pass on that if you don't mind,' she replied kindly. 'It's been a long day and I'm totally whacked. But thanks for the offer. Maybe when Connolly gets released we'll raise a glass or two together.'

Don't hold your breath.

A pained smile crossed Dorsett's lips. 'I'd like that,' he said, dropping his cigarette on the ground and crushing it underfoot.

On her way back to the city Emma's thoughts were scattered. She pictured Connolly in his cell and wondered how long it would be before the authorities set him free. Other images crowded her mind. She could still see the frightened expressions on the faces of Chris and Katie as they were eased down the ladder from the attic. Their mother was dead, their aunt Ann would never be allowed near them again, but their grandfather, Shane Buckley and their dad, Darren Dempsey would be there for them from now onwards. It was a reasonable outcome given the circumstances, one that Emma should have felt good about but her bone-weary body was beyond taking satisfaction.

Speeding through Loughlinstown, past the Silver Tassie pub, she was glad she'd declined Dorsett's offer of a drink. The only thing she wanted right now was to put her head on a pillow and sleep. Just thinking about it induced a long yawn. She turned the volume up on the car radio in the hope that it would help keep her alert and awake. Joss Stone was belting out *Tell Me 'Bout It* when her mobile cut in, snapping her thoughts back into focus. She slowed down and pulled to a halt on the road's lay-by. The caller was Bob Crosby.

'Emma, where are you?' he asked, urgency in his voice.

'On my way back from Carrigmore Stud. I filed the story.'

'Yes, we got it, and it's fine, but something's come up.'

'Ah, for Christ's sake Bob, it's almost midnight. Give us a break.'

'Sorry, Emma, this concerns you! We've just got word that Diana Elliott and Elizabeth Telford have been found dead.'

'*What?*' Emma said, almost shouting. 'That couldn't be; I was with them earlier. What the hell are you saying?'

'Details are sketchy. According to my "insider", the women were found in the Elliott conservatory. Apparently it was a suicide pact.'

'Jesus Christ!' Emma said, feeling as though she'd been punched in the stomach. 'What about Margot Hillary? She was with them.'

'She's unconscious. They've taken her to Loughlinstown hospital. They're trying to save her but they don't rate her chances.'

'Oh my God! I'm hearing this but I'm not believing it. I'd better get to Elliott's house, see if I can talk to—'

'No, Emma. If you show up there, the cops will nab you.'

'Nab *me*? What're you talking about?'

'You were the last person to see them alive.'

'Was I? Damn it, yes, I suppose I was. What am I supposed to do?'

'You're near Loughlinstown, yeah?'

'Yes, I just passed through it.'

'Go to the hospital, check on Margot Hillary.'

'Right, good idea, I'll do that.'

Emma no longer felt tired. It was as though someone had suddenly infused her body with a shot of adrenaline. She pulled the car on to the road and made an illegal U turn at the next junction. Three minutes later she pulled into the hospital car-park.

Margot Hillary was in intensive care, only family and close relatives allowed near her. Claiming sister-in-law status, Emma was ushered through without question. She saw Norbert Hillary sitting alone in the centre of the waiting room, his body bent forward, one hand pressed to his lips, the other resting limply on his knee, his eyes staring blankly at the floor. He failed to notice Emma as she sat down next to him.

'Hello, Norbert,' she whispered. 'Dreadful news. I'm so sorry.'

Hillary removed his hand from his mouth, straightened his posture and looked at her. He tried for a smile, failed to come close. 'Good of you to come,' he said in a faltering voice. 'It's touch and go with Margot I'm afraid. They're doing what they can to save her but … it's not good.'

Emma took hold of his hand, squeezed gently. 'What happened?'

'Well, as you know this was their monthly get-together. Margot told me; she actually told me it would be the last First-Friday meeting. I never took what she said to mean … well, you know, *literally* … the last.'

'Diana said something similar to me. Maurice Elliott warned me that she was acting a bit strange but I never thought for a minute … I never dreamed that—'

'Of course you didn't. Who would think such a thing? Margot told me you'd been invited to join them. She liked you, you know, might not have shown it but she did, felt guilty about accusing you friend, the detective. Truth is, she felt guilty about so many things. The deaths of Iseult and Nuala were a shock to the system. It brought back memories of the pool.'

'You mean Brendan Edwards?'

'Yes, Emma, she never forgave herself for what happened that morning in the pool. That tragedy represented the beginning of the end for Margot. The other women shared an equal guilt. The deaths of their closest friends brought home to them just how reckless, how stupid and irresponsible they'd been. Tonight's meeting was supposed to put matters right. But, damn-it-to-hell, I'd no idea that they ... that they wanted to end it all. This was their grand finale, a swan song like no other.'

The words coming from Norbert Hillary had choked in his throat. Emma made no immediate reply; she watched as he removed his glasses and cradled his head in his hands. The sound of a clock on the wall above the door that led to the intensive care unit, underscored the feeling of despair. Emma was about to speak again when a young Asian doctor, wearing pale greens, came into the room and stood by the door. 'Mr Hillary,' he said quietly, 'could you come with me please?'

Hillary replaced his glasses, got up and hurried towards the doctor. The doctor guided him through the door to the ICU. Before the door had closed completely, Emma heard the doctor say, 'I'm so very sorry Mr Hillary, we did what we could but—'

Emma heard no more. She didn't need to.

Margot Hillary was dead.

Diana Elliott and Elizabeth Telford were dead. All members of the First-Friday group were now deceased.

CHAPTER 51

It was 2 a.m. by the time Emma inserted the key in the door of her apartment. Like a marathon runner who'd hit the 'wall' and emerged the far side with renewed vigour, she'd passed the point of weariness. Probably something to do with her body clock thinking it was a new day. Just as well really; she wanted to write a comprehensive article on the Ann Buckley affair for the *Post* while events remained vivid in her mind. Sure, it could wait till the morning but she hoped her words would have more resonance if consigned to paper straight away. First, though, she needed coffee. She was still on a high and the coffee would help keep her up there for a while to come. She was making her way to the kitchen when a pair of hands reached for her.

She screamed.

'It's only me!' Connolly said, putting his hands around her waist. 'Didn't mean to scare you.'

'You bastard,' Emma yelped. 'Scared the shit out of me.'

'Not exactly the welcome I'd hoped for,' he joked, turning her around to face him. 'It's so good to see you. Good to be home.'

Emma pummelled his chest with her fist playfully before falling into his embrace. They kissed, a long, hard, passionate kiss. Coming up for air, she said, 'Don't ever do that to me again. If you knew the sort of a day I've had.'

'I *do* know the sort of day you've had. Crosby phoned me before you arrived; told me all about your trials and tribulations.'

'He told you everything?'

'Yep! Every last sordid detail.'

'Good. So, tell me, how'd you get out? Jailbreak, was it?'

'Yeah, I tunnelled beneath the walls just so I could get home to you. No, nothing so romantic I'm afraid. It was all legal and above board. It's been pretty obvious for some days that I had nothing t

222

do with the killings. Chief Superintendent Laz Rochford cut through the red tape. The old fart was probably feeling bad about how he treated me when this case broke. He had the DPP sign the form for my release a few hours ago, so here I am.'

'Here you are indeed. God, it's good to see you. Have you any idea how much I've missed you?'

''Bout as much as I missed you.'

After another prolonged kiss, Emma broke away and finally got to brew some coffee. All thoughts of writing the article for the *Post* were shelved. Instead, they sat and discussed all that had happened since the murders began. They talked about the five women who had met on the First-Friday of each month. They talked about the dire consequences of their actions and how Ann Buckley had used the women's plans for her own ends.

'I can't believe Ann would have sacrificed Chris and Katie,' Connolly said. 'You saw how she appealed to the judge for them? If that was an act then, by God, she should be on the stage.'

'She *is* good.' Emma agreed, 'She's had plenty of practice. She'd been lying all her life, lying to her sister, lying to her father, and lying to those sweet kids.'

'It's amazing. You saw her at the graveside ... crying her heart out. Don't tell me that was just an act?'

'Yes, it was! In retrospect it seems especially depraved. Her father told me about a bizarre incident in Ann's childhood; I'm no psychiatrist but I'd say it's possible it had a bearing on her actions. But who knows what goes on inside someone's head? One thing's certain, her display of spurious emotions was perverse in the extreme. In fact, everything she's said and done is a total sham. And I believe she *would* have got rid of the children. She'd felt slighted all her life and had become cynical, bitter and twisted. But here's the extraordinary thing: she has this scary ability to cloak the evidence of her psychopathic disorder from those around her; to all intents and purposes she appears as normal as you or me, but beneath the surface she's rotten to the core. Her craving for power, status, and recognition knows no bounds. In the end, she would have done anything to get her way. She's been planning her revenge for years, probably since that incident in her childhood, and she couldn't care less who she used, hurt or killed, to achieve her ends. Sam Cline was just one of the pawns she used along the way.'

'How was she able to exercise such influence over him?'

'Ann let him believe she loved him; she probably hinted that he would be her man when she became mistress of Carrigmore. She totally controlled him, exploited his vulnerabilities, wound him up and set him off so that, in the end he would do anything for her.'

'Looks as though he did.'

'Tragically, he did. Through him she was able to blackmail the women. For her, the money was purely a means to an end, a necessity to finance her operation. The same with the ransom money for Chris and Katie; money in itself was never the issue. It didn't bother her whether her father paid it or not. The kidnapping was purely a device to remove all claimants to Carrigmore. The ingenious part was that Darren Dempsey, whom she also planned to kill, would be seen as the killer and the blackmailer.'

Connolly sighed. 'Well, at least Dempsey will get to see his kids again. That's about the only good thing to come out of all this horror.'

'Yes, but I also came out ahead.'

'How do you make that out?'

'Well, I was spared the prospect of working for Maurice Elliott. That would have been the biggest mistake of my life. For the immediate future I'm glad to be working for the *Post*.'

'Know what, Emma? I think you've done enough work for the *Post* for one day. I think it's time you went to bed, my lady ... got some well deserved sleep.'

'Sleep? You want me to go to bed ... to *sleep*? You've got to be joking.'